THE ALCHEMIST'S SONG

THE ALCHEMIST'S SONG

DAVID WYN ROBERTS

GREAT PLAINS FICTION
An imprint of Great Plains Publications

Great Plains Fiction
An imprint of Great Plains Publications Ltd.
3-161 Stafford Street
Winnipeg, MB.   R3M 2X9

The publisher acknowledges the financial assistance of The Canada Council and the Manitoba Arts Council in the production of this book.

Cover illustration: Monkey figure with violin, representing the four elements, earth fire, water, air, from the 15th century alchemical manuscript *Aurora consurgens*, sometimes attributed to Thomas Aquinas.

Design and typography: Taylor George Design

Printed in Canada by: Friesens

Canadian Cataloguing in Publication Data:

Roberts, David Wyn
The alchemist's song
ISBN 1-894283-01-5
I. Title
PS8585.02945 A72 1998   C813'.54   C98-920153-8
PR9199.3.R52693 A72 1998

Acknowledgements

Leslie Gardner in London offered unfailing encouragement and widsom. Gregg Shilliday, publisher of Great Plains Fiction in Winnipeg, showed finely-tuned editorial radar. Mark Morton's sensitive editing brought light to the work. Without complaint, Mary, Dylan, Julian and Bailey endured months of distraction. To members of Adam McLean's alchemy forum I am grateful for uplifting dialogue and for the transcription of Erenfus Orandus' 1624 translation of Nicholas Flamel's ***Exposition of the Hierogryphicall Figures***. Some of the words on pages 76-78 are taken more or less from Aldous Huxley's essay Miracle in Lebanon. For five paragraphs on pages 126-127 I am indebted to my colleague Anthony Jenkins and to The Globe and Mail. Acknowledgements both humble and profuse belong to Carrington for the burning letters and to TKLH for keeping alive the spark. Thanks also to photographer Robert Tinker for cropping-out the open zipper and to Quincy Troupe for allowing me to re-phrase some words of Miles which appear on pages 130-131. Finally, this story is dedicated to the memory of my father, Howard Roberts, a fine tenor, and to my friend Steven Seywright who didn't sing, but danced.

CONTENTS

Mair: Hydoedd y byd a hedy,
Hin y fron, bydd heno fry.

World's width you wander in your flight;
Be with my love, wild wind, this night.

Dafydd ap Gwilym (1354)

PROLOGUE

Shrouded in the pitch sepulchre of night, I was a vespertined wisp of a boy, unseen as I nestled among shadows and slipped below the pine-slivered decks of Exy on my way to the old man.

Now Exy was a slate barge: well scrubbed, shining, and slightly plump when I espied her, lying low, emptying her scuppers and priming for a haul up the Menai Strait bound for Germany, Bad Godesburg.

Just as oceans of stars lap the shores of time, she carried me up that sweeping strait like Moses and the bulrushes so I might husband in the birth of those wondrous, gold-tipped horns — musical they were, of tempered brass and forged in fire and sweat from the cauldron of the earth's first elements.

Besetting on my best seven-league boots I cut a walking staff and first made overland on the mottled track through Cambria. I mastered this leg in six days on the strength of chicken eggs, snowdrop roots and spring tea from the bark of yew. In Caernarfon I lollygagged by a tailor and haberdash and buggy-eyed saw the wealth of the place as a stitchman measured silver-buttoned trousers, the tailor asking His Lordship on which Welsh side, aswy or addas, he preferred to dangle his warm cloister.

When first I boarded Exy I stowed behind sacks of pork rind and Jamaica sugar and slagged in the straw of the pigpen. And as I lay below decks like Romulus, like Remus, under a pair of great-titted sows, the mate slid open the midships quarterhatch and I saw the stars blow past. Soon I imagined looking down, down into a great pool of stars which became a deep and bottomless pool of sleep, and in dead heavy slumber swam through the stars each and all.

And when fright settled in my craw, as the aftertaste of a gamey-bird too well-hung, I drew breath deep and surrendered to The Almighty. Even when Exy's cabin boy came to feed the sows and to cluck at them, and a great pig stepped on my hidden thigh, and a piece of straw tickled my hidden ear, and the pig's bowels erupted and dropped warm turds on my half-hid forehead — I did not move nor breathe nor vomit.

And without resort to untruth, when that pine-planked Exy put in to Bad Godesburg, her decks drenched in miracles, I took my chance before moonrise to dive into the waters, to swim, and was glad to stub my nose on a rock in the dark crawl to shore.

Now into the cobblestone village, heart weightless as a lark, I made straight as a treacle-tarred cat through the Market of the Suckling Pigs and past the Street of the Children's Game to the old man's house. Filled with a hundred fears I tapped my staff on the oak-slat door. I noticed the smell on my skin was not wholesome — it reminded of the old pisser behind the Twt Hill Vaults tavern in Caernarfon, where blunt-pricked men stagger forth with their crying hymns to the night. I felt near starved and there was still a dry smack of blood from my nose. But the nails of my boots made not one scrape till a pair of eyes came at the door and it slid open a jigger.

"This is the house of God?" I asked, hiding my disappointment that the house was not great but was, rather, by outward appearance, the humblest of the most humble of dwellings in the town. The old face which appeared at the door's blast winced and gave a start, and I looked over my shoulder as a barrow bumped past behind me.

"I've come a long way," I cried. "A messenger from the forest-men at Mon in Wales. They said you might help find the red stone."

The door levered a crack and swung wide.

"Come," said the old man, and he pulled me in. The two of us remarked on one another, each sizing carefully the sight of the other. And I passed to him a heavy bag holding shards of Bible-black North Wales slate, which the Druid-men of the forest offered as a prized gift for the smelting.

The elder inspected the contents, smiled, and slunk the bag on the floor.

"How many pockets have you, lad?" old Gwynt, the horn-maker, asked.

"Pockets?" I said.

"For all the gold," said Gwynt, laying a bowl of warm barley before me and a flask of cold tea.

"If I have been taught well enough at all," said I between mouthfuls, "then the gold is not for mine own. The ore is for the furtherance of God's great work in the world."

"And who says what might be God's work?" queried the old man, whose crown was bald, smooth and sun-baked, but with long curls of white hair falling from the sides of his head to his shoulders.

"God," I told him, casting a look deep and straight into his ancient, wrinkled eyelids.

"Aye," smiled Gwynt. "You'll rest and then we'll talk. I'll make a place for you. You're whole born, my young Weal. I believe I've been a long time waiting for you. Your name?"

"Bleddyn."

Soon commenced measures to ensure my head, heart, and quickening were to snuff.

There were times the man would assemble pins, thimbles, glass balls and beads, coloured cloths of many shapes on a table. I was to memorize them all as an hourglass emptied. "How many things and what were they in the upper right-hand quadrant only?" asked Gwynt, and I recited them back with perfect clarity. "In the lower right?" And so on.

Once, the old one took me to Cologne, pressed a florin to my hand, and told me to meet him below the clock tower three days hence, at noon. When the old man thinking to fox me returned to the tower upon the fourth day, the sun high and bright, he marvelled as I popped from the shadow and dropped two florins in his hand.

And it was with great care, one sun-blasting day there in Bad Godesburg, and it was with great reverence, that Gwynt lovingly drew a book from a cellar hiding-place and shewed it me for my hungry study. It was neither of paper nor parchment but seemed to be made of the smoothed-out rinds of tender saplings. The binding was of beaten copper and engraved with strange letters and figures.

Skilled toil had engraved the pages, which bore beautiful letters, dutifully coloured, fair and neat. On the binding was drawn a staff, two serpents entwining. Lower down was a cross on which was nailed a third serpent.

The rest of the page was filled with frightful curses and execrations against any who might read this book unless he be a sacrificial priest, a doctor of Holy Laws, or a plucker of pheasants.

"The man who sold me this book did not know its worth — any more than I did," said Gwynt. "Taken from the poor Jews, long ago, or perhaps it was hid somewhere in part of their ancient abode."

The author consoled his people and counselled them to eschew all vice, especially idolatry — wrong seeing — and to wait with sweet patience until the Messiah should come and conquer all kings and pretenders on Earth and with his people rule eternally in majesty. I could see that all this was written by a very wise and learned man.

On the next pages the mysterious author taught, in common language, the transmutation of metals, so as to help his captive people pay taxes to the local authority. Alongside, he provided illustrations of the vessels, and detailed the colours and other matters, excepting always the primus agens whereof he did not speak but only painted in careful cunning miniatures.

On one page was portrayed a youth with wings on his heels and a staff in his hand. Toward the youth flew a powerful old man upon whose head was an hourglass and who held in both hands a sickle — like Death — with which, full of terrible rage and fury, he tried to sever the youngster's feet.

On the next page was a fair rose bush in flower, sore shaken by the North Wind. The rose grew among a fruity garden and leaned on a hollow oak. At its foot gushed forth a spring of the very whitest water. The stream fell away in cascades to the distance after passing through the hands of countless peoples, who dug the earth to find the spring, but could not, since they were blind, with the exception of one alone, who weighed the water.

"Mark you this," said Gwynt to me, piercing an apple with a knife and pointing to the image of a King wielding a large sword. The King slaughtered a multitude of children before the eyes of weeping mothers. And soldiers gathered the little ones' flowing blood in a large vessel in which the sun and moon came to bathe.

"Mark you that the blood of the sacrificed innocents signifies the mineral spirit in all metals, especially in gold, silver and quicksilver. This is the prima materia, the fundamental stuff of life. The holy innocents represent the undefiled stirrings or out-breathings of the vital spirit."

Old Gwynt told me that once he had the book by him he could do naught else by night and day but study it.

"From the start," he said, "I understood very well all the fixings which it described. But I despaired for I did not know what was the material I must work on to make the gold. My wife, Ingot, whom I loved like myself, was greatly concerned of this, and asked me continually if she might not lift the weight upon me. I showed her the beautiful book, with which she fell in love just as much as I had done. But she understood as little as I."

Gwynt had copied with faithful hand the figures from several pages and bore them to all manner of scholar. None but a few would pause to hear the old man's words and glance at his figures. He rhumed long, tried a thousand broulleryes and decoctions, and then bolted to seek an explanation from priests at the far-distant shrine of St. Juan the Elder at Guernica y Luno.

Gwynt made me know that on the road near Leon he met an aged man renowned far and wide for his self-learning: Midian, the son of a low pheasant plucker. Midian joyed at the figures from the book. The old goister had long heard of the book but was of the belief it had been completely lost. Together, the pair, Gwynt and Midian, set out for Bad Godesburg, from Leon to Castropol and from there to Bilbao where they boarded for France. Their journey went happily and Midian explained to Gwynt many of the figures, each word revealing great secrets.

But at Orleans the learned man became gravely ill and was overcome with the most severe attack of vomiting. Finally, he died, at the end of the seventh day of his sickbed. Gwynt lit candles and had Midian's body buried at Orleans. When, many days later, he reached Bad Godesburg, he sorrowed beyond heart-strength to learn his good wife also had died.

"In my grieving," said Gwynt, "I vowed to my lost dear ones to uncover at last the secret of the book. Often did I err. But I prayed unceasingly with this, my wife's rosary in my hand, and with Midian's voice in my heart, I read attentively in the book, meditating on the words. And in time I learned that it — the way — is known not by name of the Humid Way, nor the Dry Way, but it is the Lightning Way."

The old man then raised the trap to the stone cellar and bade me join him in his cavernous workshop. His sanctum. Strewn with vessels it was: alundels, crucibles, phials, scales, bellows and burners, retorts, pelicans and jorums. There was, kept neatly all around, sundry jars and alembics with coloured powders and liquids, and sacks of saltpeter, flux, lead, and coke for burning. Everywhere were tools for bending and kneading, smelting and polishing the brass and base metal instruments which Gwynt fashioned and sold, sometimes to the best courts and musicians of Europe.

Dryness seized my throat and a great excitement pounded in my heart.

"I can tell you now, lad," the old man smiled, "as I've told no one and will not again, that finally I found what I longed for — the magister. And having learned the preparation of the first agens I had only to follow my book word for word, and could not have missed it, though I would.

"The first time," he said, running his hand unflinchingly through the flame of a white-hot burner, "I applied it to quicksilver and transmuted one and a half pounds into pure silver, better than that from any mine. Then, on the 30th of August in that same year, at five o'clock in the evening, I transmuted quicksilver into almost the same amount of gold, better than ordinary gold for it was softer and more malleable."

"But now I possess more than gold. And so today I have a great joy in seeing and beholding the wondrous elements of nature in the vessels. I can begin to impart this knowledge of quintessence to you, boy of a Walusc, for whom I have waited so long."

Then, for many weeks together, Gwynt and I laboured as one, an old man directing a younger, working, fashioning the pair of brass horns which Gwynt had designed.

"This pair, two of a perfect pair like no others, I forge for Midian and my departed bride Ingot," said Gwynt. And in the smithing of the brass, I worked beside my master at the black stone, the white, and then the red to learn each step of the more secret work: to keep the flame steady, to burn away the quicksilver, to waste nothing, to become absorbed in the coagulation and volatization, to pray unceasingly.

And between us, master and novice, there became, as we moved through the dark dissolution, the whitening, the reddening and the quickening, a love of the highest order. Our hearts lightened and found joy in the work.

One day, the 26th of October 1760, after a year of solutions, crystallizings, menstruums, tinctures, smeltings, sublimations and burnings I produced a small amount of gold at the red stone. It happened also to be the day upon which the taintless twin horns of brass were released from the prison of their moulds.

Sweating as a rain-soaked leaf, I closed my eyes tight as I waited before the red stone and smelting flame which burned steadily, a white heat in the crucible. My lips mumbled in prayer. I felt both a tightening and lightness of levitation in my belly as I opened my eyes.

"Oh, Master," I called. "Come, see."

As the old man drew near, the entire corner of the workshop brightened with the glow of the quintessence. It was as if the light of the noon sun was pouring brilliantly through a window. But there was no window. "Oh God," I cried. "Oh God, God, God."

Sudden-like, Gwynt took me at the shoulders and shook me, hard, so that my head jerked forth and back.

"Never forget," the old one warned. "Never, never, forget that there is an inward gold which produces the outward one. And the only purpose of making the outward gold is to mirror the gold inside you, so that you may more perfectly serve the One who made you. Do you understand?"

"I am unworthy," said I, lowering my eyes to the floor.

And then, excitedly: "I was with God, I have seen his love. But He is not here. He is Other."

"You are worthy," said the man. "Born whole, you are. For the gold inside your heart now, having borne witness to this, is more precious and arduous to render than this stuff which you have made, here," he said, pointing to the bright yellow drops of molten ore which flowed like water into a pewter dish from a glass vessel.

"Now that you have perfected the work, the work is with you and within you; you will always have it present, wherever you are on land or on the water. This, boy, is the true purpose, and the rare secret of the science."

Moving to the next table and lifting the second of the cooling trumpets onto the polishing wheel, I listened carefully as Gwynt made me know that the serpent-entwined staff in the book was the staff of Hermes, and that two forces — sulphur and quicksilver — govern the spiritual axis for all beings.

"You must remember that the crucified snake," said the old man, "is a symbol for the fixation of volatile quicksilver — and that this is the first bodying-forth of the spirit. The fixing of quicksilver corresponds to the subjugation of the ever-restless vital force in life, which dissipates itself in useless wishings and imaginings."

Drenched in sweat and unspeakable joy I came smiling to the table where the old man sat on a low stool, his finger on a page of the book.

"Mark this, that the cross upon which the serpent is nailed is the body," the old man smiled in return, "but not as flesh and sense. Rather, it is as an image of the cosmic law — of the motionless cosmic axis. The He which is not Here. Follow?

"And here," he said, "where the fountains spring forth amid the desert, the place from which serpents emerge, this is the state of oneness — love, never-ending," said Gwynt.

"Love never-ending," I repeated.

And then I turned from the old man, one trumpet in each hand, and dipped the lip of each bell into a dish of molten gold. Satisfied the lips were evenly gilded, I fixed the horns in a vice and took a hammer and an awl to stamp on the brass, at a point on each drying lip, the small trademark of the horn-maker — a serpent, coiled like the letter G.

I marked one. And just as I struck the second horn there was gentle thump behind me and the scrape of a stool across the stone floor.

And having turned, I saw the old man, his back nailed to the floor in death, unbreathing, and with heft as a darkened sack of coal.

Speechless, I gasped and clenched my teeth and fists. And the point of the awl pierced my palm. A droplet of my blood fell between the horns. And under the spell of Mercury I watched the rivulets of a dark stain search through the wet gold and wash against the serpentined G, darkening the stamp-mark as the crimson liquid quickened and fixed with the hot-yellow gold.

The room grew black as a mildew-like gust of air swept through. And the old man's eyes burned a steady flame as they stared into the face of God.

I, Bleddyn Wholeborn, now tell these things for they are true.

DE DIVISIONE

Grace Keeper's footsteps made no sound as she crossed the rose-blue arabesque of the Persian carpet.

Fragile, frayed, chopped like kindling for the fire, she drifted through the place as everything once-familiar seemed alien: the perfumed signature of the living-room, the brass horn on the mantle, even the Chinese tea-stand beside the L-shaped sofa in the corner.

Her husband Harry was not there. He had been dead twenty-four hours, although she thought she could hear the soothing sibilations of his trumpet wend their way through the rooms.

Outside, the great city growled at the throbbing break of day.

She rubbed her temples, tired but oddly transcendent. Through the kitchen window, dawn spread rosy fingers across the eastern sky, igniting the green of the garden. Along the brick retaining wall a row of rugged serpentine oaks greeted the morning light. Warming to the sun, birds sang, joyous, oblivious to the tugging pall of her spirits.

The key to Harry's studio, she knew, was stuffed in the underpants of an asexual Oxford Street mannequin at the foot of the stairs one level below. The figurine wore an ill-fitting kaftan and with both hands held a Blessing trumpet — raised almost to its lifeless lips.

As Grace unlocked the door she could smell Harry. And stale cigarettes. The space was cluttered — it was his domain: a pile of vintage Slingerland drums, musical scores, papers, receipts, Quetzalcoatl wood carvings, a wine rack. In the midst of it all was a banged-up baby-grand Steinway. There too, in the corner, was the case which held his custom Hart trumpet, the one she'd stowed away in his absence just a few hours before.

The safe swung open easily. Its contents, unlike the chaos of the room, were neatly stacked. With a hand as wet and cold as a pike fished from a pond, she reached in, fumbled through the topmost documents, contracts, letters, a bag of homegrown, until her fingers stubbed an old package. Then, with a gush of adrenaline she tugged the plastic-wrapped manila envelope and pulled out a finely diagrammed sketch of the legendary twin horns — the Framptons. They were drawn as mirrors of each other, which is truly what they were: brother and sister, darkness and light, weightlessness and heft, innocence and perdition, cinnabar and vitriol, Bethlehem and Golgotha, being and becoming, wonder and sorrow — world within without end.

She had been overcome with an urge to go through her late husband's things, to touch, smell and hold something of him. Now she was gripped with uncertainty. Did she truly want to go deeper,

deeper to where the pages were foxed and vicariously into the secret heart of him? Haltingly, from the same envelope she withdrew a scrap of lined notepaper, scribbled with what she saw was the handwriting of Harry's father, John Holborn. It had been penned, she guessed, in the palliation ward of the Hotel Misericord, Winnipeg, 1972.

It's snowing here, fat flakes heaped on the windowsill. And beyond the frame and glass, face shining like Japan-wax, the cloaked reaper awaits his harvest.

They say I am a troublemaker here in the hospital. I got up, full of tubes, and tried to walk. Flat on my face. Beyond measurable repair I am, and this old carrion has all but failed. My skin is yellow like the sun and I light the room like a crayon: Jonquil Yellow Glossy. Soon I am gone to a place better than the one I leave for you. You know all I have to pass on is that which my own father left. Nothing more. Nor less.

For me young Harry, please, you must consign the ashes to the waters of the Menai Strait, the first and final corner of civilized Europe. Let me lie there and wash the shore. And you, linger there awhile too. Find the sorcery which comes with the jasmine night as you seek to couple together those great gold horns. And see how the music within you has been carried on winds guided by mystic beams.

Here now are the crumpled pages of dogs-breath which were left me, spelling the way in which these twin treasures came to be, through God's good graces. Fathom it, parse it, and become the one you were meant to be. Loving Ta, John.

How was it she'd never seen this? What other things had Harry kept hidden? She loosened more pages tucked inside a blackened binder. These were musty, loose-leafed sheets of onion skin —

yellowed, crumbling pages, painstakingly inscribed in an archaic hand. The delicate India ink was faded almost to oblivion. She felt like a voyeur as she flipped through the brittle sheets, catching phrases here and there — "the Lightning Way" — "a serpent, coiled like the letter G" — "tell these things for they are true."

Grace's eyes ached and blurred. Filling with a nameless dread she flung everything back in the safe and climbed the stairs. Deciphering the yellowed pages would take time. She would make tea, listen to a bit of Harry on the reel-to-reel, snooze until Harry's agent arrived, and return to them later.

A day earlier, when the Cairo police had rapped on the door of the Nile Concorde she had been half asleep and in no mood to be bothered. She thought it was a joke when they said they were so sorry but her husband had drowned. Harry was playing a morbid trick. He would waltz into the hotel room, drunk, in a few minutes. Or he would telephone from some bar or whorehouse in the soukh. But when the officials left, Grace was alone. And Harry did not come. Fear came. Disbelief. A growing agony. Knowledge. She tried to rationalize it: this is only death. This is only life.

She immediately left Cairo for London.

The first available flight was via Larnaca, clasped in a querulous October heat wave. Stepping from the plane for a quick smoke amid the tangle of travellers in the Cypriot air terminal, she sensed that no Mistral wind would rise to cool the blistering tarmac. The fans in the departure lounge were broken. There was no air. Everything closed upon her. She felt a vague apprehension among the sweat-stained horde but had no inkling she was being watched.

The Arab, however, well-composed and distinguished in his fourth decade, saw that she glittered when she walked, more slender, lofty, yet more fully flesh and blood than the photo he'd studied in the briefing file.

As she arrived he collected his tools: sight, taste, smell and touch. From one of the few seats in the building, his dark eyes darted from behind a book. He was dressed in a crisp linen suit and, without his keffiyah, his crown revealed a streak of grey-white through a rich black mane. He pretended, as he watched her, to fumble through pages of the second volume of Foucault's *History of Sexuality: The Use of Pleasure*. He knew so much about her and she knew nothing, could know nothing, unaware how all was weighted.

He consoled a gnawing, carking, conscience with the knowledge that whatever would pass between them was as unstoppable as the infinite ballet of the planets, as inevitable as the interstices between ticks of time. It was as if all had been mapped, charted, indexed: the fates tugging them to the same destination, an alchemy of hope and forgiveness, as deftly as the moon draws the tide.

Outside the terminal there was a low growl as an Iberian 767 rumbled at takeoff.

Down the runway it ambled, it seemed, forever. And then it rose with heft, almost rubbing its belly on the leaf-green palms, the bursting red lilacs, the thin-twisted olives. He cast his eyes through the tinted glass of the terminal window as the aircraft exhaust rippled tremulously above the ancient Cypriot stones.

The Arab watched as everything behind the great bird trembled with tenderness now, as if waiting to be sucked up in its trail, to be made One with Pratt & Whitney. Below darted foxes and hares. Crickets and locusts clung to their blades of grass and firmament. In this powerful exodus it seemed as if the isle itself — a nest of bougainvillea, fat Turks, thin Greeks, pecking chickens, swilling pigs, a trillion and one grains of luminous white sand — was caught up in a single seamless vibration.

And then turning once more to the woman, the Arab wondered what others in that terminal might think of her, Grace Keeper, who seemed so enveloped in her proud fog of melancholy. They would see an exotic with long, dark hair, perhaps a mulatto from Martinique, with skin the colour of blanched olives, big sad eyes, a strong proud nose and flaring nostrils.

Their eyes met only briefly but for him, in that moment, time lost all measure. His brow furrowed at the solemn and mysterious feelings ushering forth as she moved like a mirage across the lounge to the ticket counter, reconfirming her seat on the flight.

He tucked away Foucault and quickly joined the queue a few paces behind her, the widow of the famous musician Harry Holborn whose body had washed up from the Nile at Cairo. As she spoke to the ticket agent he recognized the thick and unmistakable glottis of an American Indian wrapping a tongue around English. It was the same gentle darkness of tongue that connects a Seminole with a Kiowa from the Cimarron River, or a Mandan with a Lakota from where the curving Knife meets the slow and muddy Heart.

"Pick a row number from one to seven," said the ticket clerk as he took his place at front of the queue. "Two," he heard himself say, to his almost immediate regret.

"Ha," said the ticket agent. "You're the first. Everyone picks seven."

Minutes later, as he climbed aboard the aircraft, he saw to his amazement that he had been given the seat next to hers. There was some small commotion over the trumpet case which lay on the floor at her feet. He could neither avoid her nor take his eyes from her as he stuffed his boarding pass into the kangaroo-pouch before him and strapped himself into his seat.

Soon they were airborne. Grace took a glass of juice, a pillow, blanket and blindfold, lowered her chair, tucked up her legs and turned from him without the slightest acknowledgement.

He stole glances at her sleeping figure when he could muster the courage. Stealthily he reclined his seat to her level. Inhaling the scent of her skin over stale perfume, he let himself go. Wantonly, wildly, he imagined they were in the marriage bed on the night of the wedding. His heart sang songs of love and belonging. He turned to her and sighed a thousand sighs, dreaming radiant dreams within dreams.

In no time came the descent into Heathrow.

And as if possessed of an inner clock Grace awoke as the aircraft passed over the lights of Hammersmith and Reigate. It was now she sensed his attentions in the seat beside her. But she looked the other way, and peering below saw only the shade of her own sorrow in the amber glow of arrival. The city lights sprawled, and on the edges of the vast grey city small fires of autumn leaves burned. From the air she imagined she could smell the caustic smoke mixing with the cool fall rains. Grace shuddered, anticipating the temperature change.

From a safe distance he followed her to the luggage pick-up, through immigration, and lost her momentarily in the Heathrow terminal. Then, he caught her silhouette pulling on a black leather jacket as she climbed into a taxi. But under the yellow sodium lights his eyes fought in vain against the darkness. And with any view further obscured by a fine drizzle, she disappeared as the cab pulled away.

Atrash — Deaf One, a name common enough in the Shouff and Bekkaa of Lebanon — turned slowly away. Then he picked up his pace to walk with precision to the telephone kiosk. His handlers were anxious to learn of her arrival.

The minicab from Heathrow cruised through the city's iron heart and on to Hampstead Heath Station. Grace wondered if burnishing her face with blush might add a layer of protection. She needed something: she felt her heart being circumcised with another plunge into uncharted depths.

Deciding vaguely to walk down the Haverstock Hill to her empty house, she asked the cab driver to deliver the luggage ahead. On the pavement beside the tube station she considered her options.

The drizzle turned to a thin hard rain. It splashed and danced and needled her face, running her eyeshadow, dripping coldly from her chin.

"Mind the gap," came the conductor's voice through the grating which covered the black pit of the Northern Line, the cry piercing her and prompting her to avoid home entirely.

She wandered laggardly, shivering, and tugged the collar of her jacket to fend off the chill. She pulled her hair back, shook it, gripped one thumb under the strap of her shoulder bag while wrapping the other around the solid handle of the trumpet case.

Aimlessly, she walked through the diesel fumes and the downpour until she came to rest, drenched, at the all-night café in Regent's Park Road. The Café Manna. She sat down and ordered tea, green dogberry, the leaves of mountain ash.

There was no pattern to her thoughts in this season of colic. All was fractured. All was moving and swirling incomprehensibly. And how curious it was that the rainwater, falling now in cataracts outside the mullioned window, stretched her reflection, pulling it out of pattern as well.

Sifting the tarry tea, she made a whirlpool in the cracked white cup. And lifting her eyes she gazed through the greasy pane. It was as though she was a cup with no bottom, never again to be filled. Now and then down the sides of this cup she could feel her own winnowing: at one moment anger, then numbing.

The Café Manna, she thought. How ironic that her late-night meanderings had driven her to the very spot in North London across from the flat of rooms that she and Harry once shared. Later they had moved just a neighbourhood away to the new, post-modern house. But three years ago they'd lived across the road — right there.

They had loved. Now it was over. She swirled her tea. Ran her hands along the sides of the cracked vessel, considered the beauty, the hazard of its imperfection.

Quite naturally the death notice would not use the word "dead" — the funeral directors would see to that. She envisioned an unknown necrologist scribing away in the dark blasts of night. Invariably he would avoid the active in deference to the obtuse, the passive.

Suddenly, on Saturday, in Cairo, after a virtuoso musical career which spanned more than two decades, the jazz trumpeter Harry

Haydn Holborn, 45. Best known for his matchless range and melodic phrasing, Mr. Holborn spent the latter part of his career seeking to rejoin The Frampton Horns, the world's first pair of valved trumpets, fashioned in Germany in the eighteenth century. The trumpeter, whose recordings garnered many gold and platinum awards, leaves to mourn ...

She imagined the news stories in the foreign or celebrity sections of the newspaper would be more pointed.

The trumpeter Harry Holborn, jazz fusion innovator, was found dead in Egypt yesterday, the victim of an apparent drowning. Mr. Holborn had just completed a series of Cairo concerts. The trumpeter, best known for his dynamic range, modulated tone and innovative phrasing, was a collector of antique instruments. Authorities have not ruled out foul play. An investigation continues.

Soon the telephone in the house would be ringing. She thought of letting loose the furies: the screams, wails and ululations of lament. She looked around for an audience. There was none, save the café waiter. In the end there seemed no words to express her feelings anyway.

She looked at the waiter. Likely Lebanese. He returned her look, guessing that she was eastern European, a gypsy, never imagining what she really was: a full-blood native Indian from the Canadian steppes. Her people were Mandan, having fled north from The Dakotas after the 1781 smallpox epidemic. She spoke her tongue well and proudly, English less confidently.

In the few hours since Holborn's body was found floating weightless in the Nile, deep rings had formed crevices below the hollows of her eyes, the rings dark as the rainwater on the café glass.

On the wall of the Café Manna a dead clock burned the hour. Whatever the time, she could not bring herself to care. She would not marry again, she resolved. Once was enough. She thought too of the moment of her father's passing a decade earlier, the father who lurked around the edges but who was never there.

So, each of the important men in her life had abruptly taken leave — gone to the Grandfathers — leaving her to become the woman with the greasy heart, the one to which no human could cleave without slipping away.

She drifted, recalled Harry's preoccupations, his battles with various liquid anaesthetics, his on-again off-again quest for the missing Frampton horn, how they had first locked eyes in hunger for each other.

Harry had been visiting an old music professor at his alma mater — the old nourishing mother — one of three universities in a forlorn prairie city. It was there she first saw him, on that quaint little campus on the bushy fringe of the Red, a sluggish muddy river that sometimes surprised its sloping banks. There also, in that little oasis of academe, wizened professors retired at age ninety-five while the student newspaper advertised a tour of the local brewery, foot reflexology, a concert of dual-throated Tibetan eunuchs and a hearty menu of counselling: depression and grief resolution, sex abuse and incest, AA, inner-child and Primal Scream, life signs, soul retrieval, women's drumming and the healing hearts of men.

Just graduated with Honours English, Grace had taken a job in the reference section of the music library. She first noticed the egret-like creature with long lanky bones smile at her from behind the stacks. She looked away. She looked up. He looked away.

On it went until she turned her back.

"Sowd and Symbow," crackled the voice as she wheeled around.

The egret had approached and was right there at the reference desk. Evidently the bird had a sniffle in its beak. A twisted holey piece of Kleenex-paper dripped in its palm.

I beg your pardon?"

"Sowd and Symbow — Music and the External World, d'you have it? Zuckerkandl. S'cuse me. Harrumph. Shit."

"No need for language here," Grace admonished. "You could check the author card index. Or the on-line terminal over there."

She busied herself with a stack of periodicals as a growing warmth surprised her belly.

"Do I need a password or can I buy you dinner?" the pitiful creature smiled, eyes round and bloodshot.

Grace resented the mothering instinct which came over her. The planet would long ago have been extinct if it were not for women wiping up after boys, she thought. She sighed. Her stomach butterflied. Her thighs were heavy and light in the same instant.

There was no doubt the fellow had a certain aura, a look of experience, a levity, a wholeness. He owned a handsome face, fine-featured and pale, and there were his greying temples, his eyes which had seen pleasure and pain. He had a story, this much she could tell. She caved. And they had dinner.

A few short weeks later they drove to see her grandmother and brother on the Indian reserve. Under the great canopy of prairie skies, pink cotton clouds wisping the sunset, listening to Roy Orbison and Stompin' Tom Conners on the radio, they cruised blissfully in Harry's rented Buick.

They went all the way past Labret to the Peepeekissee Reserve where Grace lived until her father, a gamekeeper from the Red Pheasant Reserve, took the family to the city. And when father had walked away, a life of the streets and low taverns took her mother. Grace and her brother Joey were sent to school with the Sisters of the Sacred Heart. But they returned each bright and bursting summer to the bantustan and grandmother at Peepeekissee. Those were her best memories, the summers of barefoot freedom, tall prairie grass and sapphire sky, summer streams. If you don't know you are poor, you are wealthy. It was only through hazard and hard work that she had been able to extricate herself from Peepeekissee.

And now she was bringing this man to see her roots, along the great black asphalt ribbon, by rolling fields of sunflower, blue flax, lentils and Canada Number One Hard Red Spring. Harry had wheeled the Buick over the border and into North Dakota so Grace could visit the Piggly-Wiggly for Pringles barbeque chips not sold in the Dominion.

Light My Fire thumped on the radio. "Over there." She pointed to where one winding river flowed from the Missouri into another. "That's where the Knife meets the Heart. Where my people are from."

And from this American pit stop they had twisted back north, one big smile between them, and over the border again to Canada. When they reached Churchbridge, Saskatchewan, she realized they'd travelled too far and told Harry to cut back east toward the reserve which was nestled in a low river valley beside a good trout lake.

"Funny place-names you have around here," said Harry. "Bredenbury. Breed and bury. That about sums it all up doesn't it?"

"Huh," Grace scoffed, almost spitting. "Those are the white man's names. That's why they're so silly. The words don't work. Do you know if we came into Peepeekissee the other way, from the west, you'd go through Big Beaver and then Climax?"

"No kidding," said Harry, impressed, slowing the car to turn around. "Let's go that way then."

"This is faster," Grace smiled. "We're almost there."

Harry wore snakeskin boots and a new cowboy hat for the occasion, the object of great ridicule from Grace.

"You know Harry, with that thing my people might shoot you," she said. "They might even scalp you. They might do worse. They might play a little snooker with your balls. It all depends how big they size up. You have a choice before they cut them off. If they're big, it's lacrosse — that'd be an honour for you. If they're average, it's snooker — white man's game, all hoity-toity. If they're small, well, marbles."

Harry was unflustered.

"Those guys are tough, aren't they?" he said. "But they wouldn't do that."

He paused as they cut down into the valley.

"You know what they call a gay lumberjack?" he smiled behind the wheel.

"What?" she said, eyes narrowing.

"Spruce."

As a waft of burning poplar lingered on the bare breeze, they drove the final stretch along a gravel track to the reserve. Boxed pre-fab houses, clapboard and tarpaper, were peeling their green, white and blue paint. They pulled up to the house and parked on the grass, climbed from the car, stretched, and walked to the rear of the dwelling.

Grace wore a blue skirt, belted at the waist, and walked from the hips. Her gait was unhurried, her back and shoulders motionless.

From the veranda — a plywood stoop — they could hear the old lady, Grannie Keeper, shuffling about indoors. She was humming, speaking to herself. Grace saw Harry's Adam's apple bounce up and down as he swallowed nervously.

She had not brought other men to meet her grandmother and so the old lady knew this was, in a way, for real. There had been others, certainly, of which Grace had spoken during her infrequent visits from the city. Now Grace had made a friend of a white man, a musician, and this gave the old lady concern. There would be pain. But Grannie Keeper knew that through suffering comes new life and awakening. The road to the Great-Grandfathers winds uphill, on twisting unmarked trails in the forest, through water, fire and blood, to the second jack pine on the right.

As the lovers looked through the screen door mesh they saw her ancient spine bend, her bony hands scrubbing the mouth of the stove. "Grandmother," Grace called.

The old woman rose slowly. Turned.

"This is my Grannie Keeper," Grace smiled, giving a nervous bounce on her toes as the old woman stepped forward to greet Holborn who towered in the doorway. The old one, slim and gracious, wore a simple print dress and pink sweater, her grey hair

33

pulled back with a bow. She peeled away her eyeglasses and Holborn noticed her cheekbones, the proud arch of her nose, the smooth blue veins on her weathered skin. The old lady fixed the darkness of her eyes directly into Harry.

"Welcome to my home," she said, motioning for Holborn to sit.

"You're like a big bird," she laughed. "You were a crow in your last life? Or maybe in the next? Lots of crows round here," she said, fetching a blackened tin tea kettle.

The woodstove dominated the centre of the room, the kitchen and bedroom were in the back. There was a single bed, neatly made, a Gideon's New Testament on the nightstand. For a few moments, they sat in silence. The old woman sized Harry up. "You're a man but a boy inside," she said. "Grace says to me you blow a horn?"

Harry spoke to the old woman about his music. She was curious about the force of breath it took to produce a note from his Hart. He promised to play her a tune later, to demonstrate what breath combined with metal could produce.

They ate simply, bread, bean soup, carrots and potato from the garden. "You love my girl?" said the old lady finally.

"Yes," said Harry, squeezing Grace's hand under the table. Grace thought at the time he looked exquisitely uncomfortable — a teenager on his first date.

"Ah-hum," said the old woman, walking to the foot of the stove, sliding open the grate and piling wood inside.

The next morning, the couple walked quietly to the lake and sat together in the sun on the rocks.

"She seems nice," said Harry.

"Mmm. She's tough but kind," agreed Grace. "She's really my only family. And Joey. My other brothers I don't see. Sometimes I wonder what you're doing with me, Harry," she said.

"You're beautiful," he said. "I was taken when I saw you. And there's just such simple life in you. I need that. Sometimes I feel like this rock. I don't feel much of anything. I can feel the music that's all. And I'm glad for that. But there's not much else."

"So what keeps you going?" she asked.

"You," he said, and then paused. "And that elusive fucking horn. Looking for it makes me sad. You make me feel not so sad."

"What makes you so obsessed about that?" she asked. "You're like Heathcliff or something. But really, it's just a piece of brass. Look at it. You have everything you could want. You're pretty famous, you're pretty rich, not too bad-looking."

Harry smiled, leaned back on his elbows and looked around him. The flowers in the grass, crocuses, were white and purple. A pair of wild trumpeter swans glided gracefully onto the lake from behind the tree line.

"I guess the horns are like those swans," said Grace, pointing. "Do you know if one dies her mate never pairs with another? She just stays loyal and lonely, singing their own song — alone."

"Yeah, I suppose it's like that," said Harry. "I'm for sure playing just one song, a one-note wonder. I don't feel I have any choice in the matter somehow. My father gave up looking for the missing horn when he gave up on life. He wanted to find it for me and he failed. When he died, he asked me to find it, to do what he couldn't do. It's like that when you're the only child."

"Let's swim," said Grace, grinning. One jump and she stood.

"Nah."

"Oh come on, Harry!" Grace took his hand, tugged.

"Nah."

Grace began to unbutton her shirt. She reached mischievously for Harry's belt.

"Grace, I don't know how," Harry confessed.

"You don't know how what?"

"To swim."

She rolled her eyes.

"I guess there are still a few things you have to learn about me, Grace."

"I guess," she shrugged, undoing the remaining buttons, shaking loose her black-and-auburn hair, peeling her sweatshirt and jeans. Before long she dove naked into the crystal lake and swam in smooth, strong strokes into deep water.

She could see Harry surveying her from the rock. As she swam away, he rose suddenly and trotted back to the house. Then, Hart in hand, he crept back to the rock and sat, holding the instrument as it glowed in the sun. In a moment, he began to blow gently.

The notes were slow, smooth as silk, and rose from the stillness until Grace could almost see the music skim across the smooth sparkle of the lake as they came to meet her.

She learned later that what she thought was one tune was really two, fused together. At first it was an old tune which came from the horn and floated across the lake, a Dutch prayer of thanksgiving, a tune Harry said he would hum as a child when he was lonely and missed his mamma. She recalled him saying this was deep within him, a song his mother sang. "We gather together to ask the Lord's blessing ...." And as Harry played this melody he began to blend it with a Welsh folk song, the two were so similar he later told her, the tempo identical: Ar Hyd Y Nos — "Joy will come to Thee at morning, life with sunny hope adorning, though sad dreams may give dark warning, all through the night ..."

Grace climbed from the water and Harry wrapped her in his shirt.

"That was pretty, Harry," she said. They sat, arm in arm, shoulder to shoulder, a long time looking across that shimmering lake. The sun warmed them.

"I can hear your heartbeat," she smiled, her head resting on his chest, the sun blasting upon the narrow outcrop of rock beside the lake, the faintest smell of wet pine blowing from the forest floor.

The water glistened like glass, the fir trees swayed and trembled so slightly, Harry's Hart cast a golden reflection as it sat on the rock in the sunshine. He touched her face, stroked her hair. Slowly, she lowered herself to the rock, her firmament, smooth with gold and green moss. The shirt fell away.

And the queen in her became buds and flowers: and she spread herself across the worn aubergine velvet, a couch woven from the forest floor as her jewelled, tapered, experienced hands reached for her lover.

From a safe distance across the room, the Café Manna's chef-du-jour and tea-cup washer, a practised observer of human subtlety, pondered her. But the waiter saw only that which anyone might have seen cast upon her face on that morning — becoming creeping day — in the Café Manna. Her lovely face reflected a drawn, pale look of worry.

Grace fired up a smoke. "The fucking unfairness," she blurted, sudden and loud.

She nodded to the waiter to show that she was not a lunatic, that she recognized his presence. He stood there behind the long grey counter with yellowing postcards of Beirut beaches and the American Grand Tetons pinned to the wallboard. He looked strong, brave, anxious to please, to do well, to be happy, to make the best of things. He refilled her tea and she half-smiled, feigning embarrassment.

He smelled of his labours: sweat, stringy lamb, rosemary, and kebab. The sweat reminded her of her brother, around the kitchen stove, many years ago.

The Lebanese could not see her thoughts. But Grace believed she could plainly enough read his as he stole glances at her and wiped the nearby tables. Here is a lady alone, she imagined him to be thinking. Well-dressed, perhaps with money. He might conjure up her nakedness, the nape of her neck, behind her knees. Yes, the lady was sad, he would think, but he could be her lover and all would be right again with the world. He was firm in the knowledge that in his presence all women would eventually succumb, a lump would rise in their throats, and each would become like the rabbit suddenly staring into the eyes of the stoat.

Grace glanced at her watch. Soon the night would wither as a bruise. And then over the whirling ditch of daybreak would come a new day. She began to scribble her thoughts on sheets of music scores pulled one by one from the carpetbag.

Sometimes she raised her eyes to the old flat across the road, the place now obscured in the greasy drizzle. Who lives there now? she wondered. Could they love as we had loved?

The waiter brought more tea. She lit another cigarette.

Once she thought of sleep but felt too weary and barren to move. Her very bones and sinews sagged with an ache, her heart a dry Sargasso.

Taking a long slow sip from the cold cup, she swallowed, sighed, and put pen to paper.

They say you must keep your routine and fulcrum of life alive. But how can I when I only kept them for you? Everything was for you, Harry. I loved life just because you made it so rich and full and now there is no one left to make jokes with or to talk about Billy Butterfield or Sad Sam Beckett or to talk about the two horns, and of work and of people.

Oh Harry, every hour I find harder to take. What point is there now? I'll go home to our favourite things: the books, the deerskin rattles, the records, the Chinese tea stand. Your old Frampton Horn. I could try and read the books but without you they will give me nothing. I only remember evenings when you caressed and played the horn in happiness and I hummed and sang. And the early days when we whispered words of love and longing together. When we played on the stony shore of the lake and made love happen. I think of these things and I cry.

I feel as if we collected all our wheat into a barn to make bread and beer for the rest of our lives and now the barn has been scorched and we stand on the wind-blown steppes surveying the blackened ruins.

She stumped out the cigarette and peered across the road to the third floor window. She looked beyond the frilled curtains and imagined the room when she and Holborn were there wrapped within each other.

That little room was the gleanings of our life together. All our happiness was over the fire in that room and in those books. Now the fire is gone. The smoke remains. No more perfume. My hands are empty. There was a face on the poster, a horn player offering a blessing with an upturned hand. And there was your trumpet on the mantle. It's impossible, my love, to think that I shall never sit with you again and hear you laugh. That every day for the rest of my life you will be gone.

The waiter returned with her change. The coins clinked politely on the table before her.

Weeks later she burned the scribbles.

And the day she burned them the smoke rose to meet the clouds.

GENERATIO

In the cobbled driveway of Grace and Holborn's Haverstock Hill post-modern, Aaron Kenyon rubbed gnarled fingers on the burnished walnut dash of his car.

The chauffeur, Felix, was curled in the backseat of the Daimler with an apparent case of trapped gas.

"It's likely colitis," Kenyon ruminated without turning his neck from the walloped leather seat stuffed with wool of virgin lambs. "We'll have you in the emergency once we've found Mrs. Holborn and engaged in the appropriate commiseration. Then we'll have you fixed, Felix, right as rain, although you should brace yourself for a rectal probe."

A rake-like skeleton of a man, the chauffeur said nothing as he remained curled in the rear seat, his displeasure for Kenyon as large as the baggy grey uniform which enveloped him.

For several hours now Kenyon had been waiting in the genteel ambience of his V-12 limited edition Daimler Century, a gift from Lord Montagu of Beaulieu. Occasionally he ventured forth and paced heavily along the pavement. But whenever he stepped out into the driveway, the wind rose, tousling the trees. There were thunderclaps and the night rain pelted in sheets.

Kenyon, Harry's long and trusted musical agent, had told Grace he would meet her at the house upon her return to London. But Grace had forgotten.

When her luggage arrived at the house, Kenyon felt relief. But then an hour passed, and Grace did not appear. He rang Heathrow. He waited another hour. He called his answering service. The title he'd ordered from the bookseller in Flask Walk had arrived but no call from Grace. He became anxious, waiting at the gate, at the foot of the drive, in the rain, fretting.

Retreating from the downpour to plop his wide backside onto the passenger seat, Kenyon flicked once more the controls on the dash, trying to blow cold air into the rear to benefit the silently suffering Felix. His thoughts turned momentarily to Harry Holborn. In Harry, Kenyon remembered his proud spine, the cock of his head and handsome face, his unkempt locks. Harry had always been unpredictable and sometimes a complainer, the manager mused. Artistic temperament and all, the aesthetic ones are nearly always fractured somehow.

Now Kenyon's mind raced. What would he say at the eulogy? While cultivated in Canada, Harry had been born in Wales, remained a citizen of the Commonwealth and felt London, and even Oxbridge, to be part of his cultural birthright. Of course the

Canadians had claimed the modestly famous trumpeter as a native son. The Canadians suffer from an inferiority and persecution complex, just like the Welsh, Kenyon mused. And while being Welsh-Canadian might be awfully boring, Harry must have been shockingly surprised to be dead.

Now, where was Grace? As Kenyon quit this reminiscence and fascination with the Daimler's dashboard his mind wandered to the automobile dealer on Regent's Park Road, and he remembered Holborn's old flat. On this asynchronous hunch he left a note at the house, rousted Felix from the rear seat, and had the driver take him to a spot behind the Roundhouse Theatre, a few paces from Holborn's old digs.

As Kenyon, bulbous nose and pancake jowls, stepped from the vehicle there came a beep from the car phone.

"What's this at five in the morning?" he muttered, pushing several buttons on the telephone at once.

"Yes?"

"Aaron?" whispered the disembodied voice on the line. "Let me remind you that both instruments are required to conduct the proper cross-analysis."

"Oh Christ," said Kenyon. "Not that pile of camel dung again. Look, really dear man. Why don't you simply abandon this misadventure? The bloody agency has been trying to turn sand into gold for three thousand years and I don't see how they'll be any farther along with us or without."

"That's where you're wrong, Aaron. We reached the point where we can burn the carbon electrodes from iron, silicone and aluminum, at the plant in Dimona. We're down to 300 second burns, almost there. We need the horns."

"Pah," Kenyon bellowed. "I can stomach no more of this stupidity, Eli."

"You've lost perspective, Aaron. Microchips made with aurum of impossible purity — they'll be the smallest, fastest on the planet. We'll lead the world in breaking the half-micron, the meso-electronic barrier — understand? Now listen. The bookseller in Flask Walk. You'll find your instructions in the Kabala. Wait for a call saying the cookbook is in, got that? Good-bye for now, Aaron. Time is of the essence."

"Don't make me kvetch," said Kenyon. "And don't speak to me of time. I either have none, at my age, or I have all eternity. You want my help? It may take a kalpa."

"What?" whispered the voice.

"A kalpa, Eli. The Buddhists. Length it takes a butterfly wing to wear away an iron cube a mile wide. It's a very long time, friend. Oh, and Eli?" he said. "Best not call me on this line again. I've a sense it's hardly secure."

With this, Kenyon hung up.

Gout and arthritis had swollen and calcified the joints of his feet. And so it took time for the old man to plod the few steps over the bridge in the blackness and rain. Springing his umbrella, he thought of the unsightly brown age spots which recently had appeared on his head, bald but for the tufts of white around his outsize ears.

It took just a few seconds before he spotted her through the grease-stained patina of glass in the all night café. Puffed up by the alacrity of his clairvoyance and the savvy of his intuition, he almost smiled as he rapped a white-haired knuckle on the window. His face an explosion of nerves, he adjusted his coat, tucked the brocade watch chain into his vest pocket, cleared his throat, and pushed through the door.

Grace looked up, seemingly unsurprised to see him.

Kenyon snapped his umbrella shut, shook it at the door, and approached Grace's table with a look of practised commiseration. He stood there, puffing, staunch as Prince Albert, searching for the best words.

"Hello, Aaron," she murmured, breaking the silence. "I'm sorry, I was to meet you, wasn't I?" She then added, straightening, "I just couldn't bear the thought of going straight to the house. How did you find me?"

"Grace," he said in a gravel voice, wearing a kind of collegial charm as he wrapped an uncertain arm around her shoulders. "Mere intuition. Now, come. This is nowhere to pass the night. It's finished. It's over. There's nothing to be done just now. I'll take you home."

She stood and stretched, brushed her leather jacket, and tried to show some courage. Kenyon noticed she wore black: tight jeans, a low-cut t-shirt and embroidered vest — black with red dinosaurs. A small gold crucifix hung around her neck. The case containing Harry Holborn's Hart trumpet was on the floor beside her.

She lifted the case and huddled close to Kenyon. They lingered a moment at the doorway.

Kenyon nudged her gently in the direction of the car but Grace pulled back.

"I'd rather walk," she said stonily. "I don't know why. Harry and I used to walk this way — it's only a few minutes."

Kenyon felt a stab from his calcified and inflamed toe. It travelled up his shin. He tried to ignore it.

"Of course," he said, waving for poor Felix to carry on ahead.

And so they walked slowly over the bridge, past the Roundhouse and toward Chalk Farm and the Belsize Park Road. Now the earth sizzled under a rain which came in torrents, the black sky was a shroud and the pavement heaved brutally.

As they walked beneath the umbrella Kenyon explained that, later in the morning, his office in Soho would be drafting a press statement about the tragic death of Harry Holborn. For the time being, the statement would slake the thirst of the yellow press. Kenyon told her the Egyptians had released the body listing the cause of death as accidental drowning. He wanted her written permission, at an appropriate moment, to make the funeral arrangements and to order an autopsy.

"I won't even ask what happened, dear," he said. "We'll get you home first. You'll be safe and sound. We'll have a hot toddy and you get some rest. I'll look after everything."

They were nearing the gate of Grace and Harry's home. Grace stopped and sunk Kenyon a long look in the eye. "It was no goddamn accident," she said coldly. "Something unnatural happened. I just know it. I can feel it."

Kenyon felt it best to say nothing.

As they took the last few steps toward the gate he glanced at the digs Grace and Harry called home. It had been built in the 1960s and was squeezed between the war-bombed ruins of several row houses: an architect's dream oasis of horizontal space and slabbed concrete.

The couple had dubbed it The Bunker. It was perfect, Grace said, save for the kitchen, which she had altered in stainless steel and lava rock flooring. Elsewhere too she added her own touches, some Navaho relics, Inuit soapstone carvings, and an eclectic panorama of artifacts from Latin America and India: blankets and brass statues. The upper level was two huge bedrooms — a master suite and guest-room. The main floor was a kitchen, dining room and parlour. French doors from the kitchen led to the back garden. On the lower level was a small studio which contained Holborn's wood-panelled office, and a workshop for Grace. Here she wrote poetry and fashioned art objects of feathers, deerskin and wire which she bent over a Bunsen burner — Dreamcatchers — she called them.

Kenyon despised the discontinuity of the place and had never felt comfortable there. But pausing for a moment on the step he decided he should give Grace a hug of the fatherly, one-armed variety, which he did, while shifting the umbrella. And as Grace opened the door to the house Kenyon flicked on the inner light, waving to Felix who was on standby behind the wheel of the car, the engine idling quietly.

"It's all right," she said as Kenyon offered to help her with the trumpet case. "I can manage."

The large oak door closed behind them. Kenyon watched as Grace dumped the luggage, slung her jacket on a hook in the foyer, and started up the stairs. A sudden conviction, in his twenties, that he had developed a malignant tumor had altered Kenyon's perspective on life for the next fifty years. Out of this intense awareness of life's inevitable closure he had forged his own meaning. He thought of this now as he saw how difficult it was for this trembling young woman, and all the green-of-gill, to comprehend the finality, and the terrible banality, of death.

And as he stood unbuttoning his coat in the entranceway of a house infused with the detritus of Holborn's existence, Kenyon furrowed his brow and straightened his tie in the manner of a sado-moneterist. He stepped into the living room across the midnight blue palmettes and red floral spandrels of the Persian. Remembrances of his dead friend once more flitted through his mind.

A famous rock and roll musician, a flutist, had sold the house to the newlyweds. In a way, Kenyon mused, since the property had passed from a player of one genre to another it had been properly Christened, although certainly not by the Vicar of Rome or, for that matter, by the Archbishop of Canterbury. But imagining the Archbishop, Old Red Legs — as the British incarnation of God's final arbiter on earth is sometimes dismissively named — brought a cascade of remembrance. This was because in brighter days, not so long ago, Harry had told Kenyon of a martini-laden encounter with Old Red Legs which happened during a mucky parlour soiree in Belgravia. The event had been hosted by a retired race car driver who had claimed fame by being the first human to cross the Sahara by Land Rover.

"Yep, we had a lot of G, much gravity, me and Red Legs," Kenyon recalled Harry smiling. Harry was fond of entertaining small audiences of friends in The Bunker. And here, where he was King holding court, he would leap about the room like a like a huge dancing bird. As the trumpeter told the story of Red Legs he took pains to mock the bishop's dispeptic duress with consonants: R and L were particularly difficult.

"I dare say I have always found sumpfing of a spiwitual dimension in your particuwar bwand of fusion, Mr. Holborn," the bishop had said. "More nuanced than wock and wole. The Cuban sessions were especially pwophetic. Now tell me, would you descwibe yourself as a wee-ligious man?"

Someone asked Harry how he had replied to the Archbishop on such matters.

"What did I tell him? I told him the truth. When I play sometimes I hear God whisper in the music. But mostly in the silence between the beats."

Then Red Legs said: "May I ask what you fink about whilst you're pwaying?"

"I guess I count the beats. Just like Molloy. You know. Only he counts farts, to pass the time. You remember, Your Grace, Molloy made a kind of nappy with newspapers. He wrapped himself in the *Times Literary Supplement* which is of a never-failing toughness and impermeability."

"Yes. Indeed, Mr. Holborn," chuckled the bishop, having read the existentialists or at least the Irish, at Oxford. "What was it Molloy reported? Four farts evewy fifteen minutes. One evewy four minutes. He said it was extraordinary how mathematics helps one to know oneself. Now tell me, your wips, Mr. Holborn, how are they holding up?"

"My whips?"

"I'd expect your wips to get numb."

"Oh, my wips. Right. The embouchure. You get used to it. So long as you're blowing air from the proper end of the instrument."

"Quite," Old Red Legs replied. "Well, as it says in the Book of Wook, you weep what you sow. And I should take a whiff of pneuma any way I can get it. At any wate love-ly to have met a jazz twumpetah who's wedd Molloy. How awfully unusual."

Kenyon removed his coat, tossed it on a chair, took a seat in the parlour. And in that interval he further considered the life of the late Harry Haydn Holborn, his superb musical gift, his hard-won fortune which had profited them both, his inexplicable end. And while he thought he knew Harry well, and John, his long-dead father, he could not just then recall how Harry received the middle name Haydn.

Harry had come from a long line of Welsh musicians and miscreants. But it was during his youth in Canada, on the bright and smacking prairielands that musical talent flourished in him like fruit for a good wine. The new world had sharpened in him a predisposed genius. There was Harry's grandfather, he recalled, a composer of minor merit who once served as organist in the local non-conformist chapel at Gornhaffan. And it may have been that the grandfather also had a Haydn in there somewhere.

Lighting a cigar Kenyon squinted through the smoke across the expanse of the parlour to the mantlepiece and upon Harry's most fabulous and beloved prize — the Frampton Right trumpet. His joy stick, Harry called it. How badly Harry wanted to unite those twin horns, the Framptons Left and Right, brother and sister.

And now he pictured the proud long-legged Grace: a Canadian Indian, university educated, Holborn's wife, lover and companion. She was an intelligent woman, not confident in the European class perhaps; but this was understandable. She had been torn away from her own primal roots and tongue. She was landless. Her voice was not, and never could be, her own. Likewise, Holborn had lived in a similar cultural flux, having been born in the Old World but raised in the New and then repatriated. His roots were in one place, his flowers grew in another.

"Grace?" Kenyon called upstairs. "Spike Hardman should be back by now. Do you know which hotel?"

No answer.

Kenyon leaned forward in the chair and focused his energy on his arms. Shouldn't trust that young bastard Hardman he thought to himself, or any drummer for that matter. And then pushing up on his aging frame, he rose. A vein in his forehead bulged.

He pictured Harry that last night in Cairo, floating in the putrid Nile. He tried not to think of it. The hooded geist with the scythe will call me soon enough, he thought. Who was to have known the Cairo concerts would be Holborn's swan song? It struck him that the trumpeter's ghost must be tired by now, dividing itself like a cancerous cell to make all the requisite visitations to those most deserving.

To be sure, Holborn had been positively self-absorbed and had collapsed into something of a black hole in the past few months despite the odd moment of joy Grace brought him. But even the marriage was no longer sufficient, for either of them really. It was as if the trumpeter's peripheral vision had narrowed. And hurtling forward in mere linearity he was preoccupied within a mission far beyond his control.

Still, it was the man's laughter and broad smile that caught Kenyon's remembrance as Grace reappeared in the room. She'd changed into a long white t-shirt with Van Gogh yellow flowers and had washed her face.

Kenyon rose and poured a couple of brandies. He noted the hour and suggested to Grace that she soon take to bed. She gave Kenyon a key, saying he should come and go as he pleased in the next few days. Then they sat quietly for awhile until she permitted herself just one small bit of emotion at the bottom of the drink.

"Oh, Aaron," she said. "He's gone. Harry's really, really gone."

"Yes," Kenyon shrugged. At a loss for words he drew some papers from his breast pocket. "Look, Grace. There's no appropriate time for this. But would you sign this? It approves a postmortem. I've arranged for a suitable surgeon in Canada to look after it. You can't trust the Egyptians with such things you know. It'll be all right."

Grace looked at him, anger rising now. "It will, eh?" she said, the bile rising. "You think so? Will it really be all right? Jesus, Aaron. Give it up."

Kenyon was struck dumb by her tone.

Grace rubbed her eyes and cast a good long look at Aaron Kenyon. He was puffed up with the methane of self-importance. Harry had once whispered to her that the old manager suffered from a rare psychiatric disorder, a complex hypochondria known as Munchausen Syndrome. At the depths of his sickness, he would routinely present himself at various Harley Street surgeries complaining of the most sophisticated physical and mental agonies. At length he would tell the practitioners the tortured minutiae of the invasive symptoms — yet all subsequent tests proved negative — there was nothing in him. The doctors conferred determining that Kenyon pursued this elaborate hoax to elicit attention and bask in the nuances of another's concern. Later, the disease evolved into Munchausen Syndrome-By-Proxy: He began to suspect the medical community was on to him and thus took to presenting a thin but healthy chauffeur to the bewildered specialists, all the while clucking about how sick was poor Felix.

His psychiatric condition, which enjoyed periods of remission, did not impair his ability to manage Lord Inc., his record business. Nor did it weaken his hold on the prize stallion in his stable — Holborn. He managed efficiently enough and with an iron fist.

Grace swiftly signed the document and as she rose to leave, she narrowed her eyes at Kenyon: "Spike's at the Coburg Hotel," she said. "Oh, and Aaron," she said. "I don't want to see anybody before the funeral. And it should be kept a private service."

It was now half past five in the morning. Kenyon felt tired, but only in the existential sense. And so, after Grace went to bed, he began to explore the house on Haverstock Hill. He leafed through a few of Harry's books. He unplugged the telephone that would soon ring without ceasing. He played a bit of Harry's latest studio work on the reel-to-reel machine and finally settled down to browse through Georg Kinsky's *A History of Music in Pictures*.

They were ultimately an unlikely pair, Grace and Harry, he thought. But a fusion had taken place between them, and what is fused cannot be pulled apart. Theirs had been a grand passion as they crept within each other's cells: into the structures, the amino acids. By all appearances, she was fine-featured and intelligent, reputed to be a gifted maker of jewelry, a poetess, a bon vivant. He had spotted the couple a few weeks earlier walking down the King's Road. It was a Saturday afternoon. There was an undeniable circuitry between them. She was flirting in the American way — barbed wire in her knickers and a brick in her carpetbag — poking Holborn in the ribs, all smiles. Harry seemed blissful, happy as he hadn't been in years, his step light, his deep-set eyes glistening through the coming wrinkles. The wrinkles were no doubt the work of those wickedly fat French cigarettes that had begun to impede slightly his breathing on the horn. Still, Harry had the tone. And the breath. Until he could enjoy both Framptons, Harry said, he would alternate between the French horn and the Cor Anglais.

"The Cor! Get me the Cor!" the drink-sodden jazzman would say, appreciating the deep, soft, tonality of the instrument. But touching as the Cor could be, mellow and full-bodied as it was, it was no Frampton. And yet it may have been the next best thing. When he moved over three and a half octaves on the Cor, Harry would become lost. His eyes would grow mad with red rage. They would strain to focus as though frantic to uncover that missing, transcendent element offered by the Frampton, the whereabouts of which there were but few clues. It was like searching for a diamond, as Harry would say in a Canadianism, in a box of Red River porridge.

For her part, sometime into the second year of their marriage, Grace had discovered the theatre, often going alone or sometimes with Holborn's drummer, Spike Hardman. She made new friends in literary circles. And though her romance with Holborn was novel and extraordinary, there may have been other men for all anyone knew, for she was young and saw herself as highly desirable. Hardman had taken a subtle interest in Grace. Perhaps Holborn had noticed. Perhaps a sense of mistrust had crept into the relationship, perhaps a green venom had secreted from the trumpeter's morbid psyche, soiling the squalid fabric of his thoughts and driving him to anaesthesia.

Or perhaps it was that Holborn grew more frantic with the seeming futility of his quest. With the increasingly loud tick of time, the compulsion only grew: a swelling obsession like a child tonguing a loose tooth, the fullness of the pain, the labial exploration of it all. Indeed the trumpeter was, Kenyon ruminated, literally hung on the horns of a dilemma, since it was his father's dying instruction that the twins be reunited. That was nearly twenty-five years ago.

Kenyon drew a sharp breath as he recalled the astonishment which rang through him in 1950 when John Holborn called him to his Montreal bedroom where, under the bed in a battered grey cornet case, he'd hoarded the lone and silvery-gold Frampton Right. Proudly, John Holborn whispered, "It's just as I told you, Aaron, here it is" — it had been in the family for years, carted across the Atlantic when Harry's family had emigrated. Of course, he recalled, it was not more than a few weeks after arriving in Canada that Harry's mother, large, cool as a rhinoceros, full of toxaemia, died with the spring flowers giving birth to stillborn twins. Within a couple of years John Holborn and his young son Harry moved west to the bright and blasting prairie lands. Soon, the father pining for family, for the horns, for treasures lost, struck a friendship with the bottle.

Kenyon, of course, knew of the twin horns' great provenance. He knew that together they were a perfect red-brass pair made about 1760 by the greatly celebrated Gwynt, successor to the master trumpet-maker Hofhausen. Certainly the pair, with opposing side-mounted valves, were of German origin even if the endowment for their production remained a mystery. One musicologist had conjectured that the horns, left and right, had been designed for classical duets, perfectly symmetrical in every way, the players standing on opposite ends of the stage to produce a stereophonic effect.

Who played them in 1760 and afterward was also unknown, although they had surely graced many of the houses of the European monarchies. About the time of Napoleon's campaign in Egypt the horns were separated, and still later one of them — it was said — briefly surfaced in the band of the Frampton-Upon-Severn Volunteers. Hence the Anglicized name. Harry had found significance in the fact that the fashioner of the horns had given them a small master crook, so that B-flat could be played both basso and alto. Moreover, they were the first brass instruments to be adorned with triple side-mounted Viennese valves. This gave them access to the full chromatic scale over nearly three octaves. Unbelievable really.

Harry had proudly kept that Frampton Right near his heart, spending much time and large sums of money searching for its missing mate. Together, the gilt pair would fetch a small fortune at auction, but it wasn't the commercial value of the instruments which motivated him. It was to appease his ear. Holborn wanted to hear the Framptons in unison, in digital stereo, on thirty-two recording tracks. Moreover, it was Harry's birthright and duty to unite the twins since it was clear the old man, who died a bitter drunken wreck, had failed.

But now Harry had failed as well. Lately, as Kenyon thought about it, Harry had begun to seriously acquaint himself with his father's alcoholic undoing, almost as if he had also given up the search for the twin. The trumpeter even mimicked his father in having cut his prematurely grey hair. It was now close-cropped and he'd grown a salt-pepper beard which accented the crevices of midlife etched around his deep, dark eyes.

When he wasn't seeking oblivion Holborn would work quietly in his studio, lay the odd licking on his horn, and rummage antiquarian book and music shops. Once a year he insisted on a fortnight trip into the Canadian wilds for solitude and bloodsport. This usually occurred in the company of Hardman or Grace's aboriginal brother. The trumpeter then would return to England

and invoke the wrath of Customs officials with frozen meat and a quantity of smelly dried leaves, culled from mulberry bushes to steep into a vapid tea. He claimed the Labrador Tea helped sustain an erection, gaining it admittance into the UK as a herbal-medicinal compound.

To Grace's disappointment Harry had come to scorn the society life which, as Kenyon could attest, the trumpeter had basked in as a younger celebrity.

"Horny bugger," Kenyon once said to him, years ago, half in jest.

"Can I use the word horny on television?" Harry had wondered.

"Dear boy," Kenyon had replied. "I cannot tell you precisely when horny crossed the Rubicon from rude slang to happy colloquialism. I am, however, certain that the term has a distinguished history. Horn may be traced to the Latin cornu. The proto-Germanic horna bloomed in Old English and was further reified to describe the hard protuberances growing from the head of ungulate mammals. There was a poet, Lowell, I believe, who, in the 1840s, extolled the virtues of Welsh non-Conformism and the Christian work ethic when he wrote: 'Blessed are the horny hands of toil' So, hold fast your protuberance and bless your horny hands."

Holborn had laughed loudly at this. Kenyon wondered: had it really been twenty years?

The old man padded across the soft Persian in the parlour to examine four ebony and ivory elephants on the bookcase. He had removed his shoes and the warm carpet was a welcome relief for his throbbing left toe. A slim volume hardback, pushed horizontally on the bookshelves caught his eye. Handwritten, it was a volume of poetry. He recognized the hand of Grace.

Well, he thought, after giving it a furtive glance, at least it isn't like the maunderings of other young sex addicts, those tedious individuals who connect everything to the groin to the scanting of the heart and soul.

His eyes moved across the page:

The waters join
Where The Knife meets The Heart
And I imagine a young man
Jumping off the pyramid banks
Bare limbs slicing the indigo
Waters of October.
Somewhere from the limestone cliff
Of words, he dives an obtuse angle
Into a time long ago,
A season of serpents, a mass
Of single-celled exuberance, cleaved by the body's
Perfect arc.
And everywhere suddenly there is generosity and sufficiency,
A stage and footlights arisen out of nothing.
And this, my sweet,
Is the Magic of sex.
Although truly we were just two tiny people,
human beings,
On a rock together at the edge of the world.

Kenyon had heard snippets of her poetry before, but never so intimately. He imagined she would have been attracted to the slightly younger men, the ones with tight, muscular thighs: dancers and actors. Yet beyond the carnal machine, behind the veracity of these words which, as he read onward, described one congress after another, there was an engaging multivalence about this young woman. Perhaps it was the survival instinct, an ancient vitality in her genes, but there was something of the earth about her — her people having crossed the Bering Straits thousands of years ago and persevered, more or less, until now.

He resolved to do for her what he could.

Kenyon collapsed in a chair for a few minutes to compose himself with random cogitations. He thought about losing weight.

The Scarsdale, perhaps. Running a hand over his hairless dome he cursed God for cutting down the trumpeter in the prime of life. This showed a moral apathy on the part of the Prime Mover. No, nothing, thought Kenyon. No God here. Nada. If God is anywhere God tends toward entropy. Only a vengeful God could have masterminded this chaotic mud heap of a world, torn by war, famine, pestilence and greed, the starvations of little nippers in Calcutta and piccaninnies in Rwanda. The Great Orchestrator, having abandoned his podium, is letting us wind down into massive disorganization. In condemning man to freedom, God demands too much of him.

Kenyon rose from the chair. Drawn by memory, or perhaps instinct, he pulled a slim volume of Dylan Thomas from Harry's bookshelf. It fell open, and he read:

> *Green and golden*
> *I was huntsman and herdsman*
> *The cows sang unto my horn.*

A queer and lonely feeling now came over Aaron Kenyon that night in mid-October. And though he could not in that instant see him, he could surely feel the tall, flinty, bird-like presence of Harry Holborn as the geist flew in, and then out, of the room.

SUBIETCTUM
CHIMICUM

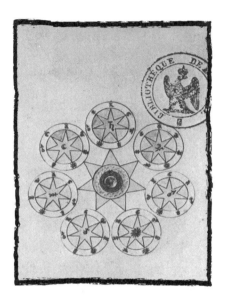

The concurrent bleat of a bedside telephone and xylophone clang of milkbottles at the window brought morning chaos to Room 222 of the Coburg Hotel.

Spike Hardman, rising naked from the quasi-coma of hangover, jet-lag, and a late night horizontal jog with a young Australian from Earl's Court, rolled over in the tangled sheets and tenderly attached his ear to the telephone receiver.

"Hey Spike! Remember the Alamo?" came a jolting Anglo-Caribbean voice from the house telephone in the lobby. "How about the Orion?"

"What?" whispered a gravel-toned Hardman. "What time is it? Who's this?"

"It's Jermaine Kidder," said the voice which proved far too bright and cheerful for the hour. "Listen, mate, remember, we played together during the jam sessions at the Orion a few years back. Ah, you do remember. Of course you do. Well it's me. Jermaine. How are things? I'm just downstairs. I was wondering if I might see you? Right now."

"Now," Hardman said flatly, staring queasily at the tawny-coloured pastels and lillies on the wallpaper of 222. "You mean, like, right now...at this moment?"

"Exactly," said Kidder.

The call to Holborn's drummer was the 1,546th action executed that morning by young Jermaine Kidder, man of exquisite promise and precision who'd come to the Secret Intelligence Service six years earlier by way of Trinidad, Brixton, Sherbourne and Cambridge.

That morning, Kidder had watched the London sunrise from the window of his highrise flat. He then checked his electronic mail. Just four messages. He had scanned yesterday's Parliamentary Hansard to confirm the government had given final reading to amendments of the Communication Act allowing GCHQ new freedom to access encryption codes for digital cellular telephones.

Kidder practised some stick-work on a drum pad for ten minutes, made toast with marmalade and washed it down with orange juice and a cigarette. He left the flat and walked down the stairs for a little morning exercise.

Stepping into the street he walked fifteen minutes to Vauxhall Close, entering a gray steel and concrete building with dark glass windows. Walking down a narrow corridor on the ninth floor he stopped at his office, a closet with a headset and video screen. He unlocked his briefcase and then locked it again while he went to the coffee machine for a cup of vanilla hazelnut creme with extra sugar. Returning to his desk he checked his electronic mail again:

two messages, one telling him his great aunt had died and another instructing him to initiate a legal entry into the deceased Harry Holborn's residence to determine the whereabouts of a particular antique musical instrument. At 08:30 he logged on and attended his dead auntie's cyber-funeral, honoured to be one of the virtual pallbearers.

A quick call to the OpsCentre revealed that Spike Hardman had arrived the previous night on a British Airways flight from Cairo. Again logging on, he quickly hacked into the computer system of Sabre, the worldwide travel registry, and found reservations for an S. Hardman at the Coburg. Kidder then secured his office and cabbed to the hotel, charging the fare to the Home Office.

It had taken some gentle coaxing but the pair met in the hotel restaurant, Kidder alert to his task, Hardman attentive to the mastication of his bacon and pancakes. A fork rang as it grazed the syrup bottle and two pairs of lips sucked at the rims of coffee cups. Kidder explained to a foggy, dishevelled Hardman his need — very discreetly, understand — to verify the provenance of Holborn's Frampton for a serious antique dealer. Hardman accepted the argument that Grace might want to dispose of the horn, but remained reluctant. He relented when Kidder reminded him that he once introduced Hardman to a lonely balance-beam gymnast from Hungary — and her twin.

An agreement reached, the two stickmen engaged in a friendly tapping contest — cutlery on china — and then parted an hour later. On his way back to the office Kidder stopped at a shop which specialized in clerical vestments.

Around this same time, Aaron Kenyon was chauffeured to his Soho offices where he arranged Harry Holborn's overseas funeral, to be held the following week, the interment following a private autopsy by a Canadian pathologist.

The headquarters for Kenyon's flagship recording label, Lord Records, was functional rather than opulent. He employed a small staff of seven including a marketing director, a public relations chief, three sales agents, a logistics coordinator and a secretary.

"No calls from Vestal Records wanting to take us over this week?" Kenyon grimaced to his secretary. This was a standing joke, since there had been speculation that Sir Richard Brampton of Vestal Records would make a pitch to purchase the select stable of artists who were signed to Lord. "Lord and Vestal: an immaculate conception?" suggested one of the London entertainment pundits. The publicity had a positive effect. Lord's stock had risen.

"No, nothing like that, only a salesclerk has been calling you, Aaron," said the secretary. "Every half hour. From that bookstore on Flask Walk. The cookbook you ordered is in."

"I don't recall ordering any such book," said Kenyon as he took the next hour to sort through his messages. There were stacks of mail, letters of condolence, and postcards beginning to arrive as news reached the world of Harry Holborn's demise. To his secretary Kenyon dictated a press statement, saying only that the family wished for privacy.

He then called for Felix to bring around the Daimler.

It was a quarter of an hour later when the smooth valves and pistons of the sedan's high performance power-unit motored through the gate and into the cobblestone drive of The Bunker. Kenyon eased from the car, banged on the large ornamental knockers of the front door and received no response. He let himself in, called out, but The Bunker was silent.

He made himself as comfortable as possible, placed a few calls, and waited until he heard a stirring upstairs.

Grace emerged at half past twelve in dressing gown, hair in a fluffy towel, deep brown rings now evident along the zygomatic arch of the eyes. She would see no one, Grace said, giving strict instructions the telephone was to remain off the hook.

Kenyon nodded absently.

"Where's Spike?" she demanded. "I thought he was coming with you."

"Sleeping it off, I reckon," replied Kenyon. "I left a message at The Coburg saying we'd be here. He'll be along soon I expect."

The flowers began to arrive. Red roses drifted in, and then yellow magnolias, lillies, starburst daisies, members of the orchid family and lady's slipper — all were piled in the parlour, where Grace occupied herself with moving them into vases. The peppery smell of spring filled the room.

"Life is short isn't it Aaron?" she said at one point, unwrapping a small paper package containing two identical red roses. The card read, in handwriting she did not recognize, simply, The Manna. How curious. And kind.

"Indeed," Kenyon ventured. "Short."

"And delicate," Grace continued. "But when you're dead, you're dead for a very long time."

Kenyon now noticed that she had changed since the night before. Her hair was tied up in a tail and she wore no make-up, no jewelry, no sari or robes of kunte cloth, only a pair of black tights and a bulky cream sweater which hung below her bottom.

Shivering, she asked Kenyon to light the fire. He struggled to do so, noticing she had changed in more than subtle nuance in the days since he had last really spoken with her in Egypt, before Harry was found on the shoals of the scum-licked Nile. As he rose from the fire, the clouds outside parted and a shaft of sunlight filled the room. And in that cruel glow Kenyon saw every crevice and crinkle on her still youthful face. She had grown older and gentler. Gone was the aggressive, sexually confident woman who believed so intently in the powers of her own will. Perhaps she was more beautiful than ever.

Not much more than a week earlier the group, nine players and their small entourage, had arrived in the Mideast. Kenyon had joined them there briefly. The junket was to be part vacation, part work, including three concert nights at Giza. Between concerts, Holborn intended to follow up some leads in his quest for the lost Frampton Left. Kenyon considered the search a futile, but harmless, way for Holborn to pass the time in Cairo.

Since the death of his father, Holborn had sifted the family legend that the twins had been parted during the Napoleonic campaign in Egypt. Usually his detective work was conducted from The Bunker by mail or telephone, but this time he planned to visit a Cairo academic, a man who had once corresponded with his father and claimed some knowledge of an old horn.

"It'll probably lead to nothing," Holborn said. "But do you know of many Arabs who follow the trumpet? That should be interesting in itself."

As Kenyon lost himself in these recollections, Grace fiddled with the coffee-maker.

"Do you take milk?"

"One lump."

She took long strides to a wooden cupboard in the corner, but paused as if she had suddenly forgotten her task. From the cool surface of the refrigerator, she peeled a snapshot of herself and Harry. It showed them, Kenyon could see, somewhere in Canada, entwined and happy. She placed the photo on the Chinese tea-stand between the L-shaped chesterfield and chair. Then, returning to the kitchen, she removed the elastic from her pony tail, and gave her long, red-tinged mane a shake. From a plastic case she seized scissors and a hand mirror and to Kenyon's great surprise began shearing her hair. Strands fell in huge wet locks as tears rolled silently down her face.

"What are you doing?" he asked.

"What does it look like?"

"Well, I can see. But why?"

"I need to do something," she said. "There has to be something I can do. And yet there is nothing to do. Strange isn't it? When someone dies. There's nothing to do."

"Well, we can try and get on. Eventually," said Kenyon. "Don't you think that's a bit, I don't know, dramatic?"

"It's symbolic," she said.

"Well, my dear, I don't know quite how to say this. But really, you don't seem ready to enter the convent."

"Oh God, Aaron," she suddenly cried. "I don't know. I just knew this was going to happen. It's the goddamn Pharaoh's curse or something stupid. It's so meaningless. Those bloody horns. He was obsessed. And now he's gone. There's so much left undone."

"Just start from the beginning," Kenyon soothed. "Tell me what happened. What you know. All the details. Everything."

Grace wanted to speak, to let the whole bloody substance of the Egyptian trip come pouring out, but she was unsure how much to tell Kenyon.

"Aaron," she asked. "Do you know anything about alchemy?"

"Alchemy?" he said, eyes glazing in autodidactic pleasure. "The craft of transmuting dross metals into gold. Practised by Paracelsus, Simon Magus and Robert Fludd. I think some Russian up in Cambridge, I forget his name, actually succeeded in converting something to something. That was back in the thirties. Why?"

"No special reason," said Grace. "Just wondering, really. No one got rich?"

"I don't think that was the idea somehow," he said. "The transmutation is symbolic. The search for the Prime Material in the universe. Rectified Aqua Vitae. Mineral Menstruums. Stinking Menstruums. Antimony. Nitre. Most of it seems to have been a ruse, promulgated by charlatans. But what about Cairo? I feel badly I was called away before the concerts got underway."

"Right," said Grace. "Well, word of Harry's music travelled fast. By the end of the second concert at Giza the Bedouins were riding in from the desert to listen. You could see them from the back of the stage, outlined against the horizon, watching. Silently watching. On the third night they staked their camels, came down, and danced in their robes in front of the Sphinx.

"He played so well — outside himself, beyond himself," she said.

"It was surprising because just a couple of days earlier he'd been complaining that he wasn't at the top of his game. There was a minor brouhaha between Harry and Spike during pre-concert sound checks, but that was nothing. He said his ears were ringing. He felt restless. Do you know he was actually talking to himself? And he kept dashing in and out of the hotel.

"It was in the evening, late, after the final gig, he just took off. Said he'd see us back at the hotel. Sometime in the week before he'd bumped into a fellow, an Arab taximan, who offered some vague lead on the other Frampton. He'd planned all along to visit that professor at the university in Cairo. He did, I think, but I don't know the details. And I don't know if the taximan was a coincidence. Harry seemed a little unsure about him, like something was not quite right. They met near a church, Coptic I think, a day or so before."

The gist of this information Kenyon already possessed, through his contacts in Egypt. The setting in Cairo, a short series of dazzling night concerts against the glorious floodlit backdrop of the pyramids, was indeed, according to Kenyon's informants, spectacular.

For a fusion player, Harry had an extraordinarily loud band, as loud as any modern amplified band, although he was no longer interested in large audiences. The rhythm section and percussion was as good as any jazz contingent in the world — the players were hot, rumbling, tight, spacial, primitive.

Holborn felt particularly lucky to have the effervescent, gap-toothed, spindly-legged Spike Hardman keeping time on drums. From Alabama, Hardman was as naturally torrid and luxuriant as a magnolia blossom. He invariably drooled spittle on the stage while his drumsticks roamed the drum skins like slow cream. Hardman refused to use electronic drumheads. He preferred an ancient set of single-headed fibreglass shells popularized by the Benzedrine and hashish-addled rockers of the early 1970s. The horn-shaped drums — standing close you could feel the breath of air swoosh from under each skin — these were his beloved. But the single drumheads forced him to perform his 'circumcision ceremony' for each performance: he ran small strips of gaffers' tape around each head, especially the larger skins to protect against over-ring, and he ripped them off, painfully it seemed, when the performance had ended.

Hardman said he required the tactile reply of each beat as it returned to his fingers from the heads of his vintage drums. Complementing this basic kit were the African drums of natural wood and animal skins: the ngoma, the murumba, kalengo, babba ganga, atumpan, duono, embuto, mujaguso. Drums of all sizes and shapes, drums with elephant-ear membranes and those that imitated the snarl of a leopard or the cry of a bird.

And Harry's horn, amplified against the pulsing rogations of the band, seemed to swoop and soar, to rise, then peter and fall. He could make it sound as though it was a freight train, an electric guitar, a drum, a mouse, a human voice.

One night during their hey-day years ago the band drew a hundred-thousand in a Roman amphitheatre. Few would forget that fetid night. In the midst of a sudden power failure the crowd of disappointed Italians, fire and ice coarsing their blood, began to stir and then riot. The band fled the stage scant seconds before the mob could tear them lick from limb.

Holborn decided then and there that the self-awareness he wanted to inspire through his music — money was a secondary motivation now — was lost on such massive, populist audiences.

"They were so keyed up that it was impossible to do much with them," Harry lamented. "When we went out to play we'd have to thrash around for thirty minutes before we could get ten minutes of real attention in order to do something. And then we'd have to thrash away for another twenty minutes so everyone could go home thinking they'd really got their money's worth."

After that original band folded, Holborn tried to resurrect a solo career, pursuing intimate studio sessions with those driven hard enough to the heart of the music to pay mindful attention. From a financial point of view Kenyon considered these studio forays a catastrophe, although he was intrigued by the essential questions they raised about the anatomy of music.

"Is there something in the sound itself which is remarkable or mystical?" Harry once asked Kenyon. "Is it the soul of the music or the player that touches the listener?"

Holborn said he had emerged from the crucible and could feel the transcendent spirit of Indian ragas flowing through him. But this was only in retrospect. "It's not like one is always aware of a transformation while transfixed within modality and tone," he said. "But it would be a good thing if one could be." Indeed, Kenyon believed Holborn's haunting style — the pleading, coaxing, and begging of the notes from his horn — was his attempt to discover his own essential nature, his own proper voice in the world.

To set up the Egyptian concerts the old impresario had travelled first to Tel Aviv and Jerusalem. Then, switching passports at Larnaca since the Egyptians are not keen to find Israeli stamps in one's documents, he zig-zagged to Cairo to finalize the contract for the Giza concerts.

The old man arranged to have sixteen tons of amplification, strategic lighting, and state-of-the-art recording equipment flown — again via Cyprus — to Egypt. The equipment would push 80,000 watts, enough for an outdoor venue. He then supervised the deployment of the stage before the Giza pyramids, greasing many sweaty palms to slip through the bureaucratic red tape. Finally, he promised the Egyptians that Holborn would record one number with a local pop-singing idol. For this, the Egyptians agreed to let Holborn perform and record within the hollow and sacred confines of the Great Pyramid Cheops. Satisfied that everything was in place, Kenyon returned to Israel and then London.

Some days prior to Giza, Grace and Harry had arrived in Jerusalem to meet with Kenyon, who knew the country, for a brief reconnoitre of the Holy Land.

It was Grace's second coming to the Mideast, for she and Holborn had been there on a short excursion some time earlier. Holborn, having once had an upsetting experience there, insisted upon staying in Arab East Jerusalem because he could not stomach gefilte fish for breakfast. He also insisted on a visit to the ancient city of Jericho — a requisite tour stop for any horn-man, Kenyon supposed. Here, though, Holborn met with disappointment: a few ragged Arab children playing football between burnt-out autos. What Harry had expected Kenyon was not sure. For some reason Holborn also drove — recklessly, Kenyon thought — through the Conquered Territories and up the coast to Akko, or Jean D'Arc as the place sometimes is known, to see the Crusader fortress.

"Was it the Knights Hospitallers or the Templars who held this fort?" Harry asked Kenyon.

"Dear man," Kenyon replied, shifting his weight from his left foot to his right. "This is a mere codicil of history, the precise nature of which I am at a powerful loss to remember. I can tell you it was a prison at one time for Baha'u'llah. The British also found it convenient to impound the Irgun at this location and hanged a few of them here in the 1940s. I believe it is a mental hospital at present."

The sky over the Mediterranean was dark with clouds so they did not linger. But further inland a brilliant sun emerged and licked their bones as they took a long detour on their return to Jerusalem, passing the Horns of Hattin and stopping near the Dead Sea. Here they watched a team of archeologists trample and scrape the ancient city of the Essenes.

"Can you imagine, Harry," Kenyon said, looking down the road toward Masada, "what it would have been like if Moses had turned left instead of right when he came down the mountain?"

"Sure," said Holborn, who was intrigued to learn the ancient sectaries engaged in metallurgy. "The Jews would've had the oil and the Arabs would've had the sand."

Holborn later was particularly moved, however, by the ambience of Jerusalem's Old City. He was profoundly meditative as they walked the Via Dolorosa and the underground flagstone street below a Greek Orthodox Church. This, legend said, was where Jesus and other prisoners of the day were stashed awaiting crucifixion, or worse.

Kenyon's thoughts were suddenly pulled from these pleonastic events, as Grace, half-way through her third coffee, began to tell him something about the Cairo trip that he did not know: that around noon on the first day of the Giza concerts she enjoyed a private tour of the pyramids.

"I wanted to see the Sphinx in daylight," she said. "So I went. Harry and Spike were going off somewhere in Cairo — sampling a bottle of Arak probably."

Despite the tourist alert — there was invariably a war or the threat of extremist terror — Grace had taken a taxi into the slum-strewn suburbs of southern Cairo, to the modest home of a guide whose name, of the all the possible names of guides who navigate the labyrinthine neighbourhoods of the Nile, was Moses.

It was all Grace could do, she told Kenyon, surfacing for a moment from her sorrow, to refrain from asking the man where he kept his bulrushes.

But this Moses, she said, was a fat Egyptian in a white singlet with an exaggerated American twang. He explained this oddity by saying he'd met his U.S.-born wife at a university in Kansas.

Moses was an intelligent man, he had assured her, but with nine children to feed had taken to moonlighting, keeping the Egyptian-style wolves at bay, by offering English-language tours of the pyramids.

"You 'Merican, miss? I love 'Merica. Most of all I love 'Merican women."

Grace was about to tell him that her late mother was Mandan and her Grandfathers members of the secret society of Itskinaks, the Horns, when the taxi driver admonished Moses for his audacity, insisting he be courteous to their guest or else he would not share in the tip.

"Aiwa. Okay," grumbled Moses, who led Grace through a maze of dusty back ways to a dead-end stable. Here they mounted a pair of sad horses who had seen better days and perhaps no tomorrow. And slowly riding past an ancient burial ground — The City of The Dead — under the smacking sun, Grace and Moses eventually arrived at the very foot of the Great Pyramid, Cheops.

They dismounted. Cairo shimmered in the distance. The grey, a mare, slowly straightened her back as she was relieved of Moses who carried more than three hundred and fifty pounds upon his own bulging carcass.

However many children he had, Grace thought, Moses himself was not in the habit of going without.

She looked around and upward, forever upward into the blazing sun, from the blond base of Cheops. The scene was deserted. But a scraping of footsteps from behind a large fallen stone caught her ear and she turned to find a rakish little man, no more than four foot ten, slyly grinning at them. He was Egyptian, wiry black hair and childish brown body in a filthy maroon t-shirt, shorts and holey running shoes. He looked like a squirrel. He and Moses exchanged some words she did not understand.

"This is my buddy Farouk," Moses intoned as he patted the horses and gestured toward the little man who continued to wear a broad and beguiling grin. "But we call him Fred. Fred Astaire," said Moses. "Because he can dance up and down these great stones."

"He says you would find it of benefit, my lady Miss 'Merica, if you come inside the pyramid," Moses offered. "We're not supposed to do this Miss 'Merica — but as you see there is no one here to catch us. There are no soldiers, no policemen."

"You come, missy," said Fred. And quickly he led the way past the tomb of Chephren to the pyramid of Mycerinus and then up — up, up, up — he danced the broad stone stairway to the pinnacle. Grace followed slowly, for the climb was scorching. But finally

69

from this vista atop Mycerinus she could see the shimmering suburbs of Cairo and, to the south, the quivering emptiness of the vast desert. Everywhere above was deep blue sky.

Fred emptied sand from his holey runners.

"Below us, far below, straight down," said Freddie. "That King was buried. He was dead along with the Queen in those days and they washed their mouths with milk and put royal jelly all around. It was called the Opening of The Mouth."

Then came the climb down to the base, where Grace and Fred met Moses, who now led the way to the largest of three smaller pyramids — the one for Mycerinus's Queen — Khamerernebty ll.

Unseen to all but the experienced eye, was a narrow passage. "You come missy," said Fred Astaire as he led Grace inside, into the blackness. "Meet the Queen."

On her hands and knees Grace followed the limbersome Fred, straight perhaps twenty-five feet and then sharply to the left and into a tiny chamber where her guide had stashed candles. Fred struck a match illuminating the rough-hewn room of granite.

"You have climbed the height of the tomb of King Mycerinus who was pious and just," said Fred. "Now is time for the queen to meet the Queen."

The anteroom rose to a ceiling of forty feet and the slightest shuffle of feet or rustle of clothing produced a crisp echo.

"Now missy," whispered Fred, his face a stoic smile, "water pours into the mouth of the Queen so that Ka — the spirit body, the twin — can come and live with her. It is the Opening of the Mouth. You listen ..."

Grace strained every sinew and in that instant the mercurial Freddie blew out both candles. In the blackness, there was, for a few seconds, perfect silence. And then amid the puff of candle smoke, the pulses of the heart, and the breaths of two humans, there came the faintest sound of what Grace thought was a ripple of water. Above her in the blackness appeared a thin crack of light, growing gradually brighter. Straining upward she was sure that she and the light had changed positions, for now she seemed to be peering down into a pool. And in the pool floated a pure white flower. And through the sound of the faint ripple of water came a whisper. It came from within her or without, she was not sure:

"I am the Near, but not as one thing is near to another; and I am the Far, but not as one thing that is far from another." And it then came to Grace in that great room in the centre of the pyramid next to the reposing chamber of Queen Kamerernebty — that the nearness was within her.

Another moment passed, and Fred struck a match and they wriggled from the pyramid as they had come. Grace shielded her eyes from the stabbing light of the sun when Moses pointed to a solitary rider on the dunes, perhaps a mile to the south.

"Come along Miss 'Merica," said Moses, who, too fleshy to enter the pyramid, had been waiting with the animals. As they left, little Fred, who lived among the pyramids, winked. "The Queen," he said. "The Queen."

They rode out to the figure on the dunes — a young Bedouin, a starched white keffiyah wrapped tightly around his head, wearing a violet robe.

"Marhaba," said Moses in greeting.

The Bedouin's dark brown face was handsome, his white teeth glistened. Grace felt a warmth run along her thighs and up to her navel. Deeply she peered into this man's eyes, how beautiful they were, innocent, penetrating, a young man of nearly twenty. Offered a seat on his camel, she accepted, leaving Moses to tend the horses. The camel bent at the knees and the Bedouin helped her climb aboard. He wrapped her in his purple cloak and whispered gently to the creature which rose and began its elegant stride over the dunes.

They rode a few miles, Grace in front and the young Arab behind, clutching the rein. They galloped and giggled as the animal loped over deep sand parapets and trotted across a stone valley. Grace admired the endless sea of sand, the Jurassic perfume of the desert air, the sweat of the boy who held her so firmly.

Within an hour, they came to a cave and dismounted.

Stretching, she shook sand from her hair. She doffed her shoes.

"Do you speak English?" she asked as he unpacked bread and a tea-kit from his shoulder bag.

"No, lady," he smiled, removing his keffiyah and passing a water bottle. "Only some."

"Do you think the Queen came here?" she asked. "The Queen in the pyramid? All that time ago?"

"Yes, lady. That time. This time. Same. No clocks here. In desert, time is God's time."

They broke bread and lingered until nightfall when the boy built a fire.

Grace saw in the firelight that the desert is a city of shadows, fleeting and changing, melting into new shapes, elements that are as old as time, the new indistinguishable from the old and the old from the new. There is no name for it. It is no longer empty but thick with human memory. At night every line of the desert pastiche rises with new significance. Every stone is the ghost of a fire pit that once warmed life. She saw too that there are fears that clutch the desert heart at night. There are places where the Bedouin will never venture after dark — haunted wells that thirsty men will not approach, ruins where the weary will not seek shelter, hollows that are bad camping grounds for the solitary.

The boy with beautiful eyes was quick and lithe, kicking out the fire and saddling the camel.

"You happy?" she asked on the ride back toward Cairo.

"Pleasure, lady, holds no time at all," he replied.

ACVATIO

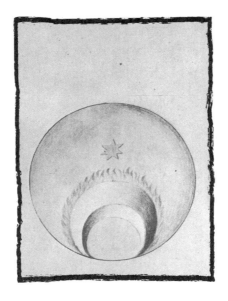

That same luxuriant Cairene afternoon Harry had complained his chops were rank and sore from a gruelling morning rehearsal. But he was awakened from his siesta in the Nile Concorde by a tapping on the door. A solicitous and effluvient Spike Hardman — arms laden with wine, spring rolls, olives, dove's dung, Dijon mustard, saltimbocca and artichoke hearts — had come to eat crow, suggesting they should head to the Cairene soukh for some bantam adventure before the evening gig.

Experienced players, Holborn and Hardman knew the importance of patching up troubles before they festered. They were able to forgive and forget for the greater good of the band.

Their tiff earlier that day had arisen in the rehearsal hall. Harry insisted the band insert into the lineup a three-minute segment of the adagio movement of Michael Haydn's *Concerto for Trumpet and Orchestra in E-major*, smack in the middle of another tune, his own spacey and roiling composition, *Solar Caustic*, during which Hardman carries the band with a solo on the atumpan.

Usually, Hardman deferred to Holborn's wisdom on such matters. This time he did not. This time the disagreement was lengthy, an annoyance Holborn attributed to Hardman's recent lack of success in assuaging a bout of arid horniness. "What happened?" Holborn dug. "Last one was rode hard and put away wet?"

Hardman argued that the splicing of classical refrains into the body of Solar Caustic was an error of grand proportion. He offered Stravinsky's *Canticum Sacrum* or *Fanfare for a New Theatre* would work instead. Louis Andriessen's *Hoketus* also would mesh, as would something by the American composer Henry Brant — all of which, Hardman insisted, met the required spatialization criteria.

The discussion was toasty.

"Will you listen Harry?" the drummer implored. "I'm worried about you. The problem is you just can't hear. The Haydn just doesn't work. The transition sucks."

"We should have talked about this weeks ago, Spike, not the day before a gig," said Holborn. "This is the way it is. You don't like it find another show. And I'll find a player who can do it."

"It isn't that I can't do it," said Hardman. "But it doesn't work, man. There's too much shift in tempo, and the transition, the shading, doesn't cover it."

"Just do it, Spikey," said Holborn, smiling, putting an arm around his friend. "Or we'll shave your ass and throw you outside to the camels" — this as he re-attached himself to a stool and lifted his Hart trumpet.

And then there occurred a moment that would go down in the musical apocrypha. Just as Holborn raised the instrument to his lips Hardman flung a drumstick, carved from Japanese ash, across the hall and in the general direction of the trumpeter. It whipped through the air, barely arcing, and lodged with a loud ping deep in the bell of Harry's Hart.

No one could quite believe it at first, least of all Hardman. And for a few seconds everyone in the room gaped in ethereal silence. Then Holborn lowered the horn from his mouth, and grimacing, slipped it under his armpit. He grasped the protruding drumstick with his left hand. He pulled for all he was worth. But the stick would not budge, so deeply had it penetrated the dark recesses of the horn.

The two players locked eyes. It was a look of antipathy, love, anger, respect and frustration all at once. Finally Hardman stood, walked deliberately across the room to his friend — and with a single quick tug — drew the stick from the bell of the Hart. He turned smartly on his heel, sauntered to his drum kit, and sat, regally, on the drummers' throne.

"Spike," Harry said, his voice a low growl, his teeth bared. "Please remind me never to piss you off again."

After scarfing down the dove's dung of Hardman's apologetic snack, the pair set off at first in a taxi through downtown Cairo. They travelled vaguely under the all-seeing eye of Sirius, The Dog Star, and splashed through puddles of human faeces slavering in the gutters, pullulations among ruins, hordes of sickly children, galled asses, and other beasts of burden bent under enormous loads.

"Come on, let's do the tourist thing, man," the stick-man appealed, climbing from the cab to walk. "See if this place has some hype under all the camel shit."

It was in a northern suburb, within earshot of a mosque where a scratchy recording of a muezzin, blaring from a loudspeaker atop a minaret, skipped and repeated, skipped and repeated, that Holborn and Hardman fell upon an ugly little Coptic church.

Until recently, few tourists had even noticed this church. But something had happened three days before. In the rose-painted narthex where the communion chalice was kept, a shaft of light had appeared on the stone. There was no sun beam, no light source, to account for it. And yet a soft warm glow had appeared every afternoon, lingered for the several hours, and then faded out at night.

Holborn, who had read of the phenomenon in the previous day's English-language edition of *Al-Ahram*, decided it was either a clever hoax or an optical illusion, soon to be explained by scientific inquiry. Or perhaps, as Grace had suggested to him, it was neither.

For Grace had told him stories of a similar phenomenon in the northern Manitoba, where summer evangelists flocked from Mississippi to convert or subvert or — as Grace said — pervert the residents of the far-flung Indian reserves. While many of the natives were sceptical of the slack-jawed proselyting, others became eager acolytes. One reserve was split between converts to Antiochian Catholicism and Manichaeism. But it was the Catholics who first spotted the face of the Blessed Virgin — her shimmery visage reflecting on the surface waters deep at the bottom of an outdoor lavatory pit, out beyond the jack-pines. The miracle sorely tested the Indian faithful, since by the time the onlookers could focus upon the stoic Virgin's beguiling face they found themselves subject to the gag reflex. This, as they ran gasping from the toilet, was interpreted by the emissary dispatched by the Antiochians as further evidence of their faith: a guttural and technicolor illustration of speaking in tongues.

The two musicians shared a bottle of Arak as they strode the last hundred yards or so down a narrow lane which led to the Coptic chimera. Here they were diverted by the sight of a boab in a long striped robe who hunched as he hauled the yellow carcasses of two black-toothed goats from a cart. Hardman was narrowly missed as a housewife tossed a bucket of slops into the lane. Four stories above hung rainbows of laundry, kaftans, nethers and carpets.

On a wall nearby perched a massive woman dressed in a tent-sized abaya. A miserable, still-gasping pheasant was being plucked silly under her arm.

Soon there were no sidewalks. And the dust and steam of the soukh, the sweat and blood, the hashish and absynth, tabbouleh, caught them up. Here the players were greeted by snotty and tubercule coughs as humans pissed and shat and grunted and worked and ate and slept, made love and died. And this swirling epiphany climbed high above the heads of the pair only to settle on the next-door neighbourhood, which once more kicked it all to the heavens.

When the musicians finally squeezed onto the steps of the dilapidated Coptic church the place thronged with pilgrims — vendors, beggars, vegetable sellers — who poured in from the Cairo streets. The crowds, which funnelled into the narrow entrance of the church, had come like Yukon gold-diggers in search of a mother lode of twenty-four carat gold — a horde of spiritual miners sifting for nuggets of manna, eager to plunder the zig-zagging vein of devotion.

Holborn had heard that in the Middle Ages a man dying in the odour of sanctity might, while his body awaited the digging of a grave, be stripped naked by the faithful, his clothing cut to ribbons and sold to believers, his ears, toes, and nipples snipped and preserved in a jar, ready for convenient veneration. Once, on a trip to Bucharest, Holborn and Grace stopped at a foot-worn chapel and had the pleasure of viewing the shriveled eight-hundred-year-old Johnson of Saint Eusebius.

But here, as Holborn and an unsteady Hardman stood agog in the centre of the stinking Coptic church, there were no relics — just light. And light could not be snipped off and dropped in a jar, not even an inch of it. Many of the pilgrims who had travelled to this Ponderosa of wonder clenched their fists in frustration: there was nothing to take away.

For others, the mysterious fluorescence in the church merely confirmed that they were privy to the truth — how wondrous to be an initiate! How delicious to bask in the certainty that one belongs to an innermost circle, to know, as Madame Blavatsky,

Elizabeth Claire Prophet, or Luc Jouret knew, that Christ did not die but spent seven years in India, that Bacon wrote the works of Shakespeare and, then dying, rematerialised as the Comte de Saint Germain who now lives in a cave near the top of Mount Shakopee with a large party of Alsatians. It must be a rare privilege, Holborn thought, to be imbued with such secrets while wallpapering the underground bunker in Montana or Cheiry in preparation for the final days.

But perhaps, thought Holborn, the venerations and obsessions of musicians were no less fervent and peculiar. Hardman, the collector of drums, was ever curious to experience the precise cadence, tenor, tension and vibrancy of every new percussive acquisition. Each new drum provided hours of fascination, of devotion.

Holborn likewise had sacrificed many hours to the hermeneutics of his instruments: his modern Hart trumpet with modified gold mouthpiece; his Blessing trumpet consigned to the mannequin, the Cor Anglais; the Frampton Right which by its nature was oriented to E rather than B-flat which he played publicly on occasion; and finally, of course, the instrument he would die for: the elusive Frampton Left, whose precise tonality he could only imagine.

Years before, fearing that he might never recover the Left, Harry had commissioned a master Swiss horn-maker named Sterner to replicate it. For several months the old Swiss gentleman in Granges-sur-Salvan had taken possession of Harry's Frampton Right, so it could be measured, tested and analysed: its component parts stripped down and reassembled, the eighteenth-century brass compared with modern copper and zinc alloys so that a series of mirror-image schematics, stencils and moulds could be prepared.

Kenyon had argued against it. He knew the commissioned work of the old Swiss craftsman was a painstaking and impossible procedure. There could never be an exact copy of the Frampton

Left because the perspicacity of the old brass could never be replicated. And although the Swiss came near to making a perfect and expensive copy, the puzzle of the Frampton's shadowy trademark remained. Dozens of times Sterner tried to reproduce the hue of the serpentined G, but he could not fathom what had blemished and altered the gold.

"I can help you possibly gentle-mens?"

The voice came from behind Holborn among the Copts. It belonged to a well-tailored Arab perspiring heavily in a grey-flanneled suit. His obsequious smile lacked one front tooth and what remained of the others reminded Harry of blackened matchsticks. His lower denture appeared to be solid gold. A chain of colourful postcards was festooned round his neck.

In one hand he held castanets, in the other, a tambourine. Several beautiful but filthy young boys, beggars, stood behind him reverently.

"Attata kallam al la Ingelese — You have come in search of miracles?" his dark eyes smiled, his pure white cap lilting to one side as he turned momentarily from Holborn and Hardman to direct kicks at the shins of the boys, scattering them to the four winds.

The man's name, he said, was Loutfi.

He was, it seemed to Holborn, just another shady itinerant, one of the many who swell Cairo's population from ten million souls to fifteen million during the daylight hours.

But Holborn took a closer look. And he decided that Loutfi had a certain ineffability. And, to Hardman's satisfaction, an interest in the drum.

They were not predisposed to trust him but with chaos among the Copts the pair agreed to accompany Loutfi across the crowded soukh and into a tiny bar for one quick drink. They settled down to kebabs and babanoug, eggplant salad and dumpling. Afterward, Hardman was drawn to the next-door shop of a taxidermist where the animals, he'd noticed, had been bent into impossible positions. "Did you see those critters?" he said, leaving Holborn to settle the bill. "I think I saw a stuffed monkey playing a lobster violin with a cobra-bow. Unreal. I'm going to check it, man."

Holborn then relaxed and sipped on a Remy while querying the Arab, a Muslim who slurped lemon-water, about the events in the church. In one corner of the bar, amid the charcoal smoke and steaming coffee, a couple of tourist girls cavorted with a trio of young Egyptian men who sparked with testosterone.

"So what do you think?" asked Holborn. "About the church — the light?"

Loutfi thoughtfully stroked his thin black moustache, smiled, and shrugged his shoulders.

Being a professional thaumaturge — trained by the masters to walk coals, to lie on beds of nails, to stuff shards of glass up his tight L'Oiel de Gabes, to go into catalepsy, to induce a trance by a mere touch on the neck — Loutfi perhaps knew best how hard a man must work to obtain even the most modest paranormal powers. He was as skilled at making miracles as making change.

"Every shaft of light," he said, eyes closed, "is a miracle."

Before long Harry took a liking to Loutfi: taxi driver, magician, guide, translator, go-between. The Egyptian's command of English was excellent. He spoke as an eighteenth century virtuousi played music with the addition of fioriture and even whole cadenzas of his own invention. And equally vital, he knew his way around the Cairene sprawl. Eventually he offered to take the musicians into the Nile Delta to see a legendary old tar drummer, a blind man named Salam-el-Salam.

And so after stopping at the Nile Concorde to retrieve Hardman's own highly-prized tar drum, the drummer, the cab-driver and the trumpeter made for the village that Salam-el-Salam had never, in his long life, travelled more than a mile beyond.

"In this village, Mr. Harry, I promise you," said Loutfi, "we will find the great blind tar man. I will show you."

Harry later told Grace that when they arrived, thirsty and dusty, Loutfi attempted to converse with the local African headman who spoke only Charinile, a branch of the Dinka language. Loutfi, putting up a brave front, smiled and gesticulated with the headman in a kind of pidgin-Dinka, a broken Dinka, which soon devolved into plain sign language and hieroglyph.

The village which held hunched figures playing sheshbesh or smoking sheeshas amid the wood smoke, and which reeked of gasoline and oil from jacked-up rusty automobiles, was in mourning. The great tar player's mother had died. No one knew how old she was, but her son was nearing a century and so her longevity must have rivalled that of the Biblical Methuselah, son of Enoch, grandfather of Noah. Still, the old man was prepared to play the drum with Hardman. He would play, he said, to honour his mother. And because playing the tar was what he had always done.

The heat was stifling. Holborn sulked, sought shade, daydreamed of the Framptons, and wished he had a whiskey.

Squatting beneath the thatch of a hut he noticed two apprentices through the opened doorway of a hut opposite. They were plying sheepskin bellows as a smithy worked a charcoal forge. As he blinked and rubbed the sweat and flies from his eyes, he could not believe anyone could work at a fire in this unsparing heat. The bellows, connected to the forge by clay pipes, fanned the flames which leaped into the air as if alive.

The smithy was working on a yellow copper pot. Seizing it with his tongs he placed it on the flames. Suddenly the place became still. The flies took refuge in coils of shit and on Holborn's sweat-lathered face. He could hear drumming in the distance but even that seemed to fade. The smith motioned for his helpers to stand back. The stillness was pierced only by the wheezing of the bellows and the low hissing of the metal. Holborn could see the smith's lips move in silence. He was praying and seemed to be invoking the spirit of fire and metal and wind — the wind which blew through the bellows, the fire that was born of the wind, and the metal that was wedded to the fire.

As he slumped and sunk his back into the wall of the hut, Harry was violently snatched from this meditation as all the coal-bummed children of the village suddenly appeared to see and inhale the strange white men. In the distance, the wings of angels shimmered in a green-white ocean mirage.

The blind tar man emerged from his hut, rubbing Hardman's tar against his weathered cheek. The old man caressed it like a lover, felt it with the palms of his hands, cuddled it, stuffed it down his loinbreech. Through Loutfi, he told Hardman it was a good tar. This pleased the young stickman intensely, who told the uncomprehending old man that he'd laid out plenty for it, nearly $2,500, in Los Angeles.

The blind man then handed his own round, brown, flat tar to Hardman and gestured for him to play. Kthak-thak-a-thak. Hardman was startled by the clarity of the sound and the fine balance of the moon-shaped drum, three fingers deep, in both high and low frequencies. He began to excite the membrane — phhhhhhhhhhhhtt, the drum trance — and for a few moments Hardman, too, was transported out of time.

CALCINATIO

Kathak-a-thak. Thump thump.

It was afternoon when Hardman banged on the door and sauntered into The Bunker, unzipped his waterlogged jacket and draped it over the banister post, brisk and aloof like a feral cat or Dominican monk.

It was typical of Hardman that when he arrived somewhere he arrived together all at once. The drummer had walked from Chalk Farm station and then tried to evade the lenses of a handful of photographers who had gathered on the pavement outside The Bunker. He smelled of rain Kenyon noticed, and something else too, something miry and primal. "Eau de trollop," Kenyon thought to himself.

When Hardman had arranged himself to his satisfaction, he presented a kiss and a small bouquet to Grace, then proceeded to enlighten them on several matters, pausing only to produce a bottle of vitamins and vial of breath freshener from which he triggered two quick bursts.

He spoke as he always did, with a peculiar mechanical diction, his words precise and staccato.

"I can't tell you the feeling I had when I heard that tar," Spike said, recalling Egypt.

"It was pure happiness. That sound completely filled me up. The desert is so empty and I felt so full. I had to hide my face. I was embarrassed to be so happy. But there was one little kid who saw me. He turned to me and looked. It was like it was just the two of us who could feel the rhythm. It was like the whole universe rippling through us, and we both shared this secret together. It was ours, and no one could feel it quite this way.

"And then, you know, that tar kept beating. It was magic, man. Everyone got more excited but in another couple of minutes I felt this impossibly shitty sadness. Right down to the bottom of my shoes I could feel it, you know? I was sad that everyone else seemed to be missing the experience, diluting it, trivializing it. Trivializing themselves in a way, because they were dancing around and vibrating and whatnot, but what they did, they did by rote."

Hardman paused to pull out an already rolled joint. With a deft motion, he lit it and inhaled deeply.

"But I stayed quiet, really quiet, unbearably quiet, and listened to the blind man on that drum. It just echoed across the desert. It was so clear and crisp yet fragile. But then that great pain, man, it was deep and profound — well, it passed away too. It was one of those really uncommon experiences. It reminds you that our joys and sorrows on this earth are fleeting."

Hardman offered the joint to Grace, who shook her head absently.

"Speaking of which, did you two see this?" Hardman asked, pulling from his bag a crumpled newspaper clipping. "This was in *The Daily Telegraph*, this morning, next to a piece about some good ol' boy who shot off his nuts when he used a .22 bullet to replace a fuse in his truck."

Grace and Kenyon read the brief news clipping.

Crash Claims Swiss Horn-Maker

The body of Rudolph Sterner has been recovered from Lake Geneva. Swiss authorities believe Sterner suffered a heart attack while driving, causing his antique Daimler to veer into the lake. A post mortem showed no sign of foul play. Sterner was well-known for producing a matchless line of trumpets, cornets, trombones, some with gold and silver mouthpieces. At the age of 80, he retired, but continued to amass one of the world's largest collections of antique brass instruments.

"That's so weird," Grace sniffed, lighting a French cigarette and exhaling loudly. "I mean Harry...and now the old fellow who made him the copy of the Frampton. What gives?"

Hardman paced the rose swirls of the Persian carpet and cast a worried glance at Grace, then offered a faint smile as if everything would be okay.

"It has to be coincidence," he said. "Although there's no such thing as coincidence. I agree it is un-bloody-canny. It's like open season on the brassmen."

He turned to Kenyon, mockingly, confident that their professional relationship would soon end. "Either that or there's too many old farts driving Daimlers these days. They should take their driving permits away at sixty-five. Force them to take a bus."

"What good would that do?" Kenyon interjected, giving

Hardman a look of disgust. "Thousands of pensioners take the bus to Brighton and Llandudno every year — living proof you don't have to drive to be senile."

Kenyon glanced at his watch, suddenly remembering the Flask Walk bookshop. "In any event, I don't drive."

With this, Hardman slunk across the room to sit with Grace, placing an arm around her. She and the band's drummer had grown friendly from the moment of their first meeting, shortly after Hardman joined Holborn's band. Although it was Harry who romanced her during a whirlwind trip to Canada, she and Hardman always had a chemistry. Grace and Holborn dithered for a couple of years but Hardman was best man at the wedding.

Even Kenyon now felt somewhat comforted by Hardman's presence there in The Bunker, for the drummer had in some ways been closer to Holborn than anyone. Kenyon also reckoned that Hardman might be able to shed more light on the circumstances of Holborn's leaving the Nile Concorde alone, and why he might have ventured solo into the black, eternal, Egyptian night.

Grace went to the kitchen to make tea and fumbled about, everything reminding her of Harry. She couldn't find the tea bags. She found some of Holborn's loose Labrador tea but no strainer. She failed to open the gas for the kettle, and dropped the sugar bowl to the floor. Eventually Hardman went in to help, leaving Kenyon to eavesdrop on the muffled conversation through the half-open door.

"What'll you do now Spike?" she asked the drummer.

"I don't know," he said. "I haven't thought about it. I've just been thinking about you and Harry. There's a '49 Harley knucklehead in pieces in my mom's garage. I guess I'll go there for awhile, work on that. I can't think of playing anymore right now. You should come down to Mobile sometime. You'd be welcome. At least it's warm there. Humid. You wouldn't have to wear a sweater and you can smell the cherry blossoms and sweet magnolias everywhere."

He placed a reassuring arm around Grace once more.

"You come when you feel better."

"Thanks," she said. "Listen. I'm thinking of going to Wales — I need to get away from here. Those photographers. Maybe I should rest a bit before the funeral, but I can't. I want to visit Harry's country. I found some old papers Harry's dad left. So I want to look around, too. Wanna come?"

"Why not?" he said. "But are you sure? I thought Harry didn't have any living relations."

"No. No family — although they were all from some little village called Gornhaffan. Maybe someone up there knows something. I need to put this all away somehow."

Grace turned from the sink. "You know, I'd forgive someone for all this, if I knew who to forgive," she said, staring through Hardman. "That's the problem. I don't know what happened. Who to blame. If I should blame Harry, myself, God ... who Spikey? Who for Christ's sake, who can I blame for this?"

For some reason her words were like a stab in the groin. "You can't undo what's done," he said. "Maybe no one's to blame. Maybe blame is ... well, maybe it's not ... oh, I don't know. Anyway, Wales huh? Anywhere special you want to go?"

"We'll try Gornhaffan. Someone up there must remember the father. Oh, and Spike?" she said. "Let's not say too much to Aaron — okay?"

They returned to the other room to find Kenyon thumbing a copy of *The Spectator*. He had given up eavesdropping and it appeared that he was trying, with little success, to become comfortable in the notion that his presence was necessary. Grace, cleaving to Hardman, readily agreed with the young drummer's proposal that the two of them should, at week's end, together take the same flight to Canada, sleety winterland, for the funeral.

Hardman told Grace and Kenyon that the other players in the band, digesting the tragic news of Harry's death, had by now arrived in London. They were in a holding pattern at least until after Harry's interment in Canada. Then Kenyon would go through the formality of releasing the players from their contractual obligations and they would scatter to the various crannies from whence they came: Cuernavacas, New York, Uren, Soweto, St. Kitts, Sobibor, Bowell.

Hardman said he might eventually go to Arizona where he could just be, like one of those Tibetan lamas, sitting in a cave. "In doing nothing — I see that everything is done."

But for now he simply helped Grace with the milk and honey for tea.

"Y'know Grace," he said, "I'd rather have a whiskey."

"Over there," she pointed to a cabinet beside the fire, which was in need of tending, London proving cooler than Egypt or Cyprus, she noted. And the house, without Holborn, felt plain icy.

"Listen," the drummer said, gulping his drink and settling in a chair. "I've arranged for a little memorial service. Private. For the band. There's a preacher I know here in London. He plays a bit of skin himself when he's not being assistant rectum or something. He's cool. Kidder's his name. I thought it would be good if he could meet you, Grace, you know, get a better feel for Harry that way."

"Oh I don't know Spike," said Grace, "I don't really want ..."

"I know it's bad timing but I said he could drop by for half an hour. Later," said Hardman. "No need for you to come to the service with the band. But you might want to meet this minister guy, you know, he should meet you at least."

Before she could seriously object Hardman changed the subject.

"I was just thinking how Harry always used to joke about this sofa and matching chair. Do you remember? He'd say, 'Have a seat in L.' And then he'd go on about how Malcolm Lowry was practically starving when he wrote Under the Volcano in that shack outside Vancouver. Dollarton wasn't it, Aaron? And across the Fraser River was a Shell Oil refinery. And Lowry would look across at night in all his splendid loneliness and see the S was burnt out on the Shell sign. And the sign would flash: hell, hell, hell.

"Ave a seat in L, everyone, lower-case 'h'."

Hardman slouched in his chair. "God, Harry made me laugh sometimes. He always knew how to break the ice. And he was a fine hornman. Good as they come."

"He was indeed," Kenyon chipped in, politely, trying to inject himself into the swing, the stoned caustic climate, of mourning. It then occurred to Kenyon as he watched this unfold, that perhaps since Hardman had been raised mostly by women, his mother and her great aunt, that he had a soft spot for the female gender. It struck him that this was an affectation from which Hardman might never recover.

And then Hardman spat it out: "I know this sounds stupid, Grace. I'm so sorry. What else can I say?"

"I know, Spikey," she said. "It's weird. I've been thinking. You know how you think you know someone and it turns out you don't know the first damn thing about them? That's how I feel. Another ninety years and I wouldn't have known him. Christ."

"Yeah," said Spike thoughtfully.

There was a long silence as Grace and Kenyon waited for Spike to pick up the tempo.

"The man could blow," Hardman said finally, lifting the Frampton Right in the air and examining it stem to stern. Harry's taped music crept in from the background as he flipped the horn around and peered into the bell, flicking the hand-crafted piston valves.

"Do you think Harry was religious?" Grace wondered without provocation. The two men hesitated.

She lifted from the tea stand the framed photo of the two of them entwined. "Harry didn't talk about it. And he didn't live a perfect life. But deep inside he believed in that little light. That little shining light. It's just so goddamn unfair, you know," she said, her mood darkening.

"Even if he didn't believe in God he believed in the good. He tried to do some good. Even when the good wasn't obvious. You know, I still can't believe it. I was hoping maybe it's all some kind of joke. Like maybe Harry is playing some stupid trick on us. You know he's like that sometimes. He's ... I don't know. What do you think, Aaron?"

When no answer was forthcoming she brought her hand to her mouth and bit her knuckle. The men did not move, wanting to comfort her in some way but uncertain what they could do. What could be added? What could be taken away?

"You can't look for justice," Hardman said rather sternly, flipping one leg over the arm of his chair as if to lighten the gravity of his words. "It just is, Gracey," he said, his timing rather impeccable. "But I have to say I can't believe it myself. One time he's here, the next ... who'd have expected?"

"What did the Egyptians say, Aaron?" Grace then pressed to know, lifting her dark eyes toward the older man.

"It's a mystery," Kenyon replied. "There's speculation it may have been robbery. He'd been lightened $5,000. Apparently he arranged to draw a cashier's cheque earlier that day."

"He had a lead on that other horn," said Hardman. "I knew it. That's what it is, you know. He got the horn and somebody ripped him off."

Hardman gingerly placed the Frampton Right on the glass table beside his chair. He gulped his drink again and began tapping fingers on the edge of the chair — syncopation was at the core of his being. He stepped to the reel-to-reel player and toyed with the volume. Solar Caustic. Harry's silky horn soothed the space of the room.

Hardman drifted.

He turned to Grace, imagined her in a summer dress, a flutter of ribbon in her hair. The bangs of her hair hung carelessly over her forehead. Her lips perfectly curved, the light sparkling her eyes and highlighting her nose. There was beauty.

When they first met, Grace had taken a liking to him immediately. He was always in the groove, and like all outstanding drummers, knew how to protect the groove inside the groove, the shebang inside the bang. He could plug the crack every time.

Hardman was skinny, pin-legged like Melville's Ahab, and now his fair hair was close-cropped and he wore round-rimmed spectacles. Yet he packed a muscular frame, and had a high, intelligent forehead, and deeply furrowed brow. Speaking, he would sit cross-legged in a chair, gesturing madly. Sometimes, listening to music, he had the most uncanny ability to pick out that lone, eerie, high-pitched note which lingers in the background. He would open his hands, cock his head slightly, searching to hold the note with one ear then the other. And then, hands outstretched, he would flick his fingers outward as he raised his arms above his head, following the note until it was lost in nothingness.

He travelled lightly and happily. On tours he slung over his shoulder a leather bag which held drumsticks, a novel by Andre Gide, vitamins and his wallet.

It was his unfortunate habit, however, to ingest ten cherry-sized multivitamins daily. He swore by them, claiming they were like a detergent that scoured arterial plaque from his system. The only side-effect was that every few days he had a putrid attack of gas — the most foul smelling flatus imaginable. This was the plaque evacuating his system, he said.

The drummer was a talent. But it took Holborn, with Kenyon's not inconsequential material backing, to rescue him from obscurity.

"When we were young we didn't rightly know if we wanted to be writers, poets or musicians," Hardman once told Holborn. "But it was the cats playing the music that seemed to get all the chicks, and so that was alright by me. I swung to jazz since everyone else was playing rock. And in the end, I just loved the openness in jazz. They say the jazz language can't express all there is to express since it's too tied to roots. But man, to me almost any kind of improv is jazz — see? People used to give me a hard time since my first drum kit was so ugly. My mom had no money. And the cymbals on that first kit especially didn't look too healthy. The China cymbal looked like someone had nibbled pieces from it. And that first band? Man, I think we were only about fourteen. We called ourselves The Fukawees, you know, after that old joke about the lost African tribe wandering through the jungle and calling out: " 'Where the Fukawee?' "

In concerts he syncopated rhythms on the rim of the snare and bass drum and extracted bits of colour by using one element of the drumset against another. When he wanted to enliven the band he played with the high-hat cymbals partly open and crackled the dotted eighth and sixteenth rhythms with unusual clarity.

"Do you know the most amazing thing about Harry and his music?" Hardman suddenly said, as the sun bled light into every corner of the room from the ceiling to the floor. "Do you know the thing that set him apart from anyone I ever knocked down with?

"He had such cool ideas about music. You know, Aaron, why he quit playing the big tables, the big concerts?"

Hardman lit one of Grace's Gitanes for himself and the smoke dragged up the walls. He was on a roll.

"It was because he didn't want to be had. You know — controlled by the industry. He didn't want to be pushed and prodded, with respect to you Aaron, by all the impresarios and booking agents who insisted on following the same tired old recipes, the same old forlorn compendiums for success. You know what I'm talking about. He despised the rush of ready-made, mass-produced culture. For Harry it was nothing more than a panic disguise for inertia. Harry believed that things like tension, mystery, unpredictability, these are the fundamentals of real life. Definition — too much definition, Aaron — this was death to Harry, the final solution, man."

"You don't say," came Kenyon's tight reply as he considered this and then offered the bait. "You are telling me that Holborn, through his music, was pushing through the hieroglyphs of language, Mr. Hardman? Is this what you're telling me? That he cut through the narrow positivist argument which admits meaning is based only on the logic of experimental verification. Is this it? Am I with you?"

"What I'm saying," said Spike, his voice rising like a crescendo on a cymbal, "is that you can make all the notations of Harry's music on the chromatic and harmonic scales that you like. You can score and sell sheet music, Aaron. You can put us on stage like monkeys. But no code or music theory can describe the true essence of Harry's experience inside that music."

"Ah, conscious immediacy. We're back to that old saw."

Kenyon eyed Hardman obliquely.

"This is all well and good," the puffy impresario huffed. "Harry and I often discussed this. We agreed that much of the world lives in a state of unconscious immediacy. Ninety percent of people on this earth must sleepwalk merely to keep alive, to pay the Inland Revenue, put bread on the table, to feed the nippers. It is the required minimum. But the Greeks had a word for this: doxa, the flatus voces — the dull opinions of the hoi polloi — idolatry.

"But you see, Mr. Hardman, there is a built-in tension. There was with Harry as well. It was almost hypocritical what Harry was doing. Ironic actually. The more innovative he became the more popular he became. He could not avoid it. And so if he was trying to communicate a particular aim, aspiration, or human secret through the music, it somehow became lost or trivialized as the music became massively popular. Indeed, it is rather as Wittgenstein predicted — an art assisting in its own elimination. The logical consequence, as Beckett discovered, is to slowly work one's way into silence: the immutable, inscrutable, whimper of nothing.

"You recall the hours, don't you, Spike, that Harry would spend in the studio on the digital sampler? In many ways this added to his undoing.

"It was the sampler's ability to lift, record, store and regurgitate sounds, notes, beats, riffs, voices and horn blasts that fascinated him — everything that made the recording business more efficient for him. For us. But it changed the way musicians such as Harry actually write music, which these days has to do as much with bricolage as with anything else. You, of all people, know as well as anyone how to put somebody else's drum pattern together with your own, to take a stolen voice and notes and sounds from other recordings and to weave and embed them seamlessly within your own. It may not be pure, and it has nothing to do with technical mastery — it is what the French dilettantes would call ecriture."

Kenyon paused to smile thinly at the drummer.

"But unlike you," he said, "Harry never saw this innovation as a threat. He pushed it forward in the vain hope something new would be forged and that listeners, his world, might be opened once more to a sense of mystery. That they would use the music rather than popularize it.

"It was his small gift to the world," concluded Kenyon. "Although he himself had lost the mystery, long ago."

Hardman reached into his shoulder bag for a bottle of vitamins.

"He did believe music is a form of worship," said Hardman, sounding mildly defeated.

"Look you guys," said Grace, stubbing out another cigarette and stirring from her spiralling melancholia. "I know you're here to try to make things better, to make sure I'm okay. I appreciate everything and all. But I think I'm going to go back to bed now."

She paused and her voice settled over the potted plants and bottled orchids. She rose then, as though some mystical scourge had been sweetly delivered unto her. "I know this much. And I've known it since I was a child. A person's spirit is alone in the silence of its source. The music just tells the world that such possibilities exist."

With all their philosophy, they could not top this, Hardman and Kenyon. And so they sat in the quiet for a moment, the three of them, Harry's horn soothing from the stereo. Hardman took a long sip of his drink and looked at Grace. If he wanted her, Kenyon mused, he hoped the drummer would be considerate in these moments of instability.

"Come along Hardman," the old impresario said, wobbling to his feet and giving a long sigh. I'll give you a lift to your hotel."

DISTILLATIO
PHYSICA

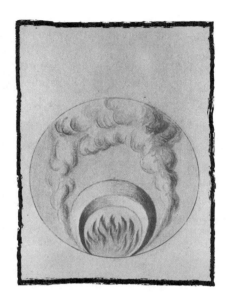

Grace was upstairs putting away Harry's things in the rarefied air of The Bunker when she came across a brochure from the Nile Concorde. She sank onto the bed as she fingered its dusky pages.

Dearest Quest. Well Come Your Honor. Every quest room are apportioned with gracioso and restfully finished. Each boast its own privvy balcony overlooking Nil. TV, telefon (near and long distant), and recordomusic is trout all rooms. Private bath with hot and coldwater running. 24 hours chamber service. there are apartements consist with 2 double chambers, one receiving toilet with commodity and one balcony overlooking Nil. Americana

cafeteria serfing dove dung with saucy Hamadryas Baboon make you saliva. At thee swimming pool you enjoyed with steam turkish coffee and drink the cheeky chick with tabac. In the evening 2 bars sets the mood for superb night dimming and dancing with musical restrooms.
She remembered the day in Cairo had promised to be golden.

They'd arrived in the deep of night, slept a couple of hours and washed up. Harry was lured to the living room of the hotel suite by the faint cry of a muezzin on a distant minaret. The sun, a red ball, peeked over the horizon.

Harry clicked his tongue and opened his trumpet case, yawned, raised up the Hart and inserted into its waiting shaft one of several custom mouthpieces made in New Orleans. Gingerly polishing the bell with cheesecloth he squeezed in the mute. Folding the cloth and dropping it into a compartment on the floor of the plush velvet case, he closed the flap and sealed the latches on the box.

He moved to the sofa and flopped down.

Dawn was becoming day. Through the closed door to the hotel balcony groaned the emerging cacophony of Cairene traffic. Specks of dust hung in the angled sunbeams of the sitting room high above the dirty world. He whistled to himself. Seventy-two hours before his death he was neither happy nor essentially unhappy — he just was.

Grace turned and smiled as he raised the mouthpiece to his lips and he licked the cold smooth roundness of its inner sanctums, pushing his tongue home to the deepest curvature. He looked to the window of the balcony, placed the horn in his lap and then left his tongue dangling out.

Wiggling and flapping this pink and nicotined protrusion, he picked dust motes from the air. Like a praying-mantis he looked, engaged in a kind of aerial ballet. Then he drew the lingua once more inside his mouth and onto the back of his upper teeth.

"Ernest Jones, Gracey," he said. "You ever read the psychological works of my Welsh kinsman?" he smiled at her, flicking his tongue in and out of the groove.

"I don't think so," she shrugged.

"You know what he called this?" Holborn grinned now, licking the brass mouthpiece and rolling his head from side to side. "It was in the glossary of his psychoanalytic papers. He called it the apposition of the mouth to the vulva.

"Apposition. Apposition my ass. It was the Welsh inferiority what wrote that," he snorted, pulling the trumpet from his lips, eyeing it with skepticism, and allowing the three middle fingers of his right hand to dance quietly across the mother-of-pearl valve heads.

He pushed his tongue against his firm palate and upper plate, slightly deformed from the physical pressure brought against his teeth through thirty-five years of playing. Holborn said there is no human mouth perfectly designed for the cold brass aperture of the modern trumpet. But, as with other parts of the body, you kick it around enough and it adapts.

Quietly, he exercised his lips. Oooh-wee, oooh-weee, oooh-weee. Ahhh-oooh Ahhh-oooh.

He stretched and tensed his eyebrows, rolled his eyeballs, tweaked to and fro on his nostrils believing this exercised the Horner's muscle delimiting the orbit of the eye and the pyramidal arch of the nose.

Raising the horn he gently pressed the cool metal to his face. He blinked, thinking for a split-second that he saw a vision, a girl, dancing, reflected on the end of the bell. Lightly as wind rustles leaves in autumn he blew a current through the instrument but did not lean so far into the maw to produce more than a whistle or low rush. Even this force of breath was enough to squeeze a flood of spittle from the spit cock, and as he leaned forward, drops of saliva dripped between his legs and onto the plush carpet of the hotel suite.

Grace donned a black kimono splashed with red dragons and plopped over the back of the sofa, near him. Reaching across, she pulled him close.

"You know what?" said Harry. "I'm scared. It's going to be a dead end. Sometimes I think it's more fun just to imagine those two babies together. What if I find the Left horn and it's all trashed up? What if it was used to span a piece of broken plumbing? What if it led the charge of the Light Brigade? What if it was crushed by a tank in Budapest in 1956? Christ, wouldn't that be something."

He walked to the balcony. There was a skiff on the river dragging nets. And a rowboat with two boys hauling trash and scrap metal from near the frothy scum-lined shore. Along the wide corniche below a steady stream of commuter buses, lorries and cars parallelled the river. They honked wildly as the city drifted to life — people and vegetable carts, masses of humanity, donkeys, horses, camels.

On the riverbank, a white-robed Arab herded a flock of tall pink flamingoes to slaughter. It was the first time Holborn had seen flamingoes outside a zoo. They stutter-stepped along the path, nearing the dinner table, their tongues a local delicacy.

He again raised the Hart to his lips. And licking the inner groove of the mouthpiece he saw in the distance, stained mauve and rose, dust blowing across the Sahara. The sand, its expanse and purity, reminded him of prairie Canada, the Egyptian desert reflecting sunlight like snow on the steppes.

His mind drifted to when he was ten or eleven. He was in a suburb of that city on those vast Canadian plains, the suburb where his father rented a small house. There were no crowds or donkeys or real humans in this suburb. Only a vast icy wasteland, the frozen edges of the world.

But it was here, in the short salient of summer, where boys fought their skirmishes on stubby square lawns adorned with pretty plastic flamingoes, mosquitoes hovering an inch from their sweating skin, that Harry first felt at home.

Over several decades thousands of immigrant families had settled in this new neighbourhood on the prairie and the mix was volatile: the Ukrainians, the Poles, the Germans, the Slavs, the

Jews, the French, all so different. Yet all lavished their lawns with the same plastic flamingoes in an effort to let go of the past and drink from the creamy cup of the future.

It was also in that suburb, a sparse, flat urban desert which formed along a bushy fringe of bending river on the cusp of the Great Plains, that he'd taken his first trumpet class from old Henrik Storgaard, a mathematics and music teacher. Harry practised the chromatic and harmonic scales from the bottom up to double high C and down. Up the scales and down. In the school corridor he would blow quietly through the mouthpiece only, which he carried close in his pocket. On his father's old record player he would listen to the horn players: Bix Beiderbecke, Billy Butterfield, Sergio Mendez, Maynard Ferguson, Miles, Chet Baker.

"One of the great secrets Storgaard taught me was not to play with vibrato in my tone," Harry said, moving to the couch, looking at his hands which were like his grandfather's hands. "Storgaard was hip, he knew how to get that sound, that special sound, near and far at the same time. At first, I used to play with vibrato since most other trumpet players did," he said to himself. "Billy Butterfield, man, I liked Billy Butterfield. And Chet Baker, man that guy was a genius.

"Storgaard once stopped the band and told me, 'Look here, Holborn, don't come around here with that Harry James or Bix Beiderbecke stuff, playing with all that vibrato. Stop shaking all those notes because you're going to be shaking them enough when you get old. Play it straight, develop your own style because you can do it. You've got enough forte to be your own trumpet man.'

"You know, Gracey, I never forgot that," he announced, his Hart still in hand.

"I cheated a bit, used grace notes, you know, the little accent before the true note in the melody. I just loved the way those guys played. Storgaard was right though — it takes work. He ripped into me one time for reading a book during band practice. I was interested in those flamingoes, so I was reading up on them —

buried in the back of the A-trumpet section, reading. Did you know they're extinct in the States? They used to be wild. Flamingoes stood for the sun-god Re here in Egypt. My dad told me they stood for Jesus, the resurrection and immortality. Huh."

He sprawled his gangly legs along the couch now, opposite her, rummaging through the daily newspaper.

"Get this," Holborn said to her, lifting a coffee cup as he pointed to an article in *Al-Ahram*, buried on page twelve:

A group of Catalonian Spaniards who claim their forefathers were badly treated by Napoleon have called on France to deposit the emperor's ashes into a remote sea. The group wants to demolish the Arc de Triomphe and declare Napoleon one of history's 'big losers' in conjunction with the phasing-in of the European Economic Community single market.

"Wasn't Napoleon in Egypt for awhile?" Grace asked.

"Uh huh," said Holborn, transfixed by the newspaper. "Around 1800 I believe. That's why the Sphinx has no nose. One of Napoleon's cannons clipped it during target practice for the battle of the Nile. Or at least that's what they say.

"You know the other thing I learned from old Storgaard was the Egyptian minor scales," he said. "With the Egyptian scale you just change the flats and sharps where you want the note flattened and where you want it sharp. So you have two flats and one sharp, right? That means you play E-flat and A-flat and then the F will be sharp. You put in the note you want, like the C scale's minor Egyptian scale.

"The stuff looks funny," he lowered his voice and said to himself, "because you have two flats and a sharp. But it gives you freedom to work with melodic ideas without changing the basic tonality. See, it's really nice to play an open horn in the middle tempos — the change, even with a mute — can be startling. The tone is a little sour but that's okay, as long as you're economical, then you get a few spattered phrases, lumpy shapes really, but it's hollow and penetrating like blowing into the end of an empty bottle."

"Harry, listen to this," Grace interrupted, fingering a copy of Trelawney's *Recollections of The Last Days of Shelley and Byron* which she'd brought from London for reading material between the Giza gigs.

"It's so ethereal. They're digging Percy Bysshe Shelley out of the grave in Italy," she said, languishing on the sofa opposite.

"He was so young when he died. Drowned. Europe was devastated. They wept in the streets. This guy Trelawney said they felt no better than a herd of wolves or a pack of wild dogs digging him up. Listen:

"They tore his battered and naked body out from the pure yellow sand that lay so lightly over it, they dragged him back to the light of day: 'But the dead have no voice, nor had I power to check the sacrilege — the work went on silently in the deep and unresisting sand, not a word was spoken, for the Italians have a touch of sentiment, and their feelings are easily excited into sympathy."

"Not the last time I was in Italy," quipped Holborn.

"Pay attention, Harry," Grace frowned as she continued to read out loud:

"We were startled and drawn together by a dull hollow sound that followed the blow of a mattock; the iron had struck a skull, and the body was soon uncovered. Lime had been strewn on it; this or decomposition had the effect of staining it a dark and ghastly indigo colour. Byron asked me to preserve the skull for him but remembering that he had formerly used one as a drinking-cup, I was determined Shelley's should not be so profaned. After the fire was well kindled more wine was poured over Shelley's dead body than he had consumed during his life. This with the oil and salt made the yellow flames glisten and quiver. The heat from the sun and fire was so intense that the atmosphere was tremulous and wavy. The corpse fell open and the heart was laid bare. The frontal bone of the skull, where it had been struck with the mattock, fell off; and as the back of the head rested on the red-hot bottom bars of the furnace, the brains literally seethed, bubbled, and boiled as

in a cauldron, for a very long time."

"This is very moving, Grace," said Holborn impatiently.

"Shut up, Harry. Now, listen:

"Byron could not face this scene. He withdrew to the beach and swam off ... the fire was so fierce as to produce a white heat on the iron and to reduce its contents to grey ashes. The only portions that were not consumed were some fragments of bones, the jaw, and the skull. But what surprised us all, was that the heart remained entire. In snatching this relic from the fiery furnace, Trelawney's hand was severely burnt.

"Charming," said Harry. "So what's the point?"

"Well," said Grace, "I guess he had a good heart."

There was a pause as Harry drifted inward.

"Grace," he said to her. "Do you remember that little initiation rite your brother arranged to make sure I was worthy of you?"

"It was my Grandmother who wanted to meet you," said Grace.

"Whatever. I suppose it wasn't just a test for me — was it?" he said, barefoot on the couch now, legs covered in newspaper, horn resting on his chest.

"No," she replied. "It was to make sure we would look after each other. Harry Holborn and Grace Keeper."

She moved across to sit beside him and Harry rested his head on Grace's thigh.

"The one thing I still remember about that first time at Peepeekissee is the drums," he said, nuzzling his head deep into her lap and stretching.

"You know I lived on the prairies for such a good part of my life and I'd never been on Indian land before then. I loved those drummers. And I learned something at Peepeekissee about drums. There was a different kind of meaning in the drum than I knew from playing in the nightclubs. It wasn't just beating out the time, keeping time, it was beyond time. Time is long. Time is hard. But the growl of the drum takes us out of time, into the silence between beats.

"There was only once before when I came close to understanding that. That was from a drummer in a club in Toronto. He was a lot like Spike. I remember he'd always be showing me shit. See, the drummer is always supposed to protect the rhythm, have a beat inside, protect the groove.

"The way you protect the groove is you have to have a beat within the beat. Like 'bang, bang, sha-bang sha-bang.' The 'sha' between the bangs is the beat between the beat, and that little thing is the extra groove. When a drummer can't do that then the groove is off and there's nothing shittier in the world than to have a drummer that hasn't got the groove. Grace, that's like death.

"But the drumming at Peepeekissee and that singing was bigger than the world and smaller at the same time," he said. "I think it was then that I saw something lasting in you, in both of us. It was bigger than both of us.

"I thought your brother Joey was an idiot, though. And I didn't know I was going to have to endure all those physical and mental tortures to become an ex-officio member of the tribe. I might not have gone with you if I'd known about the initiation."

"Right," Grace said. "You'd have failed the audition."

"Yeah. Do you remember that?" asked Holborn. "I had to sit through that infernal sweatlodge ceremony — to prove I was a man or something. There was an axe and pitchfork resting near the fire pit I remember. And there must have been twenty of those huge stones. They'd been heating in that fire pit since dawn.

"And I remember Joey came to get me from the house. It was all very formal I thought. And I was a bit scared. Intimidated. But I think I would have done anything for you then."

"Not now?"

Holborn did not answer.

"Grace, do you remember the feathers, three of them, fluttering on that scrawny willow pole near the fire?" he asked.

"Eagle feathers," said Grace.

"Uh huh," he seemed satisfied. "Oh, and man, it was so quiet that morning. And cold. Early November. A sprinkling of snow. And there were three or four guys standing around the fire and this sweet smell around the place, burning poplar. And there was the smell of tobacco mixed with cedar. It was so quiet."

Holborn coughed, convulsed.

"Got a cigarette?" he asked, pounding his chest and rubbing his ear.

Grace reached into her bag for a pair of Gitanes.

"You should quit," she said, searching for an ashtray they could share.

"So then, beside the fire," he said, unhearing, "I get close to the fire and I see these willow poles all bent in a sort of an igloo and it's covered with grey blankets and canvas and this orange and black tarp."

"I remember," she smiled.

"What was the name of that old guy? The medicine man?"

"Twohearts," said Grace.

"Uh huh. Twohearts," Holborn dragged on the cigarette, blew out smoke. "He was a Rainmaker or something, right?

"Medicine man — from the Mosquito reservation," she said.

"Did I ever tell you about mosquitoes?" asked Holborn, stretching out, readying for a mid-morning nap.

"No, Harry, but I have a feeling you're about to."

"I hate them. The females can bite up to six times before they die. The males hang around trash cans, humans, fence posts, waiting for the females to show up. The eggs are laid on standing water, they form little rafts. The larvae breathe from just under the surface through a pair of tubes like twin trumpets."

He paused, lost in thought, passed her the smoke. His mind cast back to the ancient and venerated Johnny Twohearts, whom Grace's people — at least those among them prone to superstition — claimed was the oldest human being alive. For his part, old Twohearts made no such claims but by the looks of him he might well have been: his glassy eyes bulging and red from the sight of so much of earth's bounty, his skin chafed and leathery from the rays of a million suns; his hands gnarled and corpusculent from an ancient arthritic germ.

"Twohearts was sitting at the door of that sweatlodge," Holborn recalled, his voice trailing off, becoming more distant as an Egyptian siesta beckoned. It had been a late night and an early dawn. Grace stubbed out the smoke.

"He was so little. And he had no teeth. Just like that guy, the tar drummer yesterday — out in the desert. But Twohearts was just one huge set of gums flapping in the breeze, he said it was easier to inhale the world without teeth."

Soon Holborn was in a kind of Coney Island dreamland. Grace smiled. Judging by his soft snore, Harry was very much at Peepeekissee, deep in Peepeekissee, in the thrall of Peepeekissee.

"You ready to do a little penance?" asks the toothless Twohearts, as they stand there, beside a tiny copse, on the mostly bald prairie, beside the fire pit and the sweatlodge of initiation.

As Grace had instructed, Holborn offers Twohearts a package of tobacco. Twohearts, in an outsize lumberjack shirt and Chicago Blackhawks ball cap, examines the offering.

"Oh-oh. Wrong brand," smiles Twohearts, adjusting his cap and collecting his rattle, all gums and piercing eyes. "You know our Mandan people are known for growing the best tobacco," the old man continued. "A hundred years ago down where the Knife River meets the Heart we grew good tobacco. But since we come here, now, on this side of the border the earth don't grow such good tobacco."

"You're gonna tense up, Harry, and then you're probably going to burn," was the word of prognostication from Joey who feigned a comforting arm around the white trumpeter's shoulder.

"So you want to poke my little sister?" winks Joey, coming to the point.

"Maybe I already have," says Holborn, dreaming of the shallow clearing behind the bushes on the reserve. Then to the somnamulating mind of the lightly-snoring hornman comes a voice in Welsh: 'Nos da, time for gwely, bachgen.' It is Daddy, tucking him into bed as he tosses on the sofa fourteen stories above the Nile, which runs deep, Mr. Kurtz he dead, through the black heart of Africa.

"Your lips are going to burn first," says Joey, undressing to climb into the sweatlodge. Clad only in a pair of white drawers he is almost-hairless. Joey nods to Holborn and then drops his underpants. Joey has a very long, thin penis, thinks Holborn. Joey is a very long, thin penis.

"All of us have to learn to be humble so we can walk under the ants," the brother warns. "We have to be smaller than the ants."

Does everyone have a future brother-in-law like Joey? wonders Holborn.

Inside, searing hot stones soon will be dumped into a pit at Holborn's feet and those of the others.

"When you go in, take all your troubles with you and give them all to the Grandfathers," Joey suggests.

"And when that cloth door opens at the end, you'll see white and you'll feel good. Inside, if you don't want to pray out loud that's okay. Those Grandfathers got good ears. They can hear you. If you don't make it today then you're not ready to suffer. Maybe it's not time for you right now. But remember, nobody here wants to be a lady."

Unbuttoning his shirt he looks across the clearing to where Grace and several local women from the reservation have gathered, establishing a table for the feast. There will be elk meat. Bread will be broken. He feels a slight nausea. He looks to Grace. Her back is facing him. She is raising an axe in one swift, fluid motion with her beautiful, long, strong arms, chopping more firewood. She is not like them, he thinks.

Harry doffs his shoes and socks. Unzips his denim jeans. What happens to you if you're judged a lady? A subtle signal comes from those watching the fire. It's time to cook.

The men strip naked but for Holborn who wants his underpants. Joey gives him an unforgiving look. The air, so cool in the early morning, has become thicker, a little tense, anticipatory.

Harry follows as each man walks around the fire, offering tobacco to the spirits of the four directions. He is told to be careful not to step on the 'Damascus Road' — a small ditch between the fire and the entrance to the tiny lodge in which the knowledge and visions of Twohearts will be imparted to them. The super-heated stones are rolled along this road into a shallow pit in the centre of the lodge.

Inside, the men snuggle knee-to-knee inches from the stone-pit.

A sniff of sage, smoke, sweat, deerskin and mouldy blankets.

Twohearts sits at the door, controlling his domain. Along with his rattle, he has a pouch filled with an array of ancient divining instruments and a plastic ice-cream pail of water. In a sure, melodic voice, he begins with a prayer, almost singing:

"Weave for us a garment of brightness. May the beading be the white light of morning. May the warp be the red light of evening. May the fringes be the falling rain. May the border be the standing rainbow. Weave for us a garment of brightness that we may walk fittingly where the birds sing. That we may walk fittingly where the grass is green. Oh Mother Earth. Oh Great Grandfather."

Three men outside take their appointed places, The Doorman, The Waterman, The Rockman. Inside, a pipe is passed. It is filled with Twohearts' secret blend of tobacco, sage, sweet grass and cedar.

Joey leans over with more advice: "Next time take three puffs," he says. "One for yourself, one for your brothers, one for the Grandfathers."

Yellow, green, red and blue ribbons adorn the inner roof of the white dome. Each represents spirits of the four compass points, he is told. Above, like strong bones of a human body, the tarps and bent willows form an airtight skeleton. A rumble now from outside and Holborn hears the huge deerskin drum kick up a rhythm.

Songsters growl in praise. "Ahhh-heyyy-yuh!"

Twohearts draws a long breath through those flappy gums and humbly suggests the men pray for strength.

"Some of you may be lonely — late at night, in the dark, in the quiet of the night," he says.

"Hey-how, ah-hey," come the replies.

"But the Creator will keep and guide you. Remember his words: I am the Near, but not as one thing is near to another: and I am the Far, but not as one thing is far from another."

Twohearts cranes a wizened neck out the canvas door.

"Ready for the stone," he says as The Rockman pitchforks the first cherry-red monster through the entrance. A man named Snake, a friend and blood brother of Joey, uses a Y-shaped stick to roll it into the pit. "We use rocks of love and sharing," Twohearts confides. "We don't use rocks of jealousy or mistrust because if you do your religion will surely crumble."

The first rocks are the spirits of the four directions.

"The first stone is the Eagle — his colour is yellow. We ask him to give us strength."

A second stone — twelve inches across — is pitched in through the door. "The Mouse — his colour is green. He comes from the south. He's always filled with fear, same as us. In here, we give him our fears."

Another hot stone, brown and round. "The Bear. His colour is red, from the West. He teaches us the lesson of looking within ourselves. Where am I today? We pray the spirit of the bear can heal us physically.

"The North is white and the spirit is the spirit of the Buffalo. But not because of the snow. The Buffalo gives us wisdom, knowledge, understanding.

"The most important thing of all is sharing," says Twohearts. "That's the number one thing. We people have always had to rely on each other and share with each other. The reason I'm glad we have this sweatlodge is that it brings us near the things that build up within us. Things build up and we can share them with the spirits."

He lifts a tuft of sweet grass from the ice-cream pail and flicks a few splashes at the men.

"The water represents the Love of the Creator which constantly flows to us."

The last stone is rolled into the pit.

"We use the fifth stone for Mother Earth. She's the one who gives us food and clothing and all the material things we must be thankful for."

Even before the cloth and tarpaulin door is closed the men are dripping with sweat. The temperature has jumped double digits with each new stone.

Twohearts raps on the door. A signal with no words. The Doorman seals it tight as a goollie's bum. And then he stands guard outside.

Holborn finds himself cast into utter blackness. Twohearts' voice rises in song and prayer. His small deerskin drum taps an echo to the giant drum still thumping outside. Ten men arch their backs against the willow skeleton and murmur prayers into invisible directions. Outside, others join in song and praise. The heat is searing. Songs. Blackness. Blazing heat.

"The darkness represents us," says Twohearts, his voice rolling and lilting. "That's how our life appears to be — darkness. But at the end, suddenly you're able to see the man through the confusion and darkness."

The big drum hammers outside. Inside, men murmur prayers from all directions. Songs. Heat rising. A momentary lull.

Then, crash!

A first wave of water from the ice-cream pail hits the stones glowing pink at Holborn's feet, the only point of focus for him in this misbegotten darkness. Drops of hot water splash against his shins, followed instantly by a rising furnace of steam. Lips, necks, ears, nostrils burn. Bones sag. Twohearts passes the rattle — the headbanger — to Snake, who prays in his native tongue. Snake gives it to the white horn man. Splashes of water make more steam. "Ah-hey!" "Ow-ow." More water. No air. A Bible-black inferno. The Headbanger goes to Joey the penis and it follows around the circle for who knows how long. Each man prays in turn. The thunder of the big drum. The staccato of the rattle. Pink stones. More water. Crash! Steam. Lips burn. "Ow-ow." "Ah-hey."

Amid the din, prayer. And then Twohearts raps a boney fist on the door. The Doorman peels away the skin of the entranceway and a swell of cool, crisp air drifts slowly — too slowly thinks Holborn — into the lodge. The Waterman passes paper cups into the sweat. Holborn enjoys a large gulp.

"You offer water to the Grandfathers first," says Joey the penis brother-in-law. "They are thirsty to hear from you."

"Screw Grace," thinks Holborn, who is a sight: tongue hanging out, drenched in sweat and steam, sweltering. Twohearts casts a wary eye around the tent. All appear to have suffered.

"Before the Indians got this sweatlodge," Joey pants, "this is what we used to do when we felt sad." He points to scars slashed above his nipples.

Cherry, a massive mastodon, says that he hopes no one will jam out. How can he know what Holborn has been thinking? "And I don't think any of us need to wear gotch. We all got penises," says Cherry. "The Grandfathers won't be embarrassed."

Holborn's underpants fly out past The Doorman.

The pipe goes around. There are some smiles between the men during this intermezzo. Fatigue sets in and Holborn's mind wanders. He feels taut, stretched, as if he's been nailed to the axis of the turning world. A few sighs. A prayer. Each man looks at the other for a sign of weakness.

Twohearts raps on the open flap of the door.

"More stones."

The Eagle, The Mouse, The Bear, the Buffalo, The Great Beloved Mother Earth. Blackness. Sparks. Drums syncopate with the rhythm of blood rushing past Holborn's temple. Prayers. Drenching, searing heat and splashes from the fire. The second round is longer, too long, and Holborn wants to quit. But because of Joey, he won't. Twohearts raps on the door. A cool breeze. Cold paper cups. Water. Air. An offering to the Grandfathers. A shudder.

Cherry says the sufferers must stick together for the final two rounds. The men slump back against the willow skeleton of the dome, their bones too weary to support them. Twohearts begins to explain the first mysteries of the world.

"Don't look at him," warns Joey. "It's not polite. Your ears work better if your eyes are closed."

"I know that," spits Holborn.

Rocking to-and-fro in a corner of the lodge, Twohearts launches into the secret tale of beginnings — never to be repeated outside the lodge — and it gives them inner strength.

"Some say Twohearts gets his bewitch medicine from under the water," the old man says of himself, as though he were not present. "It is true. One day he is driving horses down to drink — hey. He has a bath in the pool but the warm water makes him drowsy — hey. He is lying in the shallow water eating tubers of cat-tail rushes and Twohearts goes to sleep — hey. He wakes up in the green depth of the pool in the middle of an underwater lodge — ah-hey. Face-to-face on each side of the door are two big fish with their mouths hungry, open. The opening is in the shape of a big turtle. Around the lodge sat underwater medicine men — ah-hey. They are in the shape of frogs, snakes, water dogs, turtles and other creatures. And the Sun God, streaking down through the dark green water in a shaft of light orders the water witches to give Twohearts whatever medicine he wants. In this way he gets not only bewitch medicine but he gets medicine to make bewitch fail — unbewitch medicine. He gets medicine to cure sickness and to give success with women — hey. Any kind of medicine. Some say Twohearts kill people with bewitch medicine from twenty miles away. This a lie. The power of the Creator is Near and Far. The range is fifty miles — ah-hey-yah!"

"Ah-hey-yah!" comes a chorus of weak laughter as the suffering lean away from the fire-pit and the willow skeleton digs into their backs.

Twohearts shakes the headbanger.

"But unbewitch medicine is powerful. With unbewitch medicine Twohearts can find things. Lost things. Misplaced buck-knife, second cousin Lorraine, answer questions. This is the power of the famous Twohearts' unbewitch — hey! But this power is a gift to Twohearts by the Creator to manage for him. The Creator He watches Twohearts and he watches us all. He is Near, so near he is just on the other side of the sky where the birds fly. He also is Far, so far He is the twinkle in your very eye — ah-hey."

More stones and the lodge is once more sealed in night, once more in blackness. Crash! The water makes the stones sparkle like a pile of auburn leaves. At the bottom of the pit, stones from the first round have turned ashen, but the second stones are still pink. Bang! A fresh stone splits from within. Its two halves tumble apart.

Around the pit all is blackness, dizziness, prayer, praise, groans and sweat. Eyes burn from salt and steam.

In the sweat the Grandfathers are playing tricks. Squinting upward into the black, Holborn watches as the dome turns grey. Beyond the grey — through the grey — he can see a small circle of white. There, above his head, a dream within a dream, appears a crystal pool of cool clear spring water. Now the pool is inverted. Now it has sunk below the fire. In the pool's reflection Holborn sees them all, no longer suffering but playing like children around the edge of the water. Even Joey. Holborn wants to dive into the pool. He edges closer. He leans into the fire-pool. An unseen hand pulls him back. Is it a pool? Is it fire? The drums mark the passing rhythm of eternity. Lips and nostrils burn with sweat and steam. All is sweat and steam and dreams. Twohearts raps a fist on the door. He signals they are near the end.

Craning for air, Holborn can sense the end is near. Better make up for his laziness now. He decides to give it all he's got. But how can he do it? Only the spirits can carry him now. Alone, man is nothing.

The rattle comes around. Holborn says a loud prayer for Grace and for himself and their life together. "Ah-hey," the men agree. "Ow-ow."

More stones. Round four goes on forever.

The rattle comes again and it is Cherry's turn to pray. He prays and prays. He pants. He prays. Cherry prays for each member of the circle, for everyone in his extended family right down to his second cousin Lorraine.

In English, he ends.

"I pray my brothers will forgive me for taking so long in my prayers." He sighs. Bless you Cherry. Okay. Ow-ow. Ah-hey.

Twohearts raps on the door. The Doorman peels back the great foreskin of the dome. And this time he peels it half-way over the lodge. The suffering are enveloped in the chill of the morn. It is finished.

Each man shakes the hand of the other. And in turn, from within this inner circle, they crawl outside, Harry first, Twohearts last.

The air is so sweet. It is the same day as earlier, bright and crisp and beautiful. But now it is brighter, crisper, mortal. The meadowlark sings more sharply. The cedar smoke, so sweet. And this grassy earth is so firm and cool between Holborn's toes. As the no-longer-suffering stride around the perimeter of the lodge they cast a knowing glance at one another. Ten beings have suffered and shared secrets together. They are friends.

Harry looks around and Grace appears. She glitters when she walks. And ignoring Holborn's nakedness she takes his hands in hers. They look into each other's eyes, satisfied, complete. And there — high above, two hawks dance across the heavens beyond the trees.

MELANOSIS

Clumps of thickening mist enveloped the rhododendrons as Felix parked the Daimler behind a rubbish tip in the heart of Hampstead Heath.

The old impresario squeezed from the back seat, quietly closed the door, and disappeared into Flask Walk. As he walked through the dim lane, planning his navigation across the cobblestone's uneven surface, his calcified left toe throbbed as if tightened in an Iron Lady.

And as he pushed his way into the dowdy antiquarian bookshop the top of the door grazed a suspended cow-bell, its clanking prompting the bespectacled book dealer to look up from behind his counter. Kenyon doddered past him through Anthropology, Cosmology, Empiricism, History, Iridology, Ontology, Theology.

"You have my book? My cookbook, was it?" he asked, as he brushed past the shopkeeper.

"Cookbook, yes," said the shopkeeper with a wink, following Kenyon down the isle.

"Something special, a recipe with a tinge of saltpeter, balneo and coke. I think you want to try ... yes, here we are, the Kabbala. But watch the saltpeter, makes you droopy it does."

Reaching into the heart of the section on Judaism the clerk withdrew an English-Hebrew translation of the Kabbala and handed it to his customer. Kenyon opened the volume to The Book of Concealed Mystery and glanced at the two lines of marginalia scribbled in the gutter of the book. He purchased the black, leather-bound volume, in cash.

"I would advise you to read it in one sitting," said the clerk, dropping the purchase in a brown paper sack. "And then read it again, for meaning."

"Very good. Thank you," smirked Kenyon.

As he lumbered to the car Kenyon teetered sideways. He was overcome with sudden nausea, almost sea-sickness. He was afraid if he fell, he would fall hard.

Safely in the car, he reread the marginalia and instructed Felix to Camden Town. The driver gunned the motor and hydroplaned along narrow roads heading southward. It was warm for October and there was a smell of slow rot in the air, of mould and compost. When they reached the Grand Canal, Kenyon tucked the book under his arm and walked warily beside the locks.

Birds mocked him from the trees as he slumped down the footpath that ran beside a dozen tethered houseboats, his adrenaline rising. When he found the Mystique, one hundred and eighty tons of bobbing steel, he edged across the gangway and, with a glance over his shoulder, disappeared through the narrow doorway.

A well-dressed man sat in the pilot-lounge, Israeli folk music playing on a small stereo. "Aaron, my friend, Shalom!" he said. "Come below, to the saloon."

It took Kenyon a few seconds to register who had addressed him.

"Are you daft, Eli?" said Kenyon, flopping in a chair, winded. "Ordering a meeting? Face to face? Have you lost all sense? What if I — "

"Never mind, Aaron, you weren't followed. I have ensured our security."

With a precise sweep of his hand Eli invited Kenyon to survey the barge. "Not bad, eh? I mean it's not exactly a mooring on the Seine but it's still comfortable. Now tell me, how was Egypt? You know the saying: he who has once drunk from the Nile shall always return."

Kenyon did not answer.

"When was the last time we actually saw one another?" Eli said. "Was it the Cavalry Club in Gezirah, 1960? I believe it was. I was a mere child in Cairo, the City of Victory, on my way to the Promised Land. You know, they say the Cairenes were, perhaps still are, the eyes and ears of the Egyptian security service. Their communal retina is on every corner, outside every door and shop. It's as if the whole city is one great slumbering, watchful animal, eh?"

"Just like the nation of Israel, which will never transcend history?" snapped Kenyon.

"No, that's right, never," said Eli. "It's burned into the collective memory. Because there is no difference between memory and history. There can be no forgetting. No forgiveness, no letting go or casting away."

"And therefore no serenity, no peace, no hesed," Kenyon nodded. "The world is bigger than Israel, bigger than the Jews, the Palestinians, the Hutus, the Serbs. But what do you do? Lose it all in hatred. And you follow your father as if he were El Shaddai himself. A big shot in Ha-Mossad, are we now?"

"Will you have a drink, Aaron?" said Eli, evading. "Chivas is all I have."

"No. Thank you."

"Oh, come. Have a drink," said the younger man, as if it were an order.

Ignoring Kenyon's protest, he poured a good portion of scotch into a cheap pair of glass tumblers. "Do you know? My father told me how brilliantly you operated in Cairo in your heyday. When did you join the service? Was it really back in 1948? Oh, I'm sorry, I forgot. You trained, you had great potential, but you never joined. It was Egypt then, that was your undoing wasn't it? How curious. Fifty years.

"A lifetime has passed, Aaron. I remember my father telling me. You arrived in Egypt while he was still the number one there, and he said you were so well briefed that on your first night you commended the maitre d' at The Kharshuf for adding a '36 Figeac to his wine list. You penetrated the ruling circle of Nasser's Egypt with ridiculous ease. You were conveyed like an honoured visitor to the inner circle of Egyptian society life. There is nothing the Egyptians love more than ostentation, is there? And your system was so simple. Get them together at a party, give them a fine meal and plenty of whiskey — which most of them love but can't afford — and they soon start talking. It's surprising how much one can squeeze from even the most casual conversations. And of course no one knew you spoke Arabic."

"You know that's all a big lie," said Kenyon. "What is it you want?"

"By the way," said Eli. "Have you toured Petra?"

"You know I have not," said Kenyon who could feel the shoals and reefs of dangerous conversational waters prickling about him.

"Ah yes, of course," Eli kept digging. "That was part of your problem, wasn't it, Aaron? It was the great rite of initiation into the service back then. A hike from the border across the Jordanian desert to the abandoned city of Petra. Thirty miles. What would it have taken? Four, five days? Dangerous though. The trail passes through moist wadis where a hiker leaves footprints. How many agents were caught by the Bedouin battalions guarding that section in Jordan? I heard at least a dozen men disappeared at various times on the journey to Petra. You never tried it, eh?"

"You know I did not."

"Yes, that was the source of your troubles. No promotion into the service after that. But I heard you were good. My father said you had great potential. Potential unfulfilled."

Kenyon's mind flashed back nearly fifty years to his elite training regimen. The reminiscence came in a flood. "You never know when you are going to have to run," one instructor had barked as the recruits learned codes, surveillance, assumed identities, infiltration, handling weapons, self-defence. Agents would be told to watch a film, and then suddenly the projector would be turned off. "You have exactly one minute," the instructor would say, "to describe the scene in the upper left corner of the last frame, only the upper left corner."

Many times the trainees were taken out on the streets of Tel Aviv and told to follow a veteran agent. They were told never to do the things spies and detectives do in bad movies and sometimes in real life. Don't sit on a bar stool and eye the quarry over the edge of a newspaper — better to strike up a conversation with some girls, joke with the waiter, or befriend a drunk. "Do anything to fit into the landscape!" they were told. "Don't stick out!"

Kenyon finally took a long sip of the Chivas before him. There was silence. Eli could see the older man was lost in remembrance. He waited, watching.

Kenyon recalled the times he was given false papers, taken to the arrivals gate at Lod, and coolly conned his way past unsuspecting passport control officers, and the practice runs when he had slipped, undetected, into military installations and air bases in the fledgling Jewish state. The discipline was tough and unforgiving: preparation for the real thing.

"Always obey orders," came the warning. "Obey the orders one hundred percent, not ninety-nine percent and not one hundred and one percent, but exactly one hundred percent. Do precisely what you are told to do, not one minute sooner and not one minute later. Mind your own business. Don't take an interest in what other agents are doing. You have your job, they have theirs. Just make certain you do yours. Think only when you are ordered to think."

There were training assignments that stretched his endurance and patience. Instructors watched as he negotiated a complex itinerary through Israel, making countless bus changes, cab switches, walking past certain points at exact times. He was sent on bogus missions and left standing in the street watching for someone who never came by.

Then, 1949. Cairo. An emotional roller coaster. No amount of training or psychological testing could fully prepare him for the hazard of a real operation. Kenyon so feared being unmasked that he felt a surge of gratitude when anyone — chambermaid, hotel clerk, news vendor — accepted his pretense. He was careful not to be overly courteous or too effusive.

His assignment, such as it was, was to memorize the hieroglyphs inside the pyramid of Mycerinus. "In ancient Egypt," his Israeli handler told him, "the priests had to feed the divine Ka so it could grow and fulfill itself. The sacred food was the semen of the father in heaven, which the priests produced as a white powder, refined from gold: ghost gold. We want to replicate their process."

Sceptical, Kenyon thought he was being sent on another training mission. Yet he completed his instructions and memorized the hieroglyphs in a matter of minutes. As he was about to leave Cairo he saw no harm in telephoning his old friend Levi, Eli's father, who operated a sheep-slaughtering plant in the suburbs. It turned out to be a near disaster, for his call, traced by the Egyptian security service, almost fingered Israel's number one operative in the Middle East.

"You scored high Aaron — but not high enough," said Eli, finally, sipping his scotch.

"There were doubts about your capabilities after that. You were weighed in the balance and found wanting. But you shouldn't feel badly. Only fifteen percent of the recruits manage to finish it. And you've been a good mule here in England all these years. Life hasn't treated you too shabbily, has it, Aaron?"

Kenyon did not respond, but turned his eyes to the window of the craft, to the treetops and birds which seemed menacing.

Eyes narrowing, Eli handed the older man a small white envelope.

"I am sorry for your trumpet player," said Eli. "It could not be predicted. But we need both instruments. Now that these horns have been flushed from the dust-bins of history, we need the pair to conduct a proper cross-analysis. It's like trying to get a sufficient DNA sample from criminal evidence — with only one horn there wasn't enough of the ghost gold for conclusive testing."

Kenyon snorted, sceptical.

"Our technicians," continued Eli, flushing with impatience, "are convinced that once these samples provide an atomic blue-print we will be well on our way to refining the most perfect gold for a new generation of nano-processors. An argon laser will direct the vaporized ghost gold onto the active areas of the gallium arsenide device. We'll have processors fifty thousand times faster than the current microchips, but only if we can replicate the gold on those horns. And think, Aaron, what we can do with these new chips: we'll put the most powerful computers in the world into tiny cameras, listening posts, satellites. It will revolutionize our work."

"Now look," Eli continued. "I am taking over the last phase of this operation. You should know this is a combined operation with Shin Bet. We have activated two teams: Heth, which was in Switzerland until a few days ago, and Ayin, which is here."

"So it was you, in Switzerland ... the old man Sterner?" said Kenyon grimly.

"Not a matter for your concern, Aaron," replied Eli. "Here is a chance to redeem yourself. The next phase of the operation is vital. We need the girl to be distracted for awhile. Forty-eight hours or so. Sufficient time for a team to conduct a surreptitious entry to the trumpeter's home and retrieve the other horn. Yes, we could have taken it any time in the last forty years, but there was no point till now. Until your trumpeter led us to the twin in Cairo — well, what good would one horn do us? We'd have had just half the equation. Finally we can have both. Now tell me, what do you know of the girl's whereabouts? Quick, come on."

Kenyon swallowed, his skin the shade of a crab-apple. "Well," he said, obsequious now, wanting to wash his hands of the situation and avoid trouble. "I gather she's leaving for North Wales tomorrow. She's up there with the drummer for a few days, before the funeral. So you can leave me out of it."

"Good," said Eli. "We'll send someone to watch her. Now look, Aaron, we also require any documents the musician had relating to the horns and their provenance. This is your main task. Try and put two and two together and give me a report. And, one last piece of advice: don't let anyone do any more poking around."

Kenyon filled with resignation. He wanted out, but saw no easy way. Somewhat desperately he looked at his watch, thinking he might make an excuse and run Felix to a doctor in Harley Street to fix the trapped gas in the chauffeur's colon.

Then Eli gestured the meeting was over. "Now Aaron. We'll make contact again in a day or two. I'll make it somewhere nice and public for a late afternoon lunch. To avoid suspicion, understand?"

Eli stood towering over Kenyon extending a hand. "Good-bye for now. So nice to have seen you."

And with that Kenyon set down his unfinished drink, pushed himself from the table and hobbled down the gangway to his waiting car. It bothered him that Eli, after avoiding direct contact for so many years would risk a public lunch.

Weary, shaken, he arrived at his house on Parliament Hill less than an hour later. It was four o'clock and time for a nap. Felix's colon could wait. He dropped his coat on the shoulder of a headless semi-nude dating from the reign of King Amenhotep.

Reddening, bulbous, sweating from the secretions of bad glands, he went into the drawing room where on the mantle of the fire were a number of Babylonian haematite carvings representing a frog, a baboon, twin serpents, and a boar's head. As he rested with a whiskey in the leather lounger, his swollen pods upon an eighteenth-century Tahitian stool, Kenyon could not refrain from thinking of the twin Framptons. God's commandment to Moses, after all, was to "make thee two trumpets" not three, or one, or forty-four. He had Felix prepare a mustard plaster for what he felt was an imminent viral episode. He also called for a bowl to soak his plump, pink, and calcified feet in the soothing sibilations of Epsom salts.

Yes, yes, yes, he relaxed. The curved metal trumpets of the Nordic bronze ages, the Lurer, as they were so aptly named, were always found in pairs. The twin metal trumpets in ancient Afghanistan were played simultaneously, as are horns in the crannies of India and Tibet. And Kenyon had read somewhere that the same was true of the wooden trumpets of Lithuania, Romania and Chile.

After mustard and Epsom he retired upstairs. He'd instructed Felix to wake him at six for an early evening meal before Grace. Seating himself in a paisley nightgown, he held his wobbling head in his hands and tried not to think of his unsettling meeting with Eli. But he suddenly felt his chest constrict — a host of medical possibilities raced through his mind: acute cardiomyopathy, a myocardial infarction, pulmonary arrhythmia.

He prayed for serenity. It did not come but within a few minutes the imaginary chest pains moved down to his rectum, close enough to the prostate for concern. Tomorrow he would call upon one of his physicians in Harley Street.

He reached to his night table for *Gray's Anatomy* and reclined toward sleep. As Kenyon lowered his hairless dome onto the silken pillow of his Victorian four-poster he realized how tired he was, tired in the metaphysical sense. Ah — bed. Beautiful bed. Bed bed bed bed bed. He closed the book on his finger and allowed his mind to wander. He would not think of Eli and what, perhaps, was to come. Rather, he would return that evening to The Bunker full of brass and charm and entertain the two North Americans with his waxy tongue.

His eyes closing, he imagined how he would impress or annoy Hardman — it didn't matter which — by descanting learnedly upon the many circumlocutions which had been purged from modern usage.

"Do you know," he would begin, "that despite a grand and hearty sloom, I awoke feeling totally forswunk, thinking, mistakenly, that it was sparrows-fart. Ah, you may hurkle, but I shall flurn your snirtles, being more concerned with respect to my own wofare, if you can parse my meaning.

"Oh my little colonial bedbugs," he would regale them, sitting in the L of the parlour. "What, pray tell, may I creem before your swippered eyes? Hang-on — pass me the snotterclout before I sneeze. Ah! this snurl has me feeling a trifle treaf, frightfully frampard, to the point, indeed, where I am no more than a branglesome, fratchy, hickery totish, tethy, trunch. Err this, or I am a smidgen cross and peevish with you for your lack of respect. For all the things I have done for you in particular, Hardman, and you pay me no regard. Never mind. For you mistake me for some low Goyster. But tonight before the cock's craw thrice crumbles, we shall have a dram. A dram before cockshut, a plate of maw-wallop, and then we shall all repast for at least a few more slooms before mirkshade and a flyover to the ditch they've dug for Harry in Canada."

Kenyon chuckled himself to sleep.

PVTREFACTIO

Harry Holborn stares up, up into the effulgent surgical light, his eyes unseeing, as the bouquet of death, so sweet and so stale, curls over the clipped nose hairs of Dr. Robert Negroponte.

A clerk had unzipped the white plastic body bag, sliding the lifeless form onto the stainless steel table where it lay patiently in the subterranean morgue of Winnipeg's Hotel Misericord for nineteen minutes before Negroponte's arrival.

The physician assembles his tools and then photographs Holborn's face with a Polaroid. He dons thin latex gloves over his black-haired wrists and makes a cursory examination: the eyes, the inside of the mouth, the ears, the hands. He takes a swab from each orifice and from under the fingernails. With a casual forefinger he lifts Holborn's penis for scrutiny. The impetus of so much of a man's fawning or shame, the sight of the flaccid organ in death is not especially remarkable.

Negroponte pins a small microphone to the front strap of his apron and begins recording. He has learned, from an anatomist friend at the university, that a well-known publisher of medical textbooks is soliciting post-mortem transcripts for a new imprint: Forensics: Theory and Practice.

"We have before us the subject H. H. Holborn, jazz musician, pulled four days ago from the River Nile. There is no entry wound, no bruising, no apparent blunt trauma injury. I will analyse the vitreous humour from the eye, the stomach contents and bile for poisoning, drugs and alcohol intake."

Scalpel in hand, he slices, in one sleek motion, the cavity from the pubis to the breastbone. There is no quivering, no flinching, no cry of protest from the cadaver as he then cuts outward to the shoulders like a Y.

There is little blood. A gentle stream of water washes over the corpse and is sluiced off in a gutter rounding the examination table like a moat. With a saw Negroponte makes parallel cuts through the rib cage, nipple-wide.

As if removing a grate, he lifts out the entire rib block. Then, with a quick snip, he removes the respiratory tract: palate, windpipe and lungs, gripping the tongue like a handle.

The thoracic organs are removed as a unit, separate from the abdominal ones. On a cutting block the colour of avocado flesh, he dissects the organs, keeping small pieces — green, red-brown and grey — in a Mason jar for further study. The remainder he plops into a green plastic trash bag.

A mottled, pinky-grey mass of lung is set aside for closer scrutiny. Negroponte notes the lungs are heavy. It appears the dead man's last inspiration filled them with the turbid water of the Nile.

He makes a written note. Each organ is weighed and examined. The liver looks like a sloppy, purple rugger ball, the gall-bladder a greeny-red sachet, the spleen a wrinkly potato chip — like Pringles from the Piggly-Wiggly, he thinks.

Negroponte reaches again for the tongue — an enormous organ only the tip of which Holborn used for the staccato transition between notes. He eyes it for evidence of seizure. With his fingers, Negroponte probes Holborn's vacant airway until he reaches the U-shaped hyoid bone, feeling for a break which might indicate strangulation.

Making an incision along the hairline from ear to ear, he deftly peels back the skin from Holborn's forehead. Then, taking up his hacksaw, he cuts off the crown of the skull like a hard-boiled egg, exposing the brain in its filmy sac, the dura. Rupturing the membrane, Negroponte bottles some fluids and removes Holborn's brain. It is sliced and diced like a tomato. Electrodes are attached to a few small pieces and placed under a microscope.

The pathologist continues to dictate into the recorder.

"As we infiltrate the lower cerebellum we are cognizant of the theoretical work by Altizer and Vahanian which suggests the Neural Cellular Assemblies associated with cognition have a dynamic component."

He activates the electrodes and peers into a electron microscope as the current passes through the synaptic meat of Holborn's brain.

"In this instance the afferent sensory data appear to arrive at the surface of the olfactory bulb in dispersed form, with the signal from each sensory neuron forming a Gaussian spatial distribution of activations on the surface of the outer membrane.

"There seems also a global reafference involving the local coeruleus that may set the general gain of the network here. Whether it involves general attention or is insufficiently specific to be semantic at the NCA level is unclear at this juncture, but I have excised the inferior olive for later microscopic examination.

"There also appears in this subject to have been some over-firing of the Purkinje cells which would generate inhibitory signals to fine-tune the motor commands of the three right-hand fingers and tip of the tongue," Negroponte concludes. "So we see as in everything, there is an explanation. It is not artistry but the physical composition of the subject. This Mr. Holborn was predisposed in his ability to render musical notes through a horn. The body, matter, governs the correspondent sound."

Negroponte transits the tip of the probe a millimetre deeper into Holborn's grey matter. What this triggers in the dead tissue cannot be seen by the physician: a cellular equivalent of the cosmological big bang. In an instant, the electric current fuses two deuterium nuclei in cells which formerly governed memory, creating a helium-4 micron bubble. The man is extinct, rigour is evident, but in accord with the second law of Deuteronomics, the data of a life has not yet vanished. Indeed, it can never be erased. In this quantum moment the impossible is made possible. For the instant is a pearl-bearing shell, sealed at the bottom of the ocean of a human heart. And at the rising tide of judgment all the shells cast onto the beach will be opened for pearls.

And so in this millisecond the billion or so cells in the micron bubble do not see themselves lying in pieces on an autopsy table in Canada. These cells are in Cairo, lunching with Loutfi the light, the cunning linguist. The customers flock in, some in fezzes, some in hats, others in turbans. A waiter wipes the tabletops with a towel. Lamps light the dim corners of the stone-walled room. The bar flashes with reflections of Dewars and Johnnie Walker.

On the street laughter reverberates like a call to prayer. Holborn and Loutfi watch a shrimp seller from Upper Egypt enter the bar. He is followed by a woman with two gold teeth selling peanuts, an Indian palm reader, a man offering to shine customers' shoes, a kebab vendor who is also a pimp, and a Tunisian stamp collector who carries a cassette-player blaring "Climb Every Mountain."

In a mirror across the rear wall Loutfi sees his own flushed face and his gleaming eyes. He raises a drink to Holborn's health and rinses his tender wisdom tooth with a rabbit-like twitch before swallowing.

"We're a very conservative family, Mr. Harry. I'm the first to taste alcohol."

"But you're not drinking booze," says Holborn.

"To me, in such a place as this, everything tastes of spirits," Loutfi replies raising his glass of lemon water. "I inhale it through the very pores of my skin." He pauses.

"Wish I could do that trick," says Holborn.

"In Canada it is very cold I suppose," Loutfi continues, staring at the ice-cubes, wiping his brow from the heat.

"Yes, very cold," says Holborn.

"You have snow."

"Yes, Loutfi. The Inuk have hundreds of names for snow. Snowflakes. Snow made rough by rain and frost. Powdered snow. Crystalline snow — you name it."

"Snow," smiles Loutfi, shivering and looking about. "And balls?"

"Balls?" says Holborn.

"Snow balls," says Loutfi.

"Yes."

"And you have clubs — like this — where you drink with ice-cubes?"

"Not quite like this. When I was young I played the horn in a lot of clubs in Canada and the States. We called them bucket-o'blood clubs in those days because people would get drunk and fight."

"Bang, Bang! Shoot-em-up-cowpoke. Get on little doggies," intones Loutfi, revealing his knowledge of the ways of the West.

"With fists."

"Ah. And you played your horn during these fights?"

"I played because I love making music Loutfi. When I was a kid, musicians kept telling me I could play but I wasn't vain enough to believe it."

"It is good to have not much pride, Mr. Holborn."

"Let me tell you something," says Holborn. "One time we were playing at the Oogieboogie, that's a club in Toronto, Loutfi, and there was a dancer there named Cleopatra."

"Cleopatra?" says Loutfi, his eyes widening.

"I think her actual Christian name was Irene," offers Holborn.

"The Christians gave her a name, Mr. Harry?"

"Well sort of, anyway, she was finer than anything, Loutfi. She was so rare that men would send her roses every night. Everybody wanted to — to be her lover. She was an exotic dancer and we used to play behind her. Anyway, one night I was passing her dressing room and she called me in. Now I have to tell you, Loutfi, that woman had a fine bottom, long legs, a head of red hair that shone way down her back. She was tanned, which is something in Canada, and about twenty-three or twenty-four. I guess I was about seventeen."

"Yes, so you have miracles in America as well?" grins Loutfi.

"Anyway, Loutfi, she tells me she wants me to hold this little mirror under her — here, see — between her legs while she shaved her hair. So what was I supposed to do? I held the mirror while she did it and I didn't think anything of it. The bell rang backstage and the intermission was over. I told the drummer what happened and he looked at me very strangely and said: 'So what did you do?' I told him I just held the mirror for her. And he said 'That's all? That's all you did? Yeah, man.'

"I said, 'Yeah, that's all I did; what else was I supposed to do?' The drummer just shook his head and started pissing himself, and then he said, 'You mean with all the sex-fiend mothers in this band she lets YOU hold that goddamn mirror?'

"You had someone's mother in the band, Mr. Holborn?" asks Loutfi. "Your drummer went wee-wee and you pervert the name of God? This is not good Mr. Holborn."

"I know Loutfi, but the drummer, let me finish, he starts looking around for someone to tell. For quite awhile after, the whole band looked at me kind of funny — oddly. I thought it was just show business, right? You know, you help each other out."

"Show business," mutters Loutfi.

"I guess later as I thought about it, that wonderful woman having me hold that mirror for her, and me looking at that sweet sight — what could have been on her mind? I never found out. But she had her radar on me in that sly way women look at men who are sort of innocent. It's like they're wondering how it would be to teach you all they know. But I was kind of moronic about women then and I didn't know when I was being hit on."

"Hit on, Mr. Harry?"

"This happens, Loutfi. Oh, jeez. But that was the sixties, man. Everybody was stoned. Now it's business. I remember not so long ago when jazz, western jazz and fusion, the stuff I like to play, well, it was in its heyday. We used to play in Europe, places like the Domicile in Munich and the Bazillus in Zurich. Then they closed, and we got the message. So instead of staying inside the American traditions we started to experiment with folk music and other influences. It goes down okay in the small clubs like this one we're in now. Maybe we should come here and play, Loutfi, what do you say? We'll turn this little place of yours into the Egyptian equivalent of the Akwarium in Warsaw or the Unterfahrt in Munich. What do you say?"

"I don't know, Mr. Holborn. People here are very traditional and...Unterfahrt? What is Unterfa-"

The pair are interrupted by an arrival at the table. Towering over them is a scholarly-looking man in a silk business suit. He carries a worn leather valise. A single stripe of white hair runs through the centre of his black, neatly cropped mane.

Loutfi jumps up in greeting. "Marhaba," he says, bowing slightly in deference.

"Marhaba," the man smiles, waving his hand to dispense with formality.

The waiter appears instantly with fresh drinks. Loutfi the light, big guppy of little pond, gulps and stares into the eyes of the leviathan.

"Welcome to Egypt," says the skunk-haired Arab in impeccable English, extending his hand. "I have been eager to meet you, Mr. Holborn, since Loutfi first told ..."

Negroponte removes the probe, satisfied with his examination of the brain's electrolytic response to the stimuli, and the cells of the corpse revert to their inert state.

At the end of this procedure Negroponte weighs the remains of Holborn's brain and deposits the bits in a green trash sack. After replacing the crown of the skull and pulling the face back into place, Negroponte seals up the trash bag and drops it into the body cavity sewing it shut with a large needle. He takes a culture sample from Holborn's ears, turns off the microphone, doffs his gloves and apron, and heads for the shower.

Refreshed, he sends the Mason jar and cultures to the laboratory.

While waiting in his office for the lab results, Negroponte begins to manufacture the written autopsy report that he will forward to Kenyon. At a certain point he thumbs through The Koran:

Thinketh man that We shall not assemble his bones?

Yea, verily. We are able to restore the very tips of his fingers!

FERMENTATIO

Dead leaves drifted across the pool in the garden of The Bunker as Grace, a cipher of loneliness in a thick Icelandic sweater, spat blood-red pistachio shells onto the floating Cabomba lillies.

She tried to phone her brother Joey at the Peepeekissee Reserve in Canada. She cupped the receiver of the portable phone, began pacing the perimeter of the pool, and strained to hear the faint ringing. It would be ten at night in Peepeekissee. The number was changed, a recording said. When she dialled again she heard only the recorded voice of Chief Guy Lonesome, saying the tribal office was closed during non-business hours.

The moment she hung up, the telephone rang and she rebuked herself for not leaving it turned off. "Hello?" she said. "Hello?"

"Your friend Mr. Hardman has been in an accident," said a flat, disembodied voice. "Please come quickly — to The Manna." The line went dead.

She hung up, dumfounded. The world was abandoning her. The rug had been pulled. Nothing was certain. Panic set in, that old gut-wrenching fear.

She called a minicab, brushed past the photographers outside The Bunker and sped to Regent's Park Road. At the Café Manna, behind the counter with postcards of the Grand Tetons, the Lebanese chef, still smelling of sweat and rosemary, smiled his best lecherous grin. Wide-eyed, Grace stared at him breathlessly, then followed his eyes as they shifted to the rear of the shop. Sitting at a table, shaking a match after lighting a smoke, was a familiar-looking Arab man — the one from the airplane, she remembered, at Larnaca. The one with the skunkish stripe in his hair.

"My most beautiful Madame," said the skunk-man, rising slowly, his chromium wristwatch shining, his suit impeccable. "May I impose upon you? I have some information in which I believe you have an interest. It concerns one errant member of a pair of twin horns."

Grace sat at the table. The waiter instantly brought tea.

"My name is Atrash," the man said, lowering his eyes. "And this," he said indicating the waiter with a finger wave, "Is Faisal, the manager of this humble, vile, and worthless establishment which does no justice to your present and eternal beauty."

"Yes, we have met," she said of the waiter. "And you. I remember. On the airplane from Cairo. What's going on here? What do you know about Harry? Look, I've just about had all the goddamn mystery and intrigue I can stomach. Someone called me about Spike. Where is he? What's happened to him?"

"I am sorry. A ruse," the Arab said, adopting a prisoner-in-the-dock expression. "There was no accident. I believe he is safe and sound at his hotel. I needed a way to speak with you — you see?"

Grace glared at him, the colour draining from her face, bile rising in her belly. She was confounded, brimming with heartache, mysteriously impelled.

Atrash produced a cellular telephone, dialled, and passed it across the table.

She cradled the receiver as it rang. "Hotel Coburg — How may I help you?"

"Mr. Hardman, Spike Hardman please," she said. After a few clicks the sleepy voice of the drummer came on the line. "Spikey, it's Grace... are you... is everything all right?"

"Well for sure, Grace, just catching a few zees, what's up?"

She thought she heard a woman murmur in the background. She relaxed. "Oh, it's okay, Spike. I'll see you later. Eight."

Turning to Atrash, her eyes narrowed. She felt the stirrings of a nameless dread pounding like a timpani, a chemical abstertion flushing her veins of the adrenaline which had kept her going until now.

"What do you want? And what do you know about Harry? And the horns? What do you know?"

Grace glanced at her tea, a cracked white cup, realizing it had been just twelve hours since she sat in the same empty café, the clock burning away the crust of shock and uncovering a derma of anguish.

Atrash collected himself, mustered his humility. "I wish you to know that I am a great admirer of your late husband and his varied musical styles," he said. "I had the honour of hearing him play one night at Giza. I think the music was made of heaven. And I am so sorry for you in this time of grief. We were hesitant to contact you, but I had Faisal send flowers so that you might know we are friends."

Grace immediately scuppered this rhetoric. "You lied to me, to get me here. Lied. Why? And who the hell are 'We'?"

"This will be clear to you in the fullness of time," said Atrash.

"For many years I have devoted much time to researching the history of Frampton horns," he said. "That is, until recently when certain political agendas forced me to leave Cairo and return to the place of my birth in Lebanon, the village of Bint Jbail. Although my return was not voluntary, it turned out, in some ways, to be most felicitous. But before I say more, I beg of you, there is someone you must meet."

"Who?"

"Come," Atrash gestured to a narrow doorway in the rear of the café, "He is waiting for you — upstairs."

A leaden weight pressed upon Grace's thighs. Her feet felt chained to the floor. There was no reason to follow this stranger. She could not trust him. But neither could she afford not to trust him. Slowly the lead weight lifted. She was beyond caring for herself any longer. She needed answers. She found herself on her feet.

Atrash led her through the portal and up a narrow set of stairs where the woodwork along the handrail was festooned with Islamic patterns, stained ivory and dusty mother-of-pearl. Down a long corridor they went, at its end a massive mercury-backed mirror in a hand-carved frame. To the left was a small door with many locks, opening to a massive room where the windows had been blackened with crepe.

As her eyes penetrated the darkness, there, in the centre of the space, sat a white-bearded man, venerable, regal in his bearing. The figure was dressed entirely in white robes.

"My lady," whispered Atrash. "This is my grandfather. A chief and holy man from our village in Lebanon. He wishes a few words with you."

The pair stood at the door while the ancient man began to whisper in a low, even tone. Then the sheikh's voice rose several octaves and he broke into what sounded like a long growl on a horn. In the poor light, Grace could have sworn that the old sheikh didn't rise to his feet normally: he seemed to float up and then lower his legs to a stack of cushions beneath him.

The old man gestured for the pair to come near. Atrash took Grace by the elbow and led her to a cushion beside the old man.

She could not say, looking at his whipcracked face, how old he was — eighty, a hundred. But he had a tall forehead and the most startling bright eyes that stared through her as if plumbing the depths of her soul. Grace was transfixed.

The old one calmly raised his hands until they were parallel with the floor. He then clenched and unclenched his fingers violently. Grace wondered if she saw liquid stream from his fingers.

Then he spoke, in crisp, perfect English.

"Eighteen-fifty-six," the old man said to her, eyebrows rising, waiting for a reaction. She nodded.

"1856. In Lebanon there is a place named Naqqoura, near the border with Palestine, on the coast. It was a low night and you could see the moon carving a circling rhythm over the sea. A roof of stars took shape as night curled deep around the village. Darkness rose from the cedars. On the edge of the stone path a man, Narish, was greeted by two riders and two pack mules. They are the British Viscount, Angelsey, and his footman — a man named Gareth Holborn — an ancestor of your late husband," the old sheik explained slowly.

"The three rode seven leagues north along the coast road to the caves at Cape Blanco or Ras-el-Abiad. Here they tethered the animals behind a copse as one gave a low whistle. Dawn was burning away a shroud of mist. A boy rose from his watch over a small flock to greet them. "Wallah. Marhaba," he whispered, moving to feed and water their weary animals. To escape a brief dance of rain, they climbed down a narrow footpath overlooking the sea and into a cave which ran far into the ground. They joined a dozen Bedouin. Save for the lapse of a few thousand years these might have been the sons of Joseph come down from Egypt to haggle over a sack of corn. Can you picture this?"

Grace nodded, wondering if this ancient figure was speaking from his own experience. As she tried to fathom the meaning of it all, the old man continued.

"They had coffee and a pipe. And for twenty pieces of silver and a side of goat-meat they took possession of a bone. Not any bone. But a ceremonial ram's horn, a shofar, which had come some years before from the camp of Napoleon himself. It once belonged to the Jews in Akko. Now with the bone, and led by Narish, the Viscount and his footman set off into the Bekkaa and up into the Shouff."

The old man sighed, and clearing his throat he continued:

"They had come to the edge of the Druze fortress of Bint Jbail. Angelsey camped in a field at the eastern foot of the castle hill. The slopes to the north were deep in snow all the way to the ruined walls of the fortress, and even below the Bedouin tents a few snowdrifts glittered under a full moon."

Grace offered the old man the thinnest of smiles as the younger man, Atrash, broke in to speak.

"The village he speaks of, Bint Jbail, is my home." he said. "High on a hill. You see, in the flood courses of Rayyan the riverbeds are naked and worn smooth, as writing is etched on stone. And so we built in Bint Jbail because God has built a house with a high roof for us and we must try to reach its height. Now, the legend is that Angelsey and the footman sent a message upon their arrival that they wished to speak to the headman, known as the "Deaf One" — and that Angelsey would bring a gift.

"I — we," Atrash gestures to the old sheikh who is almost levitating on the cushions, "am a Druze. Like your own dark-skinned people in America, we are a remnant of a proud people. Our faith began in the thirteenth year of the caliph's reign, the same year as the destruction of the Church of the Holy Sepulchre in Jerusalem. We are Muslim. But we see no need for the hajj to Mecca or for the persecution of Jews or Christians."

The old sheikh cut in: "And of course we revere the words of the great Prophet, peace be upon him. But the scriptures serve only to point toward the Higher Power. Apart from that, they are empty. The are voluminous so they might be accessible to seekers at every level. A man rises in the scale and finds stepping stones to higher stages, until finally the end is reached. When that happens, the end alone remains and all else, even the Prophet's scriptures become like dried-out bones, fit only to be cast into the desert sand."

"We are simple, pious unitarians, believers in one God," said Atrash.

The old sheikh spoke softly now but clipped and directly. Grace again wondered whether he had been there, so long ago.

"With his footman and Narish, the Viscount Angelsey visited a home in Bint Jbail, a home made of very old stones," says the old man. "Here, they met my own father, Sheikh Abdallah Atrash, who was the local, shall we say, priest. He was eighty years old, and quite wise, my father. If only the Prophet had seen fit to allow me to inherit his wisdom!" the old one said.

"The Viscount wished to know the secrets of the Druze. He believed there may be some link, understood by chosen few, between ourselves and the Druids of Wales. But Young Gareth Holborn had been secretly meeting with a young Bedouin girl, Najoua. It seems that in the course of a few short days their hearts had been tethered together. He told of his love for her, and she had given herself to him out of her own heart's quickening."

"Forgive us for boring you my lady with such detailed history," said Atrash, who took Grace's hand. She listened, curious, cautious, fearless. "Now you must know that one cannot convert to Druzism, one is born into it," Atrash continued. "Souls do not die to be resurrected: even Jesus did not believe he came to this world for that purpose. He came to bring God's love and to drive away sin, yet it was his calling to be resurrected. Nor do we believe souls slumber only to be reawakened, although Judgment Day is the end of a long journey in which the soul seeks its best fulfilment. As well, our faith promises not a paradise full of earthly delights but a beatific vision of the Holy One. Sometimes this vision comes mystically in this world. Why it comes for some and not others I cannot say. Perhaps it came for your late husband in his final moments."

"What do you mean?" asked Grace. "You know something?"

"My lady, bear with me I beg of you," said the young skunk-man, gracefully opening his hands to her. She was almost expecting a demonstration of stigmata but there was none.

"Like our brothers in Islam we stand under the Shari'a, the code of law," he said. "But we interpret these laws allegorically. Rather than pray five times a day to Mecca, we see prayer as a movement of one's soul to the unity of God. Prayer becomes a constancy, a state of being. We love God, only God — who directs us through this world in humility.

"And now, I will tell you a secret," said Atrash, smiling. "The villagers of Bint Jbail kept twin horns — The Frampton Horns, although they were not called such at the time — in a beautiful silver box, which was inside another box, a rough wooden box, in the khalwa, the chapel. About once a fortnight over a period of many years, the horns were taken from these boxes along with some other objects. The faithful then would be invited to heap scorn upon these objects as a reminder that we hold no idols before God."

It was the old man who continued now: "Before leaving our village the Viscount Angelsey proposed a trade: the Jews' Shofar for the brass horns. It is our tradition to exchange gifts with guests. And so Angelsey offered what he had — the Shofar for which he paid twenty pieces of silver — in exchange for the horns of brass. After long and careful deliberation, my father and the village elders agreed. It was time for Bint Jbail to rejuvenate its icons so the humble peasants might scoff at something novel."

The younger skunk-haired man interjected: "Just as the transaction with Angelsey was to be consummated there was a ear-piercing scream in the outer court of the khalwa. Some men had found the young footman, Gareth Holborn, with the girl Najoua in amorous embrace."

The old sheik gracefully raised one hand and it glided in a chopping motion. "Everyone remembers this," he said. "A swordsman put his blade to Gareth Holborn's throat. 'Defiler! Infidel!' Blasphemer of the house of God!' he shouted. 'Now, choose quickly infidel, whom do you love more — God or this woman?' the swordsman asked, grasping the footman by the hair while another held the girl.

'Najoua,' replied the young Gareth Holborn.

'Ha! said the swordsman. 'In this house there is no love but the Love of God.' And he drew the blade, ready to cut."

Grace turned her eyes and was about to speak when the old man interjected:

"My father told the swordsman to hold. 'Do you not see the love of God in the love this man has for this woman? Remember: I am the Near, but not as one thing is near to another: and I am the Far, but not as one thing is far from another. This is God working in the world. And the love of these two, though they be not Druzes, is more important than any khalwa. God does not allow his beard to turn grey over a puny khalwa — ask your fathers who once camped in the desert at Mina, Ghaawl, and Rayyan.'

"And so the youngsters were released," said the old man. "But because my father could not offend the swordsmen, who were right that the khalwa should not be defiled, the trade for both horns was expunged. Nonetheless, in order not to offend his guests, it was deemed that Angelsey should receive one of the brass horns in exchange for the ram's bone, the Shofar. For to keep God in your heart, you must give God away. In this case, half of God."

"Now my lady, Miss Holborn," said the younger Atrash. "Please, I have a proposal for you..."

PURGATIO

There was a stick of remarkable Turkish incense, Rose Durbar, burning in The Bunker when Kenyon and Hardman called upon Grace that evening.

   ·   They were followed, not long after, by the ancient and hunchbacked Rt. Rev. Edward ffolliott-Nott of St. Saviour's parish, accompanied by a young man who introduced himself as Rev. Jermaine Kidder, on a visit to London from Sherbourne to research the birth registers at ffolliott-Nott's parish.

    Since ffolliott-Nott, as Hardman had assured her, had kindly offered to conduct a private memorial service for the benefit of

Holborn's band, Grace allowed them in, though not without giving Hardman the devil's eye as she led the visitors to the parlour. Aristocratic in his bearing despite his skeletal deformity, the elderly priest fairly glided across the sumptuously tight weave of the Persian while Kidder, trailing behind, appeared nervous as a dog looking for a place to squat.

The bishop had called ffolliott-Nott earlier that day instructing him to accompany a novitiate priest, a new up-and-comer from Brixton named Kidder, to visit a young widow. He was told not to ask too many questions — rather a curious instruction — but it had been that kind of hellish day. At noon he held a lunchtime service for a dozen patients of St. Saviour's Hospice. Here things slid downhill rapidly when a wheelchair bound psychiatric patient had insisted on exposing his testicles to all who were interested, and even those who were not. This caused great distraction as the priest moved from the Creed and the Intercessions through to the Penitential Rite. And then after the service came the unusual request from the bishop.

Now arrived at The Bunker, the clerics were introduced to everyone and Grace promptly ambled off to the kitchen, soon followed by Hardman who left the old impresario and the clergymen to discuss the finer points of aesthetic experience.

"No ice?" Hardman said, fumbling through the freezer.

"There should be," she said.

"There isn't. Got any nitro?"

It had been Holborn's practice to immerse his horns in a tank of liquid nitrogen every few months. "The tone has more belly after my babies are Christened," he would say after the horns spent a night in minus 273 degrees at The Ice Works, a London laboratory catering to professional brass players. The extreme cold was brilliant for the metal, soothing stresses created during manufacture. The old Swiss trumpet-maker Sterner had recommended this procedure. Harry's lone Frampton had responded marvellously to the treatment, as had the mannequin's Blessing, the Cor, and the Hart.

Hardman stirred his drink and approached Grace, seeing the pain in her coal-fired eyes. They transfixed upon one another, unspeaking, and the electricity which had always trembled subtly between them began to vibrate. He cupped her hands in his and then hugged her, comforting.

"I'm sorry for bringing these guys, Grace," he said. "It was the minister, suggested he'd like to meet you. We'll get it over with quickly."

Grace pulled away, unable to think of anything but Harry and of this strange mix rising within her, anger and pain, hunger and guilt. First the anger that he had left so startlingly. Rudely. To rip himself away, or to be ripped away, when the future held so much hope and promise. She did not know the answer. And now here she was, left to entertain these misfits — although not really misfits — but Harry would have known what to do, the small talk, oh, she hated this. A cup and saucer slipped from her hand and smashed to the floor.

Not a word, not a sigh, escaped her lips. Her jaw set, her face drained of colour, she simply walked to the basement door, and then slowly stepped down the stairs. Hardman watched her descend, then bent to pick up the shards.

"Everything all right?" called Kenyon from the parlour.

Downstairs in the secluded studio Grace again drew a handful of Harry's papers — letters, documents — from the open safe. She slumped to the floor, pressing the treasured papers to her forehead, but the tears would not come. She was dried up. And she saw how it was possible to hate everything in this anger. The red rage within her was consuming. It emanated a kind of styptic breath that withered away all hope and beauty. But there also was a narrowness to it. The anger. She felt she was two creatures: gross and bestial as her wrath consumed all other passions; desiccated and fleshless as she strove to keep alive the tiny coal of rage in which she now lived, and moved, and had her being.

As she ascended the stairs, steeled to face the music, she found Hardman and the young priest, Kidder, chatting in the parlour. They quickly nodded and ended their conversation.

"Hey," Hardman stepped in first. "You okay?"

"Yeah. Okay," she said coldly, joining the others for tea. "Just about okay."

Grace leaned forward to the glass table where someone had set the Frampton Right and lifted the horn into her lap. She twisted a lock of hair along her index finger. And out of impatience, in an unconscious effort to drive away these unwanted guests, she pushed out her breasts, and stared at the young clergyman, Kidder. He crossed his legs, nervously. She believed he might be trying to mask an erection.

The young man coughed, and turned to his black leather briefcase.

"May I?" he said. "I know this is a difficult time for you," he continued, giving Grace a glance and reaching for a Bible which he passed to old ffolliott-Nott.

ffolliott-Nott took his cue, cleared his throat.

"I don't know if you agree with me," the elderly one began, "but people often think and speak of God when human knowledge has come to an end, or when our resources fail. You know, it's always the deus ex machina that we bring onto the scene — either to solve our problems or to strengthen our weaknesses. It's almost as though we are trying to reserve some special space for God. But I prefer to think of God not on the boundaries but at the centre, not in weakness but in strength, and not in death and guilt but in man's life and goodness. And so I thought, well, I thought I'd offer some small reading at the memorial service that Mr. Hardman has asked me to conduct at the end of the week for your husband's musician friends."

Grace nodded, turned the trumpet in her hand, palms sweating.

"Perhaps you know this passage, from the Old Testament, Numbers, Chapter Ten."

And the Lord spoke unto Moses, saying make thee two trumpets of silver; of a whole piece shalt thou make them; that thou mayest use them for the calling of the assembly and for the journeying of the camps ... And if ye go to war in your land against the enemy that oppresseth you, then ye shall blow an alarm with the trumpets; and ye shall be remembered before the Lord your God, and ye shall be saved from your enemies. Also in the day of your gladness and in your solemn days and at the beginnings of your months, ye shall blow with the trumpets over your burnt offerings, and over the sacrifices of peace offerings; that they may be a memorial before your God: I am the Lord your God.

Overcome with fatigue and short-circuiting from the emotional stress, Grace uncrossed her legs. The Frampton fell to the floor with an excruciating boing, even through the wine-glass rosette of the Persian.

"Oh, God! I'm really losing my grip," she said, gritting her teeth and bending to retrieve the horn.

Hardman mercifully began to chat with the young man while Grace turned to Kenyon and they hastily examined the instrument, which appeared unharmed.

"You know, Jermaine," said Hardman, rising to adjust the stereo volume, "I don't much believe in God."

"God either is or he isn't," the young clergyman said earnestly, the white of his collar contrasting with the black of his face and borrowed vestments. "He's either everything or he's nothing."

Kenyon glanced from the trumpet to the priest, surprised that a devout cleric of the Church of England would say something so docetic.

"I tend toward the Buddhist view," said Hardman. "A person is a new entity each moment, mathematically speaking, and so we can't expect our present being to be preserved in heaven. What I am is largely gone the next moment — now — and so we can't expect God to preserve this full flavour forever. Not that God exists, anyhow."

"And how can you talk about nothing, at least in the Buddhist sense?" ffolliott-Nott upbraided. "You can't talk about it. You can't even think about it. If you do, it's not nothing. At least with God, he's here. You don't have to look anywhere. He's here."

"He's here," young Kidder repeated, louder.

With *Solar Caustic* drifting from the reel-to-reel tape machine, Kenyon immediately thought ffolliott-Nott was referring to Holborn. His eyes darted about the room in disbelief, his hands almost commending the Frampton to the carpet for a second time. But there was no one. And then he realized the priest was speaking of God or something, and that he had been lost in the Horse Latitudes, the Sargasso Sea of it all.

Kenyon was mildly nauseated. "Another bloody optimist," he said to no one in particular, but turned toward Kidder now, to the fresh-faced young priest from Southall, or East Coking, or Brixton.

"Optimists," Kenyon continued, "believe we live in the best of all possible worlds. Pessimists, of course, fear the same thing."

Kidder smiled nervously, eyeing the Frampton.

"Do you not think, Mr. Kenyon, that everyone has a need for transcendence?" said the old hunchbacked priest, casting a hardpan. "Is there not a transcendent-shaped hole in the human heart, which God seeks to fill?"

"Perhaps," said Kenyon, wiggling, puffing, threatening to rise from his chair. "But I doubt it. Why should the Christian God be any truer or more beautiful than any of the other gods? If you're making the argument for the existence of God from the aesthetic you've a tough sell, look at Bosnia, Kampuchea, Kigali."

"Oh, I agree," said the old priest. "There can be no doubt as to suffering. Look at your own suffering."

Kenyon thought immediately of the calcification — he could almost see the crystallizations adhere to the joints of his aching toe. Sweat began to anoint his body.

"I don't know if your suffering calls for a remedy," said ffolliott-Nott. "But there must be an underlying cause. Christian theology, all the world's religions really, suggest this cause is the fundamental disproportion between the necessities of your heart and the satisfaction it finds."

"Ah," replied Kenyon, head wobbling like a ship about to go down. "So the confirmation of hell proves that God exists. Very good. And if some human beings, Beethoven say, or even a genius such as Harry Holborn, if they create something in artistry, they might, if they're lucky, move up a rung — from hell to purgatory. Lovely."

"It's nothing to do with luck, Mr. Kenyon. Hell and heaven," clipped the ancient priest, "are only symbols of man's spiritual life. The experience of hell means complete self-centeredness. Your mention of Beethoven is apropos. Some would argue that it is only since Beethoven that music has addressed itself to men; before him it was concerned only with God.

"But since God cannot violate human freedom," the cleric continued. "You are free to choose torment without God rather than happiness in Him. You have a perfect right to hell, if you like."

"And if I don't particularly like hell — but happen to be born in Rwanda?"

"The human heart can never be satisfied; it is always in potentia," said the priest. "Riches, the satisfaction of our physical desires, these can stupify the heart's need. But they can never satisfy because the soul is afraid of emptiness."

The senior cleric turned to Grace, straightening his back.

"It is God's love that makes Him vulnerable. And so in a sense, God, too, is incomplete. And so he has called your husband to join Him, to help Him complete the divine nature, to fulfill His divine love, to be a co-creator in the story beyond this world. And you may have faith your husband is in God's loving care," ffolliott-Nott said to her.

"I am here to tell you this is assured. Even in the apocrypha, and very Zen-like, Jesus said: 'Split wood, I am there. Lift up the stone and you will find me there."

Grace nodded, more from politeness than agreement, and offered an uncertain stare. Then she said: "But he wasn't there."

"What?" said ffolliott-Nott.

"Jesus," she replied. "Isn't that the point? They split him on the wood, but when they lifted the stone he was gone."

"Well, yes, but..." said ffolliott-Nott.

"Here's what I want to know," said Hardman, reaching for a vitamin. "If God is so damned perfect already why does he need Harry? So He can be more perfect? I mean, I know Harry's a good metal player and all and would likely round out the heavenly brass. But you know, perfection is perfection, and even with the best pair of chops you can't get any better than that."

"Likely the best way to think of the incompleteness of God is to combine the idea of complete, for now, with the possibility of further novelty through the input of our unpredictability," said ffolliott-Nott. "Imagine God creating the world and setting up a kind of improvised jazz session where he deliberately chooses not to know the ending. Or perhaps he knows the ending in a general way but not all the details: the decisions you and all the other players will make along the way. This is our freedom of will."

"You're saying Harry chose to go swimming in the Nile, despite the fact he couldn't swim, and that his whole life led up to just that moment, so he could fulfill a tiny part in God's game?" said Hardman.

"No." said ffolliott-Nott. "And yes. We make decisions. This is our freedom of will. If God foreknows and foreordains every little detail then our freedom is an illusion. But if something happens which will surprise God, as it were, and give him enjoyment, then God is capable of growth into greater perfection."

"And what cruel enjoyment will he derive from the ministrations of Harry's dying?" said Hardman. "What do you think Jermaine, um, Reverend Kidder?"

Kidder squirmed in his chair, loosened his clerical collar. He reached slowly across the table and raised the Frampton, examining it carefully.

"I think," he said without lifting his eyes from the horn, "that God is so great he doesn't even need to exist."

There was silence throughout The Bunker for a long time. Hardman was rendered speechless by Kidder's diligent preparation for his role.

"I think we're in danger of losing this in semantics," said ffolliott-Nott with an air of finality.

"Maybe, but you still haven't proven anything," said Hardman, turning to the senior cleric. "Nothing."

"Nothing is precisely the point," said ffolliott-Nott.

"We must imagine God as having a consciousness, just as much as we have. Consciousness presupposes the 'nothing' that exists between the end of one thought and the start of another. So, just like the spaces between musical notes, those divine nothings must exist. They are the dark which makes shadows in the light. I like to think of God as having just flung out a vacuum and then thrown in matter — which is all creative energy."

Hardman again reached into his bag for a fistful of vitamins.

He swallowed four walnut-sized atoms and lifted his leg over the arm of the chair. He shuffled about uncomfortably.

"In the end, it is the duty of humans to live life to the very fullest to the very last breath," suggested ffolliott-Nott, as Hardman let loose a powerful egg-like emission.

"This, I think we can safely say your husband has done, and we can look to his life with celebration," the priest continued, smiling at Grace and covering his nose with a handkerchief, eyes watering.

"His duty, eh?" said Grace, unimpressed.

"Here," said ffolliott-Nott, fumbling through his book. "It's here somewhere in Ecclesiastes, ah: 'The end of the matter; all has been heard. Fear God and keep his commandments; for that is the whole duty of everyone."

"And where does it say it was Harry's duty to check out before he'd finished his work?" spat Hardman suddenly, rising now and rubbing a small tattoo on his shoulder. "Or before he could find that horn? I think Harry's music pointed to that God beyond God.

You know, the old one's kind of croaked by now. Like a doornail. And Harry accepted that. He didn't cringe at the notion of freedom. Fuck duty. Fuck subservience to some absentee landlord. Seize the day. Tell the truth. Be real. Let your balls flap in the wind."

There was a momentary lull when someone in the room might have put a word in edgewise, Kenyon, for instance. But even he did not. ffolliott-Nott adjusted his vestments.

And it was, finally, with one quite deadly vitamin emission, gas so vile as to gaggify, that Hardman dispatched the two clerics, one from Stoke and the other from Trinidad by way of Epping or Wapping, once and for all.

The Rose Durbar had long worn away, it seemed. The clergymen rose and wished all a good evening. As the door closed, Hardman caught the eye of Reverend Jermaine Kidder, who winked and accompanied ffolliott-Nott into the darkness as they retreated from the smooth, cool, concrete confines of The Bunker.

SEPARATIO

Rising into mist through the soft, aqueous light were the stippled mountains of Snowdonia. Below, veiled in a lean drizzle between peaks dubbed the Three Elephants, was the tiny village of Gornhaffan.

Through friends at Vestal, Kenyon had chartered a chopper for Grace and Hardman. As steel blades swooped them through the sky, the pair cast bloodshot eyes onto the rugged hills sloping toward a yellow estuary. The pasture around the village wept with a lush and verdant green. The Welsh air was sweet, chloroformed and resinous, in sharp contrast to the previous night in The Bunker where things had hung rank and stifling as a crypt.

Before leaving Haverstock Hill, Grace retrieved the Sterner from Harry's studio and set the Swiss copy on the mantlepiece in the parlour.

The Frampton, meantime, she polished with cheesecloth, carefully rolling it into a lambs-wool sweater before stuffing it into her backpack to keep it close during the trek to Wales.

She had cloistered with Kenyon and Hardman that morning in The Bunker's increasingly claustrophobic confines. Hardman loomed sickly as he brushed through the front door. Eyeballing him, Grace concluded it was the effect of last night's duty-free Arak or too many vitamins gobbled before his overnight kip at The Coburg.

Kenyon had awakened to the crude cackle goslings or quislings outside his Parliament Hill house, smacking his lips and clacking his tongue on the hard palate. He arrived at The Bunker to see Grace soon after breakfast, suited and flushed, and limped into the parlour leaving his coat over the banister of the stairs. He was carrying a cane. Even at that early hour, Holborn's horn drifted from the reel-to-reel tape machine.

"Listen," Grace barked, startling the two men. "The funeral is in three days. In Winnipeg.

"I don't want there to be a eulogy. None," she said, holding Hardman in the grip of her eyes. "And no photographers," she added, shooting a glare at Kenyon. She winced and put her hand to her belly. Fury, red-hot, wrenched through her body. She could let it consume her, she realized, or she could use it to get some answers. But it was difficult. Kneeling in her scarlet kimono, she dumped onto the floor stacks of Holborn's files on the Framptons — two massive boxes of weathered books, papers, notes and clippings.

"Now let's get to work."

The two men exchanged a look of surprise. Hardman raised a wary eyebrow. It occurred to Kenyon that Grace would be letting no more cups and saucers slip from her hands to the floor.

"Right," said Kenyon, taking her lead. "Let us proceed with business. What do we actually know? We know the Framptons were struck in Europe by Gwynt, around 1760. We know they are stamped with a serpentine G. There's a tradition, not much more than rumour, that they fell into the hands of Napoleon and were separated at that point. One of them was inherited by Harry's father — this was long after the instrument was paraded with the Frampton-Upon-Severn Volunteers. Do we know anything else of their provenance?"

Grace parted her lips about to speak but decided to keep to herself the discovery in Harry's safe. The documents were curious and, she suspected, important. But knowing they were her secret made her feel all the better, calmer, connected. And while she hungered to disclose her extraordinary meeting with Atrash, she waited, wondering first what Harry's files might reveal.

They sifted through the documents, she and Hardman squishing spandrels on the Persian and Kenyon leaning awkwardly from a chair. The files included papers once belonging to John Holborn, correspondence from Switzerland reporting on Sterner's progress in copying the Frampton, magazine and encyclopaedia clippings on ancient horns. They sorted the material in various piles: history of music, books on Bonaparte, Harry's genealogical information, including his father's military demobilization papers.

"Well, what I want to know is how the hell did John Holborn get the Frampton Right?" asked Hardman. "I mean that's a crucial question, isn't it?"

"It is, but John never told anyone," said Kenyon. "At least he never told me. I'm not quite sure how much Harry knew, except that it had passed from father to son for several generations."

Kenyon set aside a small stack of papers and clippings about an eighteenth-century Welsh trumpeter.

"Grace?" he asked, removing his bifocals, "do you recall Harry ever mentioning anything of this Welsh trumpeter named Midian? Whoever he was, it suggests here that he was a master hornman and friend of Mozart. Look — here's Mozart's dedication to the Concerto in E Flat, K 417: 'MIDIAN ASS — Wolfgang Amadeus Mozart took pity on Midian the Ass, Ox and Fool, Milan, 1786'."

"I don't think Harry ever mentioned that guy," she said. "Let's have look."

"Mmm," said Kenyon. "Well, here it says he was for a time a musician in the court of a Bohemian count who discovered him as a travelling gypsy. But Midian reviled his serfdom and escaped along with three other brass players, including a woman. This led the count to issue warrants for them, charging anyone who found them to knock out their front teeth."

"Sounds familiar," quipped Hardman. "Nothing's changed in the music industry in two hundred and fifty years. We're still serfs and niggers to self-righteous poobahs."

"You're awfully brassy, Mr. Hardman," Kenyon snapped back. "For someone who's unemployed."

Grace began to thumb through the papers Kenyon had set aside and saw that Midian had surfaced in Paris during the Revolution, becoming Kapellmeister at the Theatre des Varietes. And he had crossed paths with both Beethoven and Napoleon, Kenyon noted. Impressively, Beethoven wrote for Midian the Horn Sonata Op. 17, first performed in the Hofburgtheater in 1796. Midian had died in Wales, a peerless trumpeter, the equal of Liszt, titan of the piano, or Paganini, the magus of the violin.

At Milan's la Scala, he once played a duet — a Horn Concerto in D — with a well-known female horn soloist of the time, a trumpeter named Ingot. The event apparently caused a sensation. And they had performed upon a set of twin horns which were so melodic and versatile that the audience, carried away by the end of the performance, had washed them with more than two dozen ovations.

Midian and Ingot: Grace remembered these names from the mysterious onion-skin description of the twin horns' birth. But they could not be the wife and ancient pheasant plucker described there, for they had lived a generation earlier. So who could these people be?

"I'll just hang on to these," she said, putting the one stack of papers aside. Still, there was little in the boxes of papers, Grace noticed, to shed light on the lives of John Holborn's father, Haydn, or the grandfather, Gareth. They remained an enigmatic historical gap. Nor was there anything to explain how the Frampton Right fell into the Holborn clan's possession.

As the trio scoured the remaining documents it was Kényon who noticed Harry had scribbled in the margins of Emil Ludwig's 1926 biography of Napoleon.

Kenyon had long been fascinated by the Battle of Marengo and knew that some years earlier, in May of 1796, the Great Emperor had also laid siege to Milan. Might it have been here, he wondered as he scanned the pages of the book, that Napoleon chanced upon the twinned horns?

Suddenly, there was the reference Kenyon had been seeking. He sunk into the chair and read to himself quietly while the others genuflected on the Persian.

Kenyon struck on a passage describing the Little General swaggering victorious into the city's premier theatre, la Scala. There, in the Green Room, abandoned by Midian and Ingot who had fled at the approach of the Emperor, were two boxes lined with calico. "Lying therein," said the reference, "were twin horns."

Kenyon removed his reading glasses. His imagination pulsed. One mystery was solved: there could be no doubt that Napoleon himself had once held the horns.

What would Bonaparte have said when he spied those beauties, Kenyon mused. "Flicorno alto," an aide would say. "Aye," Bonaparte would reply, peering down into the bell of the Left horn. "There is a mystery in here — like looking deep between the legs of a woman." He would laugh, flipping the instrument around as a child at play. "Put them in my footlocker."

Kenyon asked Grace if he might borrow the copy of Ludwig's *Napoleon* and a few other papers while she and Hardman were in Wales.

They agreed to divide the most promising documents, Grace and Hardman taking everything relating to Midian, Ingot and John Holborn, Kenyon promising to peruse the documents of antiquity.

As she locked the door to The Bunker, Grace shouldered her backpack, Hardman clutched his bag of vitamins, and Kenyon squeezed into the back of the Daimler to head back to Hampstead.

Three hours later the chopper feathered to the ground in a sheep pasture on the outskirts of Gornhaffan. All around them were scarred cliffs, iron-hard and naked. There were grey-black crags, shingles, cwms and brans, mauve aretes, broken buttresses and razor sharp pinnacles giving way to sand and silvered sea. Grace, windblown, tired, her heart a stone, her brain looping and electric, revived in the Welsh air. Hardman looked as if he'd just swum a hundred laps in a pool of chlorine.

Soon a beautiful apricot light enveloped them, both soothing and caustic, like the gleam of a varnished pew. The sea grew pale, and the land, Wales, appeared blood-soaked and holy. Save the bleating of lambs there was no reception awaiting them on the slippery ground outside the village, so the couple walked ten minutes to the Angel Hotel, checking into rooms Twelve and Four.

They freshened and met in a corner of the near-empty bar where Grace spread before them some of John Holborn's military records and birth certificate.

The fingers of mist and momentary blast of sun which had greeted them was now a frenzied rain, a pluvial wash laving the leaves and grass, percolating down to the thirsting roots of Wales.

The need-to-know publican, a Mrs. Edwards who suffered elephantiasis of the breasts, brought two pints of ale as the couple stared stoically out the window. Pressing for gossip, she quickly determined their story.

"Lost your husband, dear?" she said. "Tisk tisk. Duw.

"Well, I lost mine nine years ago," she continued, adjusting her apron. "Had his life, did Mort, fair play. Was his lungs got him in the end. Too many plain end Woodbines. But crikey, it was a mess you know. The nurse from Bangor had to come over and close his eyes. And he left his ordure on the bed sheets. Well, it wasn't really him, bachgens, it was just his weary, crippled hide, his soul having left to be at peace with our saviour if you know my meaning. American are you?

"Would you know where we can rent — hire — a car?" asked Hardman, downing his glass quickly.

"What you be wanting a car for then, cariad?" smiled Mrs. Edwards, patting her hair, her hand sliding down the sleeve of her cardigan.

Grace explained that her husband's father, John Holborn, was buried in Gornhaffan and they wished to visit the grave. But it was raining.

"John Holborn? said Mrs. Edwards. "That would be the son of Haydn Holborn. Haydn served in the chapel years ago.

"You're a relation of Haydn Holborn?" she asked, her eyes narrowing to take a closer look. "By marriage, of course. Dear God. You'll want Old Mr. Pugh."

"Pugh?" said Hardman, digging for vitamins.

"Duw, yes indeed, bachgen," said Mrs. Edwards. "He's the resident historian in these parts. Knows everything and everyone. Haydn Holborn, I'll not believe it."

An ancient stone house six miles northwest of the village was the current haunt of Athraw Pugh, they were told, and they would pass the graveyard on the edge of the village along the way.

"I could have Mr. Parry from the Post Office run you up to Pugh, cariad," said Mrs. Edwards, eyeing Hardman. "But he's not free until half-four. I suppose you could try my dear Mort's old bike," she said. "It's in the lean-to in the garden."

She smiled slyly to Hardman. "It's not been fired up for some time, though, I'll warn you. Good with your hands, are you dear?" she grinned.

Hardman pulled on a jacket, wandered to the rear of The Angel and in the shed found an old US-made Indian motorcycle. Borrowing Mrs. Edwards' toolbox he set to work. Soon, the clouds parted and a golden ray of sun peeked over the Isle of Angelsey to the west of them, across the straits.

Hardman stood to look.

"Mon," said Mrs. Edwards, coming out to ogle the young drummer's taut backside. She had makeup now, pancake on her face, whitening the jowls like death, and ruby red lips like a baboon's bum.

"That's what we call Angelsey around here. The Isle of Mon. Pretty what? And over here," she pointed to a great spreadeagled oak in the orchard behind the hotel, "was a woodpecker in that tree yonder pecked and pecked while my Mort was in his death throes.

"Then, when Mort passed on," she said. "Lo, the yammering stopped. Argof. So peaceful it was all of a sudden, natural-like, you know. Mind you, the way it was yammering I wouldn't have been shocked if its little pecker dropped off, poor thing. Overwork, if you get my meaning. Another glass of ale, cariad?"

Grace spent time in the garden, inhaling the late day sun and reviewing Holborn's papers along with those of his father who had been in Palestine from 1946 to 1948, a subaltern with the Royal Engineers.

It took ninety minutes of sweat and five gallons of fuel to coax the Indian to life at about the time Mr. Parry from the Post Office was available. But they preferred to see Mr. Pugh alone. As they readied to leave, Mrs. Edwards popped out once more.

"Now there was Hadyn and then John and John's son the trumpeter. Duw I've forgotten his name now, Harold was it? That would be your hubby then?"

"Harry Holborn," said Grace.

"Crikey Moses, yes, of course. He was here was Harry Holborn, not more than four or five years ago. Very image of his dad, he was. Didn't speak Cymraeg though, pity. Said it was all Greek to him you know. Those were his very words. Of course it'll all be dead in time. Won't it? Our poor old Welsh language as well. That's right, off you go, bachs. Just a few miles past the graveyard is Mr. Pugh. You'll see John Holborn's grave and Haydn and his wife rotting together there for all eternity. Cheerio, dears."

Grace and Hardman gave the motorbike a quick rinse and it turned over quite perfectly.

"I thought at first the cylinders had seized," Hardman said as she wiped the leather seat with a damp rag.

"I almost had to stroke the engine to get this baby going," he said, proudly.

"If you stroke, you get increased compression which can be good or bad, depending on how much compression there was. But I filled the oil pump drive gear and pinion with Lactite and torqued it to the high end of the specs after adjusting the flywheels, which puts a higher load on the crankshaft. There'll be some vibration. But you know what they say: 'You Can't Wear Out an Indian Scout'."

"Shit, Spikey," said Grace, unsmiling, shaking her head. She wore a buckskin jacket, beading on the back forming a cross. As she climbed aboard, she checked her backpack. The Frampton, a solid piece of Harry, was with her still.

"Did you know Dave Brubeck was part Modoc Indian?" Hardman shouted over the engine rumble as they sputtered and smoked into the Gornhaffan cemetery, stopping to see John Holborn's grave. Tidy, it was, with a small bouquet, fresh.

"No," said Grace, absently, climbing from the rear, her hair windblown, eyes watering.

They stood at the grave quietly for a few minutes. And then zipped away from the graveyard and popped and sputtered around the leafy green bend of road toward Pugh's. A mile down the road, they turned right, through a menacing craggy pass toward the sea. The weather worsened and soon a soupy fog obscured the view of the Menai Strait.

Hardman saw menacing yellow lights appear in his rear-view. He sped, the lights followed. He slowed, the car behind slowed.

"There's someone tailing us, I think," he shouted over his shoulder to Grace. "Don't look around." She gripped him around his belt.

"Hang on," he said, accelerating around a bend as the fog lifted. Still the car, a large German wagon, black with tinted windows, was gaining on them. "Shit," said Hardman, winding out the hand-throttle as far as it would go. "These old things were never meant to go more than fifty. I'm going to let him pass."

At the next curve the car was upon them. Pulling alongside, the driver suddenly veered to the left, cutting them off and forcing them from the pavement.

The bike swerved as Hardman cranked the handlebars, caught a passing glance of the driver, and accelerated through a grassy ditch. As they came up the other side of the ditch, the bike went airborne. They landed with a bone-crushing thud but still on two wheels.

"Spike, stop!" Grace screamed as the wind was knocked from her lungs, but it was too late. They careened through a farmers' fence. The top rail caught Hardman across the hands and then whipped him in the mouth. He jammed both brakes hard, and with the front of the bike in a sharp nosedive he dropped his left leg to the ground. They spun in a large circle through a field of soggy barley.

The rain had stopped and there was a deep and eerie silence as they lay in the field, their hearts frantic. The engine on the Indian had choked and died. Steam hissed from the cylinders and crackled in the oil pan.

"Are you okay?" he asked, lying back in the crop and exhaling a long, slow arc of breath.

"No. I'm not okay," Grace said, standing, checking herself, and opening her backpack to inspect the horn, still intact and warm. Then she looked up at Hardman.

"Oh God, Spikey are you all right?" she asked, staring at his hands, blood-smeared like a perfusionist inside a heart recipient.

"I don't know," he said. "But if that was an accident then I'm the Vicar of Ipswich, as old Kenyon would say," rubbing the back of his seeping hands across his puckered mouth. Hardman smiled then, to calm her: "Who is the Vicar of Ipswich anyway?"

"Switzerland, Cairo — and now this," Grace frowned.

"How about you — in one piece?" Hardman asked again, massaging stalks of cool, wet barley against his fingers.

"I don't know," she looked away. "You make a good cushion, I guess. Jesus, that was awful. Maybe we should forget this whole thing and go back to The Angel."

"No," said Hardman firmly, angry now as he inspected the damaged front fender. He straightened the bike and kicked over the engine, which started and died.

"We're shaking things up now," he insisted. "Getting to the bottom. Someone doesn't want us to get a sniff of this Mr. Pugh — that's pretty obvious. I don't quite know what's going on, but I don't like it. It doesn't pass the smell test."

There was a long silence before Hardman tried again to start the bike.

"I'll bet he was an apple," murmured Grace, as the engine roared to life.

"Who?"

"Dave Brubeck."

"Apple?"

"Red on the outside," replied Grace. "White in the middle."

MERCURIUS
PHORUM

Mercurius phorum.

Hardman flicked off the engine and leaned the Indian onto its kickstand, his lip gashed, his hands numb and scraped raw.

They walked up to Pugh's old stone farm cottage, built partly into the side of a hill, overgrown in every direction with ivy. At the edge of the place was a cliff, overlooking, eighty feet below, the roiling waters of the bay. They made themselves presentable and knocked but there was no answer.

In back, the door of the chicken coop stood ajar. It was dark, half-lit, and it was obvious the coop had just been cleared of birds to market. The feeding trays had been winched up to the ceiling and the straw bed was caked with manure, although half the floor had been scraped clean. The acrid stench of fresh urine and the bitter chocolate of chicken droppings smacked their nostrils and seized the back of their throats. At the far end they could see a figure bent over a spade, scraping straw, feathers and shit from the centreposts. A garden tractor was parked, idling, midway down the length of the building. There was a small wet pile of dead birds near the doorway.

"Hello!" called Hardman. "Mr. Pugh?"

The figure turned slowly, rested the spade against the post, pulled off a woollen cap and walked slowly toward them. Favouring a game right leg, he switched off the tractor's ignition and made his way to them, smiling.

"Hallo, sut mae," the old man said, blinking, quizzical.

There was no answer as the couple eyed him uncomfortably.

He wiped the sweat from his furrowed brow and surveyed them for a moment.

"Siarad Cymraeg?" he asked.

"No, sorry," said Grace.

"Tasmanian are ye?" he asked.

"Canadian," said Grace.

"Ah!" he smiled. "Holborn. You'll be with young Mr. Holborn then, he's with you?" He glanced over their shoulders, brushed past them, and then led them from the barn to the house. "Gwael cany yn gwaddod — sorry for all the shit. Where's young Harry then?"

"I'm Harry's... wife," said Grace. "Harry's had an accident. In Egypt. He's died."

Pugh stopped in his tracks.

"When?"

"Saturday."

"Oh, my dear," he said, pulling her close so she noticed the manure encrusted in his fingernails and white hair. "I am so sorry to hear that, sincerely. Dear me — Duw! Don't get the news much

here, see? Come in then. Tisk Tisk. Tell me all about it, both of
you. Young wasn't he? Wouldn't have been fifty. Harry Holborn.
Dead by Christ."

Pugh was not what they expected, although what each expected
was kept in silence. He was old and yet youngish, spritely. He had
masculine shoulders and hands, but a tapered waist and a woman's
wide-gliding hips. Inside, the house was a museum of playthings.
Scattered everywhere were thousands of rounders, marbles, tops,
conkers, and bandy sticks — sheep's vertebrae from Jack Stones
and Catty, Quoits, magic lanterns, and holey donkeys from
Blind Man's Buff.

And then there were the clocks, hundreds of timepieces —
watches, brass horologes, oak and mahogany long-box clocks,
ornamented with spandrels and cherub's heads.

Hardman introduced himself and grimaced when the old man
seized his hand in welcome. Immediately, old Pugh saw the
drummer's bleeding fists, and fetched alcohol and a gauze wrapping.
But he asked no questions as he led them to the sitting room.

"Forgive my curious collection," said Pugh, as the pair's eyes
roamed the shelves that lined the walls. "I shan't explain. My
grandfather said if you want to be wise and prosperous there are
just two rules. Rule One is never tell everything you know."

"And Rule Two?" asked Hardman.

The old man smiled but said nothing. Then he shrugged.

"The collections are the work of a life-time," he noddedto
himself. "They say I'm an old eccentric. And I suppose it must be
true. Who would really care about the nuance of difference between
a pendulum and a balance spring?"

"Well, Spike here keeps time in a band," said Grace.

"Do you now? You keep time? A mere mortal? They say a
pendulum is the most perfect timekeeper there is. Although time
itself can be a friend or an enemy. One of our great poets, Daffydd,
sang 'Woe to the black face clock on the ditch side which awoke
me — a curse on its head, its tongue and its heavy balls, its yards

and its hammer. Was there a mangy-cruppered saddler or tyler more fickle?'"

Just then an old duplex-escapement clock cluppered and clanged the hour.

Before it could strike again the old farmer sat them in front of the fire with a bottle of sherry, a box of biscuits, and piercing blue-green eyes.

They explained the sad events in Cairo and enquired after John Holborn.

"Well, we didn't see much of young John after the second war," said Mr. Pugh. "He went to Canada, you know, years ago now. Harry, your, er, husband miss, was in the village here a few years ago. Came to see me he did. Wanted to know about his dad and his grandfathers. Very nice to see him. Famous trumpeter I hear, not a singer like Harry Secombe or Tom Jones. Argof."

The old man shifted his weight in the rocker as Grace fetched a biscuit and passed it into his gnarly fingers. "Do I know anything about Haydn Holborn?

"Duw. I'll say: Haydn Holborn — hypnotist, lecher, horn player."

"I beg your pardon?" said Grace. "Did you say horn player?"

"Indeed," said Pugh, his eyes glistening.

"Go on," said Hardman.

"Indeed-to-goodness I will, hogyn bach. There's some darkness here, because Haydn's mother — Caerwin her name was — never spoke of her dead husband Gareth when she came up here from Llallogen. That would have been about 1870. She passed on, bless her, only a little time later. So Haydn was left an orphan, he was. He was brought up in a loving Christian home but, being a sensitive boy and all, he was trouble.

"They say," the old man continued, shaking his head, "it was the cock fights drove him mad."

"Cock fights," repeated Hardman, flatly.

"Y Cocyn, the vile sport was called. The fairest season of the year was given over to the cocks, which was followed by days of drunkenness, bawdy ditties, fisticuffs, courting, swynking, fighting and the like. Against the law now, of course.

"The pit was a pure circle, six to eight yards round. The ground was peeled to a depth of eight inches and the floor made hard. In the week before the Cocyn, the birds were readied: the wings were cut, as were the tail and hackle, and the birds fed sweet butter and white sugar candies. Then their beaks were sharpened and they were turned into the pit to try their fortune.

"Well, young Haydn Holborn, they say, witnessed the Great Cocyn of 1874, when thirty-one birds, many belonging to Lord Bandersnatch of Ty'n-y-Cornel, met a bloody death. Young Holborn had been missing all day, and when they found him in the hayloft, peering down at the Cocyn through a chink in the flooring, the boy's hands streamed with blood. His own nails had pierced his palms as he clenched his fists at the sight, horrified, but unable to look away. Tragic, really — Duw. They say it was this brought on his stigmata and attacks of noisy glossolalia. One time the villagers had to lower the lad into an old dry well because he would not or could not stop repeating an old Bardic riddle. More than a thousand times it passed his lips. Perhaps you've heard it:

> *I'm not the pheasant plucker,*
> *I'm the pheasant plucker's son.*
> *I'm only plucking pheasants till the pheasant plucker comes.*

"Even in the well, the hoarse voice of Haydn, chanting the riddle, crept into the ears of the villagers. At night, some stuffed their ears with beeswax to drown out the incessant words. At last he stopped and they released him from the well.

"But of course it was some time later, as a young man, that Haydn Holborn became truly famous in these parts."

"He did?" queried Grace, unable to imagine how Harry's great-grandfather could further distinguish himself.

"Oh, indeed," said Pugh, downing his sherry, and then falling silent as he twisted the yellowing tumbler in his hand.

167

"Go on," said Hardman, filling Pugh's glass.

"Well, we wouldn't talk about it in my time but I know your generation has cast off the Victorian morality of that age.

"You see, Hadyn Holborn was reputed to be capable of withholding orgasm for a very long time. And he had a large mole strategically situated on his manhood which vastly enhanced his capacity to provoke pleasure. There was a local girl, Elsie Prothero, who told one of her sibs that the orgasm Haydn bestowed upon her was so violent, she fainted — it was, argofion, a marvellous, delicious sensation the likes of which she never relished before or since."

Pugh turned to Grace.

"Haydn's prowess soon caught the attention of a nearby heretical sect that first sprang up in the mid-nineteenth century. The Deaf Ones, they called themselves, since they turned a deaf ear to their detractors. Their doctrine grew out of a kind of Presbyterian neo-Platonism: earthly love is a ladder to divine love, and thus they commenced each service with a pell-mell orgy. Haydn soon became its deacon.

"That's when his working of miracles started," said Pugh, "Small things at first — fixing toothaches, cramps, bouts of flatus." Pugh glanced at Hardman. "But then his miracle curing got more grand — severed earlobes, broken hips, and the like. Some say his power to heal came when he learned to play an old cornet, an udganu or gorn, as we Welsh say, which he also played to work his congregation into sexual frenzy."

Grace took this moment to pull the Frampton from her backpack.

"Have you seen this before, Mr. Pugh?" she asked.

"Oh my," he said, examining the gold-rimmed bell. "Your husband showed me this beauty when he was here last. This is the very gorn then, is it? A piece of history. Of course, it all came to an end in 1916 when the Lady Angelsey — wife of the seventh Viscount of Angelsey — gave birth to a son."

The old man returned the horn to Grace.

"The child was a bleeder and during one of his attacks the mother was easily persuaded by friends to call for this marvellous and humble holy man — the horn-player of Gornhaffan.

"Haydn arrived at the manor house and went straight to the sick boy's bed, where he prayed in silence. Shortly afterward, the haemorrhage ceased.

"That visit," said Pugh, "transformed Haydn's situation. He was no longer a local holy man, leader of a few dozen non-conformists. Through the Lady Angelsey, he was introduced to some of the worthiest people of the land.

"Haydn's hold over the Lady became stronger and stronger. She became fully convinced that the horn-player was an emissary of God sent to provide personal guidance to the manor house."

"But what happened?" asked Hardman. "Why did he die so young? He couldn't have been fifty."

"Duw!" said Pugh. "You don't know?

"Haydn was murdered by Lord Angelsey, or by one of his men at any rate. Jealousy. His Lordship was furious, believed his wife was cuckold. It may have been so.

"But whatever it was, on December 15, 1916, Angelsey managed to lure Haydn to the manor house. Haydn's widow said afterward that Haydn had dreamed of his death but chose to ignore the warning. Ten days later, she too died, hours after giving birth to John.

"At any rate, while the gramophone was playing Yankee Doodle in the manor house, Lord Angelsey helped Haydn to cakes and wine laced with potassium cyanide. The gentleman watched and waited, but the poison seemed to have no effect on Haydn. After a while Angelsey felt he could wait no longer. He took a pocket Browning from a drawer, suggested that Haydn say a prayer on a crystal and bronze Italian crucifix, and shot his guest through the chest. Haydn fell. Angelsey felt his pulse: it wasn't beating.

"Suddenly," said Pugh, rising to his feet, excited, "Haydn opened his left and then his right eye. Angelsey was paralysed with fear. Haydn jumped to his feet and seized Angelsey's throat, foaming and bleeding at the mouth. The horn-player released his grip and ran when a servant heard the commotion and broke down the door. The servant fired four shots at the fleeing Haydn Holborn while Lady Angelsey, roused from her slumber, watched in horror. The first two shots missed but the third caught Haydn in the back and stopped him; the fourth sent him to the ground. The servant ran up and kicked him hard in the left temple. At last Haydn was dead.

"The inquiring magistrate found the Lord acted in self defence and that was the end of the matter."

"What else do you know about Haydn?" asked Hardman. "Or the horn?"

"Well the old cornet I think his son John took to Canada. It came from Haydn's father, Gareth."

"There are also some strange stories about Gareth and especially about Gareth's father — all that goes back nearly two-hundred-and-fifty years. But Gareth died the year Haydn was born — about 1870. Some say that as a young man Gareth accompanied Viscount Angelsey's father on one of his foreign adventures to The Holy Land. I think the Viscount was there in the 1850s. Now I may be old my bachgens, and Saint David will be coming for me soon enough, but all this is long before my time. The story is he was looking for some lost connection between the Druids and the Druzes."

"What sort of connection?" asked Grace.

A broad grin straddled Pugh's countenance.

"Well I can offer some scraps of the Druids, of the others I cannot say."

Standing up from his rocker, the old Welshman walked slowly, his right leg stiff as slate by now, to the bookcase. From there he pulled out a dusty tome.

"Great lies have been propagated about the Druids," he said, returning to his rocking chair. "There is today in Wales each year what they call the Gorsedd of Bards, ceremonies of the supposed descendants of the Druids. But these are only the shallow trappings of the Druidic imagination, the vestiges of still deeper secrets, for which seekers such as yourselves must continue to dig. If you do, you will find the tradition walks in open day and upon beaten tracks, exposes itself to the eye of light and has its own language. Although there have been a great many attempts to rub it out.

"Cariads," he then said, raising a finger and pointing through the window and looking off, far, far away. "The Druids lived over there on Mon, the Isle of Angelsey.

"They raised huge stones, such as those at Stonehenge. The stones were used for the destruction of snakes and other serpents which multiplied in huge numbers in those days. There were many more snakes than now, in those days. The snakes would beat themselves against these stones until they wrought their own destruction. There is a circle of such stones near here, The Stones of Grief, which are close to Menai Hirion in the parish of Gwyntchwydd in the County of Caernarfon.

"Now the Druids kept their teachings secret but taught their disciples a great number of verses. If these were passed at all it was by the lips. Only the lips, bachgens. And so what I tell you now is as I myself was told.

"Here, in these places," said Pugh, opening the book and pointing at several places on an inset map, "the Druids formed their great seminaries. They received the science of astronomy by way of Enoch, who went up to heaven as you know my darlings, and parsed the stars on his own account before returning to this world. Some say they worshipped the Sun but they worshipped God, cariads, 'One God, Near and Far, Who consisted of three essentials: Infinite in Himself; Finite to finite comprehensions; and Co-unity with every mode of existence in the Circle of Grace.'

"I would be the only old fakir around here now who recalls this, I reckon," Pugh smiled.

"You said there were some strange stories about Gareth's father," said Grace, interjecting. "What was that all about, do you know?"

171

"Well, now we're going back very far. Before your husband and before John and before Haydn and before Gareth the word was that Gareth's father — Bleddyn, his name was — studied metallurgy and the fashioning of musical instruments with a master horn-maker in Germany.

"But then he came back to Wales and lived in the forests. Some say he was a hermit. Others said he grew rich, amassed a fortune in gold and then lost it all. At that point, now an old man, he married and fathered Gareth at the age of ninety-eight. His wife, whose name I cannot recall, was fifteen. And that's how he ended his days, not wealthy, but rich in life if you see my meaning. But that's really all I know.

"And now I'm very sorry my lovelies, I have talked myself out, and your ears blue I'm certain. Time is not my friend any longer. As we say: Mae'r glaw wedi gostwng y llwch — The rain has laid the dust."

"Yes. Thank you," said Grace, who saw through the window it had become dark.

There was a long, cavernous silence. The kind of silence one could drop stones into and not hear the echo for a million years.

"Any ideas how we can find out about Gareth Holborn?" Hardman asked as he gingerly pulled his jacket over his rapidly swelling hands.

"I'm sorry, my darlings," murmured Mr. Pugh, his mind drifting. "You might try Angelsey's diaries. They are in the Gornhaffan Historical Society Records. Mrs. Edwards at The Angel will show you where.

"And you might want to speak to Mrs. Duggan in Llallogen. They say she's got expertise. In fact, they say she knows everything."

COITUS

Grace is in Twelve.

Her hands cross over her stomach holding an elbow in each palm. Hopelessness. Aching sadness. Tugging loneliness. Feet pulled up on the bed. Knees tucked under chin. Rocking. Dark bridge. Nile. Trumpets. Lips. Seeing him, seeing him, coming around the corner. A taxi. Home. Collapsing onto the floor. Into herself. Hard Red Spring. Manna. Phone-call-someone-anyone. Nile. Harry.

"Drink?" said Hardman, knocking and poking his head in the room.

Grace eyed him undecidedly: empty, weightless, spavined. A sigh.

"Yeah, okay. Five minutes."

When she joined him downstairs there was Mrs. Edwards and a crowd of Welsh tipplers in the smoke-filled bar.

They chose a strategic spot in the corner, not far from the hearth and the fire. Mrs. Edwards, white face, red lips, broad smile, brought the Guinness.

Before long the melodic voices of the regulars rose to a crescendo. Dreamlike and weepy the Welshmen sung, their voices ebbing and flowing, the song rising all the way up from their uncut toenails.

And then, swaying sadly to the music, Grace and Hardman were approached by a short, bespectacled man, mid-twenties, who was in his cups. For an instant Hardman thought he recognized the face — but he wasn't sure.

"Professor Eluein Thomas, Department of Near and Far Eastern Studies, University of Wales, Bangor, at your service," the man said, helping himself to a chair.

"American, are we? Ah — America! America! Spacious skies and purple mountain majesties and amber waves of grain — speaking of which I could use a few more amber waves in my glass. Will you have a lager?"

"It's okay, we've got drinks here," said Hardman as Grace turned away.

"You know I've been drinking lonely amounts of whiskey on a corner of the bar," the professor said, rising and returning a minute later with fistsful of lagers. "But I've switched to beer so that I may be more lucid in the morning. Lectures, you know. Top of your game and all that. Still, the Druids were great consumers of hops, and their blood runs through my coarse and alcohol-sodden veins.

"Yech-y Da!" he grinned, tipping his glass back.

"Up yours too, I'm sure," said Hardman, unimpressed.

"Mrs. Edwards tells me you youngsters have only just returned from the Middle East. She likes you, boyo." the stranger said, winking, turning and waving to the bar. Mrs. Edwards, rinsing glasses, smiled at them. Hardman flushed like a beet.

"I suppose you've come to Wales to study poetry," he said. "In the old-fashioned way?"

"Poetry?" said Grace.

"Indeed, the ancient Welsh method of training poets. Acolytes like yourselves memorize thousands of lines of poems on strictly classical, Bardic Brythonic models. Of course you only succeed in obliterating the real essence of poetry, Welsh or otherwise — the individual voice. But you are spared the collegiate whinings of endless introspection which pass for the poetic medium these days: unique whinings to be sure, but only in the way yelps of walruses are unique to their anxious mummies — am I correct?"

There was no response. Grace stared at the muddy boot print on the ceiling, Hardman at the table. Thomas took another tack.

"You know of the links between Druidism and Druzism, of course?"

"Druzism?" said Hardman, looking up. "Funny you should ..."

"Well, yes, lad. According to most scholars, the name Druze derives from the heretical missionary Muhammad al-Darazi," said the Welshman.

"Darze, by-the-by, means seam and al-Darazi means tailor. He's the one who offered Islam a seamless web of theology, one without idols, for which the Welsh word, the Druidic word, is dyrysu. Coincidence? I think not."

Thomas eyed the pair for a response.

"Unfortunately, in 1019 al-Darazi was assassinated. Had a falling out with a rather venerated pair of Islamic theologians.

"At any rate, there's a tradition stemming from Crusader days that says the Druze are descendants of the French Compte de Dreux, who disappeared in the mountains of Lebanon following the fall of the final Christian outpost there in 1291. The French Crusaders, defeated at Akko, were led by Geoffrey of Bulloigne, founder of the Knights Templar, the Foreign Legion of the time. Stranded there, the Frenchmen began wearing white turbans, fell from Christ and loosely embraced Islam. Their descendants, the Druze, are of neither faith.

"Akko," said Grace, perking up some. "Harry was asking about that place. He really wanted to go there for some reason."

"Hardman..." said Thomas, turning to eye the drummer more closely. "Jewish is it? One of our Hebrew brothers are you? You'll know then that Ashkenazi Jews of European origin score higher on standard quotient IQ tests than any other ethnic group, saving the Welsh of course. Although I should say you don't look especially Jewish."

"No," said Hardman, tapping his foot. "And you don't look particularly Welsh. I thought all Welshmen were five feet four and covered with shit, or soot, coal dust or something.

"Excuse me," he said to Grace. "I'm going for a leak."

"A leek?" replied Thomas. "You'll find plenty of those in Wales, boyo ...."

Grace nodded and Hardman made his way through the singing hordes to the men's room, Mrs. Edwards watching his tightly drawn backside all the way.

Just as he unzipped Thomas stepped up beside him. They both stood there, gushing geyser-like, eyes upon the ceiling now. A little unsteady, Thomas teetered for a moment and then casually turned his head to Hardman's crotch for a good stare.

"Hardman," laughed the academic. "Hard man. But not when you're going wee, I see."

The drummer kept eyes riveted to the wall.

"Of course," continued Thomas, "The Druze don't snip, unless it's a very special occasion."

"What?" said Hardman, fuming but unable to extricate himself from the gravitational exercise of his bladder.

"The Druze. If a male Druze is not circumcised as an infant, it is unlikely the operation will be performed later. Whereas in remote Lebanese villages, boys would routinely hide in the hills whenever the mutahhir — the ritual circumciser — appeared. They'd show their heads, so to speak, only after he left for fear their parents might engage his services."

"I see," said Hardman.

They returned to Grace who looked alone and distant at the table. Not even the low moan of Welsh hymns from the crooners of The Angel pub seemed to lighten her.

"Nor do they engage in that barbaric practice of female circumcision," Thomas continued, slumping into his chair, and smiling at Grace. "And their women are most beautiful."

"They are?" said Hardman.

"Oh, yes, and the traditional ones wear the most singular head dress in the world. A long silver or wooden horn about twelve to fourteen inches in length, shaped like an old-fashioned speaking trumpet. They look like unicorns. And over this they drape a veil, dyed with the five colours of the Druze pentangle: green, red, yellow, blue, and white."

"Same as the sweatlodge," mused Grace, thinking her words were low enough that Thomas could not hear. But he did.

"Ah, a native of the North American variety are you, my dear? I wondered," said Thomas. "Of course you're very likely Welsh," he said.

"Yeah, right," scoffed Grace.

"Oh, indeed, my dear. Let me guess, you are from what tribe? The Mandan?"

"How the hell would you know that?" Hardman interjected suspiciously.

"Yes!" said Thomas triumphantly. "I knew it! Well, it's obvious neither of you have heard of Madoc ap Owain Gwynedd or you wouldn't be asking that question. And, I suppose, this would be the true reason for your being here now — theologically speaking."

"Who's Owen ap Gwyn — whatever?" Grace queried.

Thomas sighed a deep and condescending sigh, had a long swig of his lager, wiped his lips of the froth and proceeded with what Grace and Hardman expected would be a lengthy dissertation.

Thomas took a breath:

"In 1170, Madoc, a local Prince tired with the constant warfare and petty quarrelling in the Land of His Fathers, set sail with his followers into the Atlantic upon his ship, the Gwennan Gornofio, to find a more ethereal environment.

"Prince Madoc sailed long and hard to the west until he found land comfortable for settlement. He returned to Wales with the good news and sailed again with more followers. Of course they disappeared," said Thomas.

"The great geographers of the Elizabethan period identified the land where Madoc set foot as Florida. But on his second voyage Madoc is believed to have landed in Mobile Bay, Ala-baah-ma," said Thomas, bleating, lamb-like, and feigning a southern drawl. "This was more than three centuries before Columbus."

"Oh yeah? Whatta load of bullshit — " said Hardman, sensing he was being had.

"I tell you not one word of a lie," said Thomas, downing the dregs of his glass.

"There are several reasons for believing this, not the least of which are the reports of English and French explorers who probed the North American wilderness in the eighteenth and early nineteenth centuries. They said they met with Indians who were light-skinned, had beards, and who spoke Welsh — descendants of Prince Madoc and his followers.

"There seems little doubt Madoc's settlers moved inland from Mobile, up the Mississippi to the upper Missouri and settled there, becoming, eventually, the Mandan. The evidence is staggering. Roman coins have been found along the way, the vestiges of forts built in the Welsh tradition, and even one of America's greatest but, sadly, neglected artists of the Wild West — George Catlin — left drawings and written testimony of the Welsh-speaking Mandan tribe. It all points to your forebears coming from Pwll-coch, my dear."

Grace was at a loss for words.

"There is a bronze plaque," concluded Thomas, "mounted even today, by the good fathers of Mobile in praise of Madoc."

He looked to Hardman who stared back blankly.

"But I'm from Mobile," said Hardman.

"Crickey!" said Thomas. "What a rarefied coincidence."

"I don't remember anything like that," Hardman scoffed venomously. "And there's no plaque."

"You're out of touch with your history, my boy," said the professor.

"Yeah. Maybe," Hardman said, readying to leave. "But at least I don't go around gawking at other guys in the pisser."

"What's this?" asked Grace.

"Never mind," said Hardman.

"Oh, cariads, you'll not stay and have another drink?"

"Nah — I don't think so, bud," said Hardman.

"Yeah, it's been a long day," said Grace. "But, by the way, what's the name of that ship mean in Welsh — Gwennan Gornofio?" asked Grace.

"No meaning, really, I shouldn't think," said Thomas. "Gornofio means 'to swim above'."

"See you around," said Spike, declining Thomas's handshake. The hands were too sore, bleeding still and scabrous now, oozing through the gauze.

"Pleasure was all mine," said Thomas. "Nos da."

"Meegwetch," Grace thanked him, for what, she was not certain.

The two then strolled outdoors for a few minutes where Hardman gently hugged her with one arm in the crisp night air.

They climbed to the top of a small Welsh hill, overlooking The Angel. The wind picked up, blowing their hair and stretching their dark faces. They took refuge behind a pair of huge stones and Hardman lit a thinly-rolled spliff.

"Wild story, huh?" he said.

"Uh huh," she murmured, oozing air from behind her tongue. "But you know what? It's no more wild than this situation here. Harry's gone, actually gone. And we're here and I'm not sure why. Trying to find some clue about the horns. For him I guess."

Grace leaned back and looked up into the clear cold heavens clutching a handful of dark stones by her side.

"What kind of black stone is this, Spikey?" she asked, accepting the joint from the drummer.

"Oh, slate I think. Nothing but slate around here. I think the Welsh use it for everything. Eat it, probably, in their porridge."

Grace gave no answer, but stuffed pieces of jagged rock into her coat pocket. Restless heart, her thoughts crossed the laggard wonders of the night. Yet the stars seemed chained to the sky as if the glint of dawn would never come.

One star flickered brightly, winked at her the way Harry did when he joked. Then it came to her like a stab in the belly. Her husband was dead, she would not hear his voice or see him again.

She turned to Hardman and burst into uncontrolled sobs.

"He's gone," she cried out loud. "and here I am, in the middle of goddamn Wales, looking for some bloody horn, some goddamn clue, some bloody something that could explain something that can't be explained. And he's not here. Nobody's bloody well here. Oh Spikey! What are we going to do?"

Hardman held her, his injured hands throbbing with each heartbeat.

"I'm here," he said calmly. "I'm here, Grace." And they sat quietly for a time, listening only to the notes of the wild wind blowing up the valley and through them.

After awhile she said: "How many nights and days do you think have gone by before this day and this night, Spikey? In all. I mean, could it be an infinite number of days and nights?"

"I don't know," said the drummer. "What about the big bang? It had to start somewhere."

"Well, what about before that? How many days and nights before that?"

"Just nights I guess," he said. "I don't know. I think there have been a million days. And before that there was just this wind. I was thinking about what that priest said the other day about Beethoven. How all music before him was for God. I mean look at those stars, those are for God too. Make a wish?"

"Do you know I didn't even say good-bye to him?" whispered Grace.

Some time later they climbed the stairs to the bedrooms, Hardman on the first landing at Four and Grace in Twelve.

As she reached for her key, he took her hand. "Nightcap?" he asked. "I still have some Arak."

She considered the consequences for a microsecond.

"More spirits?" she said. She looked Hardman in the eye. "I don't think so, another time Spikey — I have to sleep. Good night."

She kissed him on the cheek and went upstairs.

She slipped from her clothes and into bed. Feeling dead to the world, still she could not sleep.

Once more came the welling up of anger, the unfettered roiling of disbelief and dread. She tossed and turned as if eels twisted in her stomach. Her heart flayed her with loneliness and the ache that Harry had left too soon and that she had failed to touch, to really touch, the mysteries of him. She switched on the light, dug through the old desk for a pen, and — after raising her eyes to the moon — began writing on the back of an old letter from Harry that she had folded into her pocket.

> *I am Luned, Lady of the Fountain*
> *Commanding Britains Arctic niggers work the pits*
> *The dark slate-smoothed sheaths,*
> *Slippery and rain-soaked.*

I am Luned
Hand me the Corn
So I am free to sail on the notes, do you see bach?
Over the time-tinselled, lollygagged jumbalorum
The sea-slavish Pirate ships shall carry mugs of me
On their Jolly-Rogers

Is it hot in here Cariad, or is it me?
You, ruby lips parted like loose shavings of thin alum
Trembling and Quivering,
As jellyfish with the lash of my utopian words
There is a lecture tonight at the Cymmrodorion Society
And I shall speak.

I am Luned.
Though sometimes my passport shows a dark Ukrainian gypsy
From Trieste;
A Ukereste.

Number Four meantime was a small cage with a low ceiling, a brass four-poster, a wash-basin and lace curtains. Hardman, his hands still throbbing, gingerly poured two small glasses of clear, licorice-tasting nectar.

"You're beautiful Grace, even in mourning," he said to himself as he downed both drinks.

He peeled and replaced the gauze with fresh bandage, staring at the colour bars of the television before flipping to the news in unreachable Welsh.

He startled when he heard a quick tap. The door opened a crack and it was Grace.

Wrapped in a wool blanket, she tiptoed quietly across the floor and sat on the soft edge of the eiderdown. She pulled the Frampton from under the blanket, its bell glistening in the yellow light.

"I didn't want to sleep with you, you know. You should be ashamed for even thinking it."

"How do you know what I've been thinking?"

"Look, it's not that I don't like you. It's just that your timing's off."

"I'm a drummer, Gracey. My timing's never off."

She paused to consider this. She felt no surprise nor fright nor guilt. She was just lonely. It was as if she were suspended in freedom — a world emptied of any moral strictures, where right and wrong had no status.

Hardman rose, carried the Frampton to the dresser, and poured two drinks, passing her a glass. She sipped and placed the glass on the night table. He reached for her and with a swollen hand cupped behind her head, drew her near.

As they kissed she searched for a voice of protest and then wondered why. She tumbled into his green eyes, tentatively touched his soft blond hair. Slowly it seemed, like a falling, she found herself folding faraway into his arms. She tried to hold back the sobs. She was surprised his touch was so different than Harry. She looked at him as if he were stronger, leaner, more whole than he had been an hour, a day, before.

Hardman rolled her beside him, prone. "It's okay Gracey," he said. "It'll be all right. It's just a little horniness between friends."

He rose, turned off the overhead light, felt his way to the side of the bed. And soon they made love, or if not love, then each pierced the other's loneliness. And near the end both began to cry, perhaps because the taste of the fruit they had tried was more bitter than sweet.

LEUKOSIS

At sunrise came a tapping on the window.

Grace was lost in slumber but Hardman heard it, the sound of stones, tiny pieces of slate, tinkling on glass.

Room Four looked east. The sun's fiery fingertips spread through the room, singeing, cleansing, raking Hardman's face in a bright, fate-filled candescence.

Still, it was not the light but the unalloyed Welsh air, the over-starched sheets, the empty flagon of Arak which tugged him from one of those mysterious dreams where fantasy conjoins with reality.

He was sinking in a watery pool. And there was Grace above

the surface, alluring and inviting, tossing small pebbles through the skin of the water. She was naked, darting her tongue at him, breasts ripe as fruit, her body wet, growling and succulent — stippled with dew. But he could not reach her. He kept sinking. Tap-tap-plop. The stones broke the plane of the water and were falling past him in slow motion. She laughed. She could not see him. He could not breathe. Tap-tap-tap.

Startled, he awoke and there she was beside him in bed.

Another tap-tap-tap and now, he realized, on the window. He slipped groggily from bed, peeking from behind the curtains. A dark figure lurked in the garden below. Dressed in an overcoat, a man gestured for him to come down.

As he pulled on his jeans, Hardman looked at Grace longingly, hopefully, pricked by guilt. The door whined and whinged but he tiptoed along the corridor and down the groaning stairs. He slipped through the hallway beside the vacant front desk and opened the front door of The Angel.

He was greeted by what appeared to be the ever-friendly Jermaine Kidder: erstwhile drummer and music groupie, one-time pimp to Hardman, clerical vestment model, computer hacker, marmalade-eater and low spy by way of Trinidad, Brixton or Sherbourne.

"Hey, Spikey! How's it going, man?" Kidder smiled generously, far too freshly serene for the hour. "Tell me, how do you hold the snare stick, thumb-index or thumb-middle?"

Hardman closed his eyes, adjusting them to daylight as he shuddered in the crisp and mist-filled air. Then he screwed up his face as if he had just walked into a filthy toilet stall.

"Well," he yawned. "If it isn't the stick-man-of-the-cloth. What the hell are you doing here?"

"I have news, come."

They walked briskly to the warmth of Kidder's car where the young agent poured English Breakfast from a thermos. Even in his sleepiness, Hardman could see Kidder was different somehow, more serious, a gravity in his usual levity.

"Spike. I'm not acting for an auction house but for a security firm that protects against industrial espionage," said Kidder, straight-faced. "It's the SIS actually."

"Oh yeah?" said Hardman. "Really?"

"Yup," said Kidder. "And I must tell you, man, lots of people are looking for your trumpet friend's old horn. Including your pal, Aaron Kenyon. I came to warn you."

"Warn me? About what?" he yawned again, trying not to appear alarmed. "How'd you find us?"

"Never mind that just now," said Kidder. "I need another favour."

"Forgive me, Father," Hardman mocked, awake now. "I don't think so."

Kidder took another tack.

"Do you know Professor Eluein Thomas, Bangor University?"

"A bit too well," muttered Hardman, checking his fly. "We bumped into each other last night."

"It's a cover," said Kidder. "SIS pegs him as an amateur with Mossad links. He's been buried here in the UK for several years. Tried to run you down yesterday afternoon."

"What?" cried Hardman, incredulous, spilling tea. "That slimy son-of-a-bitch — I thought I recognized him in the bar last night. How'd you know about this?"

"His name is Tomas Avi Levin. He lives up here in Bangor, wife Miriam," Kidder continued. "He's a graduate student, covers in summer as a diamond cutter, metallurgist, sometime geologist. But his father worked with one of Israel's top agents, a man called Eli Singer, in Canada, on a hit in 1959. They waltzed into Canada from South America and whacked an Estonian war criminal in Winnipeg, made it look like he hanged himself. Later the father and Eli worked on the botched hit against Abu Hassan Salameh in Lillehammer in '73. You remember, retribution for the Munich Olympics? Offhand, I'd say the son is not dangerous. But it's obvious

The Institute, Mossad, considers the operation important if they've activated him now."

"Jermaine," said Hardman, lighting a smoke, sipping tea. "What the fuck are you talking about? Are you a — ? You're not a goddamn — " He bit his tongue — "Spook?"

Kidder gave him a filthy look. Hardman's hands burned, the infection throbbing round his knuckles.

"Later," Kidder intoned. "You'll know all you need to know. For now, let's just say we've been watching the peculiar movements of your friend Aaron Kenyon."

"Huh? Mossad, Munich, operation — who's 'We?' And what's all this got to do with me and Grace? And Harry. What do you know about Harry? I knew it had something to do with those horns."

"It may. Listen to this," Kidder said, producing a small cassette recorder. "See if you recognize the voice. Girl still has the horn, by the way?"

Hardman shrugged.

"Now Kenyon's been meeting all over London with this Israeli, Eli Singer," said Kidder, holding the recorder like a dog treat before Hardman's eyes.

"Nothing so far to pull either of them in on, conduct unbecoming a foreign national, nothing under the Official Secrets Act, but they've been meeting very publicly: King George's Park Wandsworth, and then at The Berkeley and then at the Pigalle near Piccadilly, and then The Criterion, and then The Royal Court. Really done the rounds. It's all rather inexplicable."

"I'll say," Hardman said, shifting the scalding cup of English Breakfast between his blistered hands.

"Now, what we're trying to suss," Kidder continued, "is why Eli Singer, one of Israel's best agents, breezes into the country the same time as this obscure Lebanese we've been watching. His name is Atrash, came on the same flight as your girl. At any rate something odd is happening.

"You see, we had no reason to suspect Kenyon as a mule for Israeli Intelligence until he was contacted on a houseboat at Camden Locks by Singer. And then suddenly Eli and Kenyon are doing the town red. It's almost as if Mossad wants to finger old Kenyon, to kiss him off. They're virtually inviting us to pull him in. But why blow Kenyon now? Makes me wonder if they're covering for something more important. The old pea and thimble trick: use Kenyon and the horns to draw attention from something else. But we don't know what."

"You are a spook," sighed Hardman, blowing on his fingers, looking off into the village, defeated. "And you play the skins. Fuck. That's disgusting."

Kidder clicked the button on the recorder.

"What do you make of this Spike?" he asked. "It's at the Kit Kat Club. Kenyon with one of his old drinking chums, Sir Tubby Whitehead of *The Daily Bugle*. Something about Napoleon — and we're not talking brandy. Whitehead's an expert on Bonaparte, you know. We wired the chauffeur, Felix. Listen."

"Did you know, Sir Tubby, that Serbia-Croatia has more artists, writers and teachers than it has art, literature, and schools?

"Ah, ideal conditions for all forms of cultural abscess. You end up with a situation where idealism flourishes unreservedly amid the mental unemployment of the masses."

"Indeed. Gathering the hounds at the weekend?'

"I say."

"I have been rereading, Sir Tubby, your biography of the Emperor. Delightful, I must add. I was wondering if I might trouble you to elaborate on one section in particular — to wit, Bonaparte's Egyptian campaign."

"Ah, yes, Aaron. The ambience of that period in the great Emperor's career — the puffs of cannon smoke, the smack of steel, the stench of cordite and sulphur as the Chief positions his artillery in the Egyptian desert against the Mamelukes."

"Indeed. Those very weeks."

"Mistral winds blow from the north as the ships head for open waters from Toulon. After his evening dinner he would hold sessions with academics from The Institute, the academics who tended the 125,000 volumes he had brought with him from France. Mathematics and the study of antiquities are his favourite subjects."

"And to think, Sir Tubby, of him bobbing across the desert sands, approaching the terrible face of the Sphinx? The eyes of stone meeting the eyes of steel!"

"Nicely put, Aaron. Yes, the Emperor rides before his troops, points to the pyramids in the distance, and says: 'Soldiers, forty centuries look down on you'."

"But then, Sir Tubby, he arrives in Cairo and is greeted with two bits of bad news."

"Yes, yes. Josephine has been toying with someone else's organ. And the French fleet had been destroyed. Which news is worse? We can only guess. But in his wrath, he determines to redouble his attack. He seizes all the magazines from the Turks, arms the Syrian Christians, and stirs up the Druze!"

"Then Jaffa falls and three thousand Turks surrender to the Emperor."

"A triumph, yes! But what is he to do with the prisoners? His own men have scant food. Exchange them? For what? Set them free? Then they will reinforce the fortress of Akko, which he must take next. What on earth is he to do?"

"I must interrupt, Sir Tubby, and commend your decision to end chapter seven at that point — a stroke of narrative genius."

"Tut, tut, Aaron. To continue — Bonaparte ponders for three days. Finally he decides that they all shall be slain, Turks and Mamelukes. What choice did he have?"

"I dare say the Somalis and Tutsis would not concur, ha ha!"

"Ha ha! A nice point, Aaron. More cognac?"

"Thank you, yes."

"All are to be slain — save one, a tall, handsome fellow with blue

eyes, a slave named Rustam. Napoleon gives Rustam a sword with an encased hilt, and makes him his body servant. For the next fifteen years, Rustam sleeps outside his master's door.

"Now, if I recall, Sir Tubby, Akko lies before him, does it not? But the fortress has been reinforced by the Turks and, worse, the English. The Chief has no patience for prolonged siege. He hits upon another plan."

"Yes, the tunnel trick. Thanks to his study of history, the Emperor knows of an underground passageway leading into the city, a tunnel dug centuries before by Crusaders, the Knights Hospitallers. The English forces have no knowledge of this passage, and think themselves secure. Napoleon intends to send a small force through this tunnel, a surprise attack to open the gates for his awaiting army.

"But he does no such thing."

"Correct, Aaron. At the last moment, he boldly decides that a symbol of his imperial power will say more than an actual victory. The English will be made to know that the Emperor's army could have taken the fortress but, in his inscrutable greatness, he chose to spare it. In the depths of night, he has Rustam weave through the secret tunnel, his mission to enter the city and return with some prized booty. Rustam reappears before dawn, in his arms the head of a subaltern, and a long wooden box."

"And in that box, Tubby? What was it? You claim in your book that the contents were never revealed."

"A bit of mystery improves any tale, Aaron, even a biographical one. And I might add that if I had revealed in the book all I knew, it would have jeopardized my own search for those 'unknown' contents. A quest, I might add, which I have since long since abandoned."

"Then the contents, Sir Tubby, you can now disclose?"

"Certainly, my good Aaron. When Napoleon lifted the lid he discovered a ram's horn."

"A shofar? To be blown the Day of Atonement and other ceremonial days."

"Yes, Aaron, but according to a scroll, inscribed in Hebrew and placed in the bottom of the box, that shofar was the *shofar. The one Joshua blew beneath Jericho to make the walls come tumbling down."*

"The very shofar!"

"Yes, Aaron, marvellous to think, isn't it? The Emperor thought so too, for he added it to a special caravan of antiquities and curios that had come his way as he retreated from Akko. Although a wild look of defeat overcame him as he retreated, contemplating the ultimate stubborness of Akko. He stood alone on a hill, filled with ferocious melancholy as he ordered a great noise from his troops, the roar of trumpets, cannons, chains and mail the blast of the shofar."

"Tell me about the horns — if I may trouble you further."

"Bonaparte had previously acquired two twinned trumpets while passing through Italy. Abandoned, according to an earlier biographer, by two renowned horn players at la Scala in Milan. The Emperor intended to display all his artifacts of conquest on his return to France. But alas — "

"What happened?"

"The Syrian plague began to take its toll on his rearguard soldiers. He visited the sick in hospital but the doctor pointed to fifty cases as hopeless. What could be done for the agonizing pain? Rustam, riding on the point, had met up with a party of Druze — opium dealers who would trade the narcotics for precious artifacts so that they might denigrate and spurn them during their peculiar religious ceremonies. 'Give them the horns,' the General ordered, 'The twins and the ram's horn.' And so Rustam made the exchange and his commander ordered lethal doses of opium for the dying."

Kidder snapped his wrist and with a finger clicked off the recording. There was a long silence in the car. For Hardman, enlightenment came like a blow to the back of the head. His pulse accelerated, anticipation tore at his flesh. But there was nowhere for him to roar or run, nothing in him that could tremble or cry in the air. There were wonderful green, green hills everywhere around, and inside, emptiness. Tossed on an uncertain sea, he felt alone and breathless.

"Is Grace in ... danger?" he asked, guts knotting, his hands pounding with pain.

"I dunno," says Kidder. "What do you make of it — the tape, what are they on about?"

"Well, it's obviously something to do with the Framptons. I really can't guess," Hardman said, his voice defeated, his breathing heavy. "What about Harry. What happened to Harry? Was he, you know, bumped off?"

"No idea."

"And Sterner?"

"Who's Sterner?"

"Swiss. An old brassman. Car accident three days ago."

"Right. Heard about that," said Kidder. "Dunno. But I have another little surprise for you. Come with me."

They walked to the shed behind The Angel where Hardman had worked on the Indian. Attached morosely to a stool between two burly plainclothes constables was Professor Thomas.

"Well I'll be a cat's ass," said Hardman, stunned. "I know him," he said, sneering at Thomas. "And these pleasant fuckers?"

"Local officers," said Kidder. The officers puffed their chests and warily eyed the musician who had arrived with the SIS man. "Found him in a ditch last night, drunk driving," Kidder said, gesturing toward Thomas. "They called us when they found this."

Kidder produced a mass of scribbled technical papers and a notepad with "Holborn: Framptons" written in green marker on its front cover. "Then we searched his house, found a few cypher pads, a shortwave radio — enough to warrant detainment for questioning about espionage."

Kidder looked scornfully at Thomas, no longer full of brass but contrite, fearful, as if an entire zoo were crouched in the bushes, ready to leap at him.

"You could pull a long stretch of time for industrial spying," said Kidder.

"Look, I'm no spy," Thomas muttered mournfully.

Kidder leaned toward Thomas. "I hear these Welsh boys, good men, salt of the earth they are, can whip seven shades of shit from boyos like you." Kidder grinned at the gorillas who now proudly grasped Thomas firmly in the chair.

"I'm seconded to The Institute, yes," Thomas suddenly offered. "But I'm a scientist, metallurgy."

"Tell that to His Lordship when he sends you down to Wormwood Scrubs or Brixton or somewhere juicy for the next twenty years," Kidder warned. "Nice little chap like you, you'll have a black eye and a sore arse first day, and then it gets worse."

"But I've broken no laws," Thomas protested, his voice faltering.

"Don't worry, we'll think of something," said Kidder, circling like a shark. "Now what's all the fuss over these trumpets?"

"The metal," said Thomas breaking down. "But it's not just us. They're doing experiments everywhere now. It's a race for time. Lawrence Livermore labs in the States. The Russian Academy of Sciences. The German Institute of Spectroscopy. The Niels Bohr Institute. The United States Naval Research Centre."

"A race?" said Kidder, arms folded, intrigued but sceptical, pacing the shed. "What kind of race, pray tell?"

"It has to do with refining gold from elemental sludge," Thomas said, the officers sneering at the ease with which he had been broken. "There's a substance, ghost gold. It's non assayable. It has no weight. When you cupel it from the essence there is nothing. Yet it's an element. It's there. I can't explain, it's too technical."

"Try me," said Kidder.

"There's some of this ghost gold in the horns," said Thomas, on the verge of weeping, his cover blown, his career in tatters, his future fluttering as a speck in the air.

"But the pair must be analysed together. Emission spectroscopy. It's like carbon dating — you know, The Shroud of Turin. You take a carbon electrode and place your sample on the carbon. Then you run another carbon electrode from above and you strike an arc between them. The elements ionize and give off specific light wavelengths. Well, the Russians found that in order to do this properly you need a three hundred second burn instead of usual fifteen seconds. In fifteen seconds you get the standard readings of iron, silica and aluminum and sometimes traces of calcium."

"Go on."

"Well, nothing else is read until ninety seconds into the burn, where palladium begins to read. We've done this now at Dimona. At one hundred and ten seconds platinum begins to read, at a hundred and thirty seconds ruthenium begins to read, and at two hundred and twenty, osmium. The Russians call the process fractional vaporization."

"So?"

"The race is to find the purest of the pure. That gold you're wearing around your neck isn't pure. All precious metals contain natural materials, contaminants. When you neutralize the acid and hydrogen and reduce it you should have pure metal. But with the gold on those horns, it seems you get gold and quantity of ghost gold, which is not a metal."

"Not a metal?" said Kidder. "Look mate, I've forgotten my chemistry set along with nose plugs, which I should have brought since I'm starting to smell a lot of bull droppings."

"This is the truth," said Thomas. "I'm telling you because you and I are allies, whether you know it or not.

"The horns are brass but they were tipped in metallic gold. And when you dissolve metallic gold in aqua regia, Kingly Water, which is a mix of nitric and hydrochloric acid, you convert the chloride to get rid of all the nitric. What you have left is a cluster of metallic gold. You can boil this forever at 5500 degrees and it will never dissolve to its essence — the monoatom. But somebody did create such an essence when they made those horns. How they produced it — we don't know."

"Cut to the chase," said Kidder, feigning exasperation.

"The gold on those horns has no metallic character. And under an inert gas such as argon you can heat it and the protons let go. And when the protons are annealed away, it loses four-ninths of its weight. Conceivably, if you anneal the powder over and over it would literally begin to levitate in the annealing pan, weighing less than the pan it was sitting in. When you cool it back, instead of four-ninths weight you might get more gold, perhaps 150 or 300 percent of the original weight. So you're literally making gold — absolutely pure ghost gold — out of sludge."

"Make your own gold, eh?" offered Hardman.

"And they need both horns to make this analysis?" queried Kidder, arms crossed, hands buried in his armpits.

"Yes. Simultaneously I understand there was a preliminary analysis of the one horn some time ago, in Switzerland, the same one that remains in the possession of ... of your friend there," he said, pointing toward the window where Grace lay sleeping.

"What about Kenyon?" Kidder asked.

"Aaron is a low level operative like myself. He doesn't know much except that it's imperative we find both horns."

"You have the one Frampton?"

"We have — from Cairo."

"And Harry? What happened to Harry?" Hardman asked.

"Honestly, I don't know. Drowned. I wasn't there," said Thomas. "I've been here in Wales, off and on the past few years, studying the properties of slate. The idea is to see whether we might produce some positive sludge from the slate. I was told to watch you and the girl since I could pass as a local. I was to keep you away from London for a few days."

Without another word, Kidder nodded to the puffed up constables who bundled Thomas into a van parked on the road. Hardman and Kidder strolled back to the car as the sun climbed over the peaks of the Three Elephants.

"I can't tell Grace about this," said Hardman.

"Why on earth not?" asked Kidder. "She likely should know."

"She'll freak. You posing as a priest, you know, that bullshit about a service for the band. Fuck. I should've said no. What a mess."

"A white lie," offered Kidder.

"White, red, black — it's all a lie," Hardman groaned. "And now this. SIS, Mossad, ghost gold. Jesus."

"You're tangled up in it regardless," shrugged Kidder. "Any of that make sense to you? Or anything in the business about Napoleon?"

Hardman thought hard.

"Not really. We spoke to some old chicken farmer on the coast who knew Harry's family history and a bit about the horns. They seem to be bad luck. Something about cock fights and Druids. One of Harry's grandfathers was with some Earl in Egypt looking for a connection between the Druids and Druzes. This Thomas, whoever he is, he was on about this Druid-Druze business last night, too."

"Well, there's more," said Kidder. "The Institute has had your friend's house on Haverstock Hill burgled. Kenyon and Eli Singer. Looking for the trumpet."

"What?" said Hardman.

"Yeah. The old man, Kenyon, he must have had a key for the place. Kidder paused. "We had an ambient listening device in the light fixture in her parlour." He drew another tape from his pocket, pressed it into the cassette player, and once more pressed the play button.

"Here it is. Now we just have to toss the place up a little, steal her knickers and all, make it look like a break-in. She'll think it was the resident East End mafia. We'll be laughing all the way to the fish and tank."

"Hang on. Let me see that. It's not the right one."

"What do you mean?"

"It's not the Frampton. After twenty years of watching Holborn

polish it, play it, and talk to it, I should know. It's the Sterner, the replica the Swiss made."

"How do you know?"

"The trademark. The trademark on the real Frampton is discoloured. The only detail Sterner couldn't get right. She's left the Sterner here."

"Maybe she cached the real one somewhere here. Let's have a peek-a-boo."

"You look, Eli. I can't be bothered. This entire escapade is no longer of any interest to me. It's one thing to attempt to ensure the economic security of a nation. It's another to kill someone over a bloody horn."

Kidder stopped the tape and the pressed the fast-forward button on the player.

"I won't bore you with the next twenty minutes of crashing, scraping, and general rooting around. But here, give this last part a listen."

"No, Eli, that's not it either. By god, can't you even recognize a modern trumpet? That Harry's Hart — he used it daily."

"She's taken it with her, the little cunt. We'll have to get word up there, to Wales. We'll nab it there. Same difference. Nothing lost."

Kidder snapped off the tape and Hardman closed his eyes, slumping in the seat.

"Okay, Jermaine — don't bend over in the pew. What do you want me to do?"

"How do you get that little sha-bang sound on the drums, Spike?" asked Kidder. "Is it a Grace-note? You could show me sometime."

"I don't know if I'll ever play again," Hardman said sadly. "Look at these..." he said, his hands bloodied clots of bandage.

"I noticed," said Kidder. "What happened?"

"Banged 'em when I fell off the Indian," said Hardman.

"You should have that looked after. When are you going back to London?"

"Tomorrow, I think," the drummer replied. "Then Canada

— funeral."

"Right. Stay with the girl. Mind the horn. Get those hands repaired. Then back to Canada — From Sea to Shining Sea — right-o."

IMPRAEGNATIO

At breakfast, Hardman was subdued.

He glanced fretfully through the window of The Angel's dining room to the spreadeagled oak where the woodpecker once tapped for Mrs. Edward's old Mort. What could he tell Grace? Nothing. Nothing to report. Nada. A lone bandaged hand swept slowly across the table to his fork. Why feel guilt, he wondered, if there is no God? But then who is to forgive? He wiped the corner of his mouth oh-so-slowly with a napkin. He sighed often.

Grace came down from Room Four and immediately sensed his agitation. She hoped they would transcend the emotional shrapnel of sleeping together. Of touching bones and resting in each other's warmth.

"What's wrong?" she asked, poking a sausage between sips of coffee.

He shook his head. "Sad, that's all," he lied. "Thinking about Harry."

"Where were you? Earlier? When I woke up?" she asked.

"Walk," he replied.

They picked at the food in silence and then went outdoors, the sun shining on the deep canyon between them.

Soon they set off from The Angel upon the unsteady Indian, the bike trembling and shaking until they arrived at the Gornhaffan and District Historical Society, a tiny stone cottage on the edge of the next village, the hamlet of Cwm Close.

The clerk was impressed with Grace, who, familiar with libraries, quickly found Viscount Angelsey's diaries, filed in a corner box under volumes of The History of Sphagnum Peat Bogs, Welsh Thatching and Rushlight Practices of the 1890s, and Notes on the Grinding of Curge.

Delicately skimming the pages of the dusty tomes they learned that it was in 1856 that Hubertus Horatio Kiddwelly, the Sixth Viscount of Angelsey, was on expedition at the boundary between Lebanon and Palestine looking, among other things, for a lost connection between Druids and Druze.

"There's that Druid-Druze business again," Hardman whispered, breaking the ice. "Which reminds me, do you think that guy Thomas was, you know, queer? I told you kept staring at my — oh, never mind."

"Can't imagine why," said Grace without looking up. "Oh, look. Here's the first reference to Gareth Holborn," she said, suddenly sitting erect, turning the book around on the large oak table so Hardman could examine it. He read, in bold, elegant handwriting:

21 January, 1856
We have encountered a large Bedouin encampment, which presents
a welcome sight to the wanderer of these steppes. Even the wisps of
blue smoke from the many camping fires seem to sharpen the
appetite. Women carry urns on their heads, children chase one
another between the goat-hair tents, and dogs sleeping in the shade
bestir themselves to bark savagely at the visitor. The manners of
the Bedouin are as easy, correct, and natural as those of the
aristocrat. Bedouin women conduct themselves with a surprising
grace. The footman, young Gareth Holborn, has observed that a
gazelle moves with no greater ease than the young Bedouin woman
carrying an urn balanced on her head.

"Umm," winced Hardman, flexing his infected hands, trying
vainly to keep the dust away. "And over here in this passage, it
mentions Napoleon:

In the next days came our experience of the Druzes of Lebanon,
who refer to themselves as the Sons of Beneficence — those who
help others. And so it was that after tarrying with the Bedouin for
a time, we travelled to the village of Bint Jbail where the young
Holborn almost became a headless footman having been found in
flagrante with a fiery Arab gazelle. But here, too, among the Sons
of Beneficence, we apprehended a certain treasure, a pair of Twin
Horns reputed to have once been held by Napoleon. These Horns
were held within a large wooden box in which a silver box was
contained, along with statues of a Phoenician calf and phalluses
and conches. Now, many heathen revere statues and objects,
imagining themselves to be worshipping an image or attribute of
God. But the curious citizens of at Bint Jbail acquire such objects
only to treat them with contempt and scorn.
They were easily persuaded, therefore, to part with one horn in
exchange for a lowly Shofar, which we assured them was much
revered in our own land.

Hardman turned to her.

"What the hell do you make of that Grace?"

"I don't know," she replied, realizing again that this confirmed the words of Atrash. "It must be the Framptons. It can't be anything else. I can't believe Harry didn't know this. There's powerful medicine here I think. But I want to see that Mrs. Duggan in Llallogen. I think it's about twenty miles."

They sketched notes of Angelsey's diaries and, with the Indian rumbling beneath them, set off for Llallogen.

Sunshine had broken the cloud by tea time and the sight of the village was rejuvenating as it lay there, nestled neatly in a cleft between great craggy mountain bugles and bryns. They stopped at the top of the hill, stretched their legs and had a smoke. Grace stared at the drummer.

"I think I'm cracking up," she said in a flat tone, distant. "Maybe I'm already cracked. And everyday I feel more and more angry. I'm just angrier than I've ever felt in my life. Last night in my dreams I literally saw red. I guess I'm mad at Harry for dying. I'm even pissed off at you, Spikey," she said. "And I don't know why."

Hardman said nothing. He gazed down into the village.

Again they boarded the bike which putzed and banged down the hill into the high street where there was a pleasant white-walled house with a glorious garden of snapdragons and lilies. At the gate was a cluster of middle-aged men and women, crowding around an ancient and laughing old lady. They received directions here, cruised through the village and up the south incline past some savage crags before taking a lumber road to the left. They followed five hundred yards to a clearing and turned again to the left, where there was an old stone house with outbuildings, the centre of a working farm.

Mrs. Duggan was toiling in the flower garden. When they introduced themselves, saying they had been sent by Mr. Pugh, she welcomed them quite openly.

"My dears," said Mrs. Duggan, a hearty woman of fifty, with short brown hair, a wide bottom and a green thumb.

"I can tell you everything I know about Gareth Holborn, father of Haydn Holborn, but it's better if I take you. This very house, you see, is where Gareth and his beloved, a slip of girl named Caerwin, once lived. I've been here fifty years. It was dead as a doornail when my own father bought the place, but the smell of history lingers still. Come."

The walked a good half mile up the steep hill to a little church at the edge of Llallogen. A bare slate tombstone marked the grave of Gareth Holborn beneath a huge oak in the corner of the churchyard.

"It was the summer of 1869," began Mrs. Duggan as the three sat on a low wooden bench, facing the grave. Grace clutched her knapsack, hugging the bulge of the Frampton.

"They say two farmers met on that road leading from Llallogen to Gornhaffan, just up there.

"One, Thomas Pearce, was well-to-do. The other was younger with sharp, keen features, his complexion almost sallow enough for a foreigner. His name was Hughes. They were travelling over Dafydd's Hill, from which we've just come.

"Can you see the view? Snowdonia over there. All the hills here that day were bathed in glorious sunshine. Indeed," she said, lowering her voice. "These hills were calculated by the Almighty to inspire much better thoughts than those which flowered in the minds of these men.

"Because from the high point they could just catch a glimpse of old Cambria Farm, my home now, but which was then occupied by a widow, Mrs. Probert, and her only daughter, Caerwin. The husband had not been a successful farmer and died in distressed circumstances. Everyone believed the widow would sell the farm, which, during her husband's illness, had been promised to Pearce for a very modest sum.

"But then Gareth Holborn, a young man who had been brought off Angelsey and across the Menai Strait by her brother, moved onto the farm. He managed well and the property once again became profitable. He devoted himself entirely to his work and to the widow's interests. Kept to himself."

"His relatives?" Grace asked. "His parents?"

"I'll come to that my dear," said Mrs. Duggan. "Certainly after Gareth had been with the widow and Caerwin for two years, they came to regard him more as a friend than a servant. The mother was pleased that Caerwin's sentiments were even more favourable than her own, but the stranger — for he kept himself a stranger still — carefully avoided all sentiment and never spoke of his past life.

"In his heart, I believe Gareth felt grateful to them both for not prying to know his early history. But Caerwin grew romantically curious. One spring day, under the weathercock, they kissed. And on that same fateful summer day, cariads, I hope you won't mind if I call you cariads, on that day the two men — Pearce and Hughes — approached the farm, and talked. And they both saw Gareth Holborn as the enemy. If it had not been for him, one might have had the farm and the other the girl. After many consultations they decided to be rid of him.

"The next day was a market day and Gareth Holborn went to transact business for the widow in the village. It was in the evening when he left town for home. Soon he was overtaken by his two neighbours. There was an argument. He begged to be allowed to continue. But nothing he could say would satisfy them. He must take off his coat and fight, which he did, and would have beaten them if it had been a fair fight. But while one caught his attention, the other, as planned, dropped his watch and purse in Gareth's coat pocket.

"His purse?" Hardman repeated as he rose from the bench and idly tossed a few shards of slate against old stone wall which closed the churchyard. He gave up when his hands began to throb.

"Then they made him put on his coat," Mrs. Duggan continued, "dragged him back to Llallogen, and accused him of robbing them, artfully suggesting that if the one friend had not come in time Gareth would have killed the other. Young Holborn protested his innocence. But when he was searched the watch and purse were in his pocket. He was quite dumb with surprise and his silence was presumed to evidence of his guilty conscience. He was committed to the Great Sessions which were held at Bangor on the 23rd of August."

"Great Sessions?" asked Grace.

"The court as it was called then," said Mrs. Duggan. "He was visited frequently at the gaol by Caerwin and her mother. And then the trial began. The prisoner was a stranger and his accusers were sons of respected men. They swore the same story as they had told the justice of the peace. The prisoner was found guilty of highway robbery with violence.

"His Lordship, Justice Horace Berriman, donned the black cap and asked the accused if there were any reason why the sentence of death ought not to be passed upon him. Gareth Holborn said in a firm voice: 'My Lord, it is useless for me to oppose the evidence your worship has accepted. I trust the day will come when my innocence will be proved and that my lady and her daughter' — here his voice faltered — 'will know that they have not befriended a common highwayman.' Caerwin apparently made something of a scene here, but he continued: 'I have prayed earnestly to God that he will reveal my innocence or not let the grass grow upon my grave.'

"His Lordship passed sentence and the prisoner was sent down to be hanged in mid-September."

"Holy shit," blurted Hardman. "You mean they hanged the guy? What a family, those Holborns."

Then Grace interjected. "Mrs. Duggan, I'm curious. Was there any evidence Gareth Holborn had a horn or a trumpet at all?"

"It was just before the fateful day in mid-September that Gareth, wishing to cleanse his conscience, whispered to Caerwin that he once had purloined a trumpet. Not just any old trumpet but a very special one. It was, he said, one of the two great horns once held in the company of Napoleon. The horn, which he had laid an eye on as the servant of Viscount Angelsey, was one of a perfect pair. Dipped in gold round the end it was. He had taken it from the Frampton-Upon-Severn Volunteers to whom Angelsey had bequeathed it as a gift. It had a sound so full and sweet he was smitten, compelled to thievery. He told Caerwin that it took six days of wild blowing in the copse and gorse below Mount Snowdon before he was able to achieve so much as a peep from it. Having made his confession, he said he believed the Almighty had forgiven him and that he too had forgiven those who bore false witness against him. Caerwin, sadly, was too distressed at his plight to attend to much of his story.

"But there was another confession that day as well, cariads. Young Caerwin told him she was with child, and so there was much wailing and lamenting. He told her where the horn was hid and that she should pass it to the child when baby bach was old enough to be told of its father's fate.

"And so hanged he was, at age twenty-nine, on that day in mid-September, 1869, not for the theft he did commit but for one of which he was guiltless.

"It was a morning of bright, beautiful sunshine. But as the hour of execution drew near, it became very dark. The lightning and thunder were dreadful and it seemed a shame to hang a man in such weather. Women and children were too terrified to leave their homes. The storm was general and the damage up the Welsh coast that day was appalling.

"After the execution the body was given to two friends of the widow who had asked for it. One was a carpenter and had made a coffin. The hearse was drawn up in the pouring rain and the tail boards opened. The body was brought here to this churchyard. Caerwin was torn, they say. She wanted to bury the horn with Gareth, but it was his request it be passed to the child.

"The priest, a pale, young fellow, looked for the shelter near a sapling which grew at the head of the grave here. He took off his hat, dropped it carelessly onto the ground, and proceeded on to business. One or two watchers winced slightly when the holy water was sprinkled on the coffin. The holy drops were quickly washed away by the river of water flowing into the grave, but they left little round black spots on the wood of the casket.

"During a lull in the rain, the gravedigger scraped up some soil and threw it down after the coffin to deaden the fall of the clay lumps. Now the fall of clay on a convict's coffin doesn't sound any different from the fall of the same thing on an ordinary wooden box, but one person there — Caerwin — would have felt every thump jolt her heart.

"And yet the most remarkable thing of all. Despite all the wind, which blew from the heavens and lashed the coast with rain and thunder and wetted the parched earth, despite the wet, the grass, cariads, never grew over the grave of Gareth Holborn. And now you see by your own eyes it remains so today, as if scorched by fire or lightning.

"Caerwin took the name Holborn and moved to Gornhaffan to have her baby — Haydn she called him — but she died soon after. At least that's the tale told by my own mother who heard it from a woman in Gornhaffan before Caerwin died. But now you've heard it from three women so that likely makes it an old wife's tale," she smiled.

The two North Americans were at a loss for words.

"What about Bleddyn, Gareth's father?" asked Grace.

"He was not," said Mrs. Duggan.

"What do you mean? I thought Bleddyn fathered Gareth when he was over ninety."

"Poppycock. Who told you that?

"Mr. Pugh," said Grace.

"And old Pugh had tales about the virtues of Druidism and wild yarns about the cock-fights, didn't he?"

"As a matter of fact..." Grace was cut off.

"In Old Mr. Pugh, bless him, the rivers of memory and fancy sometimes flow as one. But not many people around here will gainsay him. We don't like to speak of babes born out of wedlock in these parts. And they'll never speak a word, at least not to strangers, of babes being born to brothers and sisters. Bleddyn was the Grandfather."

"What?"

"Aye," the woman said. "Bleddyn Holborn, raised by the Druids it's true, made a fortune in Germany somehow. When he returned home he lived a pious and prosperous life until at last, in mid age, he had children, off a young wife. Twins they were, Ingot and Midian. And then he died — of joy — he always wanted twins. And the two puppies, gypsies they became, rode over Europe in a caravan and played matched horns. Gold-tipped they were, a prize from their father so the legend has it. They even once played in the opera house in Milan so it goes. Very talented. But in 1796 they both were very badly wounded. Each lost a leg when Napoleon bombed the city in his Italy campaign. They were returned to Wales, penniless, injured, and with only each other for comfort. Some joked it was a miracle Gareth was born whole, each with the opposite leg gone, see? In chapel they said Gareth was adopted. But everyone here could see he was theirs. The fever took them both to the grave not many months after Gareth was born."

"The horns?" asked Grace, eager to find if Mrs. Duggan's story would correspond to the other accounts.

"Lost in Italy I imagine. At least that's what I told that charming Professor Thomas and your husband's solicitor."

"What?" said Grace, suddenly in disbelief. "Harry's lawyer? What lawyer? And Thomas?"

"They were here not a fortnight ago. Mr. Thomas and Mr. Singer. Said they were conducting research for your husband, in trust."

"Thomas..." Grace repeated.

"I knew we couldn't trust that prick," Hardman chirped, trying to appear as surprised as Grace.

Grace shook her head, trying to piece together what they now knew. Bleddyn Holborn, her fingers counting off the generations, helped the mysterious Gwynt fashion the twin horns. Then Bleddyn's children — the twins Ingot and Midian, named after the wife and mentor of Gwynt — lost the horns to Napoleon at la Scala in Milan. Later, if what Mrs. Duggan said was true, Ingot and Midian produced Gareth Holborn. It was Gareth who accompanied Viscount Angelsey to the Holy Land and later stole one of the horns from the Severn Volunteers — though how the horn had gotten from Napoleon to Angelsey in the first place, Grace could not imagine. From Gareth — hanged after being wrongly accused of stealing a watch — the Frampton passed to his lecherous son, Haydn, the miracle healer. After Haydn was poisoned and shot in a fit of jealousy by the next Viscount, the horn passed on to the next-to-last Holborn, John, Harry's father.

Grace nodded, her brow furrowed. It made a precarious sense, despite a few remaining gaps. She gripped the Frampton in her backpack tightly. But what of the other horn? As far as Grace could tell it had been kept all this time by the Druze in the village of Bint Jbail. Another chat with Atrash was necessary, this time one of her own arranging.

A lone starling bolted from an oak beside the grave and pulled Grace from her pondering. Mrs. Duggan beamed at her.

"Is there anything else I can tell you, cariads?"

IGNIS
INNATURALIS

The next morning Grace and Hardman swooped back to London in the Vestal chopper, each lost in their own hushed and cloistered world.

It gushed brightly that day in the great city, the buses gassed and gambolled, and Hardman, during the drive in from Hendon, faced the acute realization he had seriously banged up his hands by failing to wear gloves on the Indian. Grace, guided by an unseen hand and a nagging reluctance to be home alone, had Hardman drop her off at The Manna.

She gave Hardman her key for The Bunker, stepped from the cab, and clutched her backpack which held the Frampton.

Opening the door of The Manna, she nodded to Faisal, the waiter, sorting cutlery behind the counter, framed by the postcards of the Grand Tetons. In the corner at a rear table was Atrash, smoking a cigarette, sipping his espresso, reading Foucault.

"My dear Ms. Holborn," Atrash smiled sadly, rising and offering a seat. "Do come and sit." Faisal brought tea.

Grace turned squarely to face him. She took a deep breath. "What happened to the other horn from Bint J'Bail?" she asked, her voice steady. "And tell me now what happened to Harry in Cairo. You saw him didn't you?"

"Let me ask you a question first, my lady, if I may," said Atrash, caressing the smooth surface of his cup, running fingers through the skunk of his mane. "Your late husband's great-grandfather, Gareth Holborn, somehow obtained the Frampton Right from a certain Viscount Angelsey, or rather from the Volunteers he had entrusted with it. How?"

"He stole it," said Grace.

"I see," said Atrash, his face stretching into a thin smile. "The Viscount acquires one of Napoleon's horns from the Druze in exchange for a shofar made from a ram's horn — only to have this great prize, the Frampton, spirited away by a lowly attendant."

"And what happened to the other horn, the one kept in your village?" Grace stabbed back.

"Ah," said Atrash. "It was kept in our village for a time, though not in the khalwa. That place was reserved for the Shofar, in the silver box within the rough hewn box."

"And then? After that?"

"That horn, the Frampton Left, was kept among the villagers. It was passed from father to son among many families. Someone even bought an old beige trumpet case for it. Although I never learned to play the instrument — indeed, I have never raised it to my lips — I often wondered what became of its twin, the one which fell into your husband's family. And thus, as a young man, I made it my pastime to inquire after the horn we gave away. After hearing Mr. Holborn's playing I convinced the my people that he should be the rightful owner of the one from our village. So as you see, your husband, your late husband, God be with him, and I have much in common."

"With one difference," said Grace. "The horns belonged to Harry's family all along. Two hundred and fifty years ago a man named Bleddyn Holborn actually made the Frampton Horns. Under the teaching of an old brassmaker named Gwynt."

"Ah-ha," Atrash clipped, flicking a cigarette ash into a nearby tray. "Yes. I'd often wondered about their origin. Dreamt about it. Speculated. Cogitated. They are so magnificent. I'd hoped your husband would tell me when we met in Cairo."

He paused, stumped out his smoke.

"Your husband, Miss Keeper, died well. Although I am sorry it occurred at all — it was none of our doing. I think you'll find the Swiss horn-maker was a hit, killed purposely. Your husband's death was accidental."

"What do you mean?"

"I was there."

"So you... you were there? In Cairo, when..." said Grace, paling and then flushing red, peering into his dark eyes as she wavered between incredulity and rage.

"I had Loutfi arrange a meeting," said Atrash. "In a bar, the day before the final concert at Giza. There, I offered to give your husband the Frampton Left from my village. We agreed to meet the next night at a warehouse on the Nile dockside to conduct the transaction. The people of Bint Jbail were content to have Mr. Holborn take the Frampton Left. God unites all things, and my people sensed a divinity in bringing together the twinned horns. As well, the original role of the horn in our village — an emblem of material vanity to be ritually scorned — had faded as the passing generations grew over-accustomed to its presence."

"Contempt breeds familiarity?" said Grace, her nerves settling.

"So to speak, yes," replied Atrash.

Grace lowered her eyes, and stared for a moment at the rings of coffee staining the table.

"But Harry was robbed," she said suddenly. "Why did he take $5,000 from the bank?"

"Of this, I have no knowledge. Myself, and my people, we asked for no fee from Mr. Holborn. Perhaps you should ask Loutfi. We used him, yes, to bring your husband to us in Cairo, but I can only surmise that he had his own financial gain at heart."

"Loutfi," said Grace grimly.

"We were about to turn over the Frampton Left at the dockside warehouse but things went terribly wrong. Loutfi, or at least your husband, did not know that their car had been followed by others, men motivated by — who knows — greed, avarice, pride, fear. The motivations of all wicked deeds."

Grace lowered her eyes, placed a hand on her forehead and clutched the sack with the Frampton Right tightly to her belly.

"What happened?"

"Your husband arrived with Loutfi and climbed from the Peugeot. I was waiting. The Frampton Left, the one from my village, was in my hand, in its case. There were many smiles, much goodwill, and a feeling of — may I say gaiety and anticipation — brought a blessing to everyone. There was joy in your husband's eye as I handed him the trumpet case, and he placed it on the floor to open it.

"He gasped when he saw it, he was so happy. Very gently he reached for the instrument as if it were his infant child. Lifting it, he looked more closely. He caressed it, rubbed it on his cheek. He knew instantly that it was genuine. Then, my lady, he gave us the largest, most complete and utter look of happiness I have seen worn by any human face. There were many hugs and words of thanks as we once more explained our reasons for giving up the horn.

"I asked him to play.

"And so he raised it to his lips and was about to blow, when strangers crashed through the warehouse doors. They came from nowhere. They were masked, four of them, armed with Uzis, And they demanded the trumpet. Your husband bolted for the open door. He ran across the quay and there was a struggle. I did not see everything. But I believe the horn fell into the Nile. Your husband paused. He jumped. Seconds later he rose with the Frampton Left in his hand. Only his head was bobbing above the water and he was sinking. Then the horn was on his lips and he drew a breath and blew. I could see the glistening gold of the horn reflected on the water. The sound of that note was ethereal. He had the look of a hunted animal but he also appeared curiously at one, as if some broken spirit had been mended. That is all I can say."

Trembling, Grace could find no words.

Atrash sat close, taking her hand.

"The water was not deep. He almost reached the shore before he went under for the last time. I don't know how it was done, but the strangers recovered the horn while I pulled Mr. Holborn's unbreathing body into the bulrushes and contacted the authorities. Loutfi by this time had disappeared. Your husband could not be revived. I am no coward, but I did not stay. There would have been many questions."

"There still are," Grace nodded, familiar tears suddenly unavailable as the knowledge came sweeping over her. "Who were these men? And why was the horn so important?"

The waiter, Faisal, come close. "You must believe us, my lady," he said. "I was not there but I know Professor Atrash — he does not lie. If he says it was an accident, it was. Please, I also am so very sorry about your husband."

Atrash cast his eyes into hers.

"As I said a few days ago, when we last met, I have a proposal for you my good lady. If you are still interested I think it still possible to recover that horn, the one lost with your husband. I have seen that sometimes miracles happen in this world. And they happen under the most unusual circumstances, in the unlikeliest places, such as here, for example, in this unworthy and wretched kebab house of the Druze.

"Now please, hear me. Your husband made a replica, a Sterner, it may be called. If you will consider it, we may conduct some business."

"What kind of business?" Grace mumbled, her deep dark eyes covered by one hand. Her insides barren, she felt the lump of the Frampton through the canvass backpack drawn tightly to her stomach.

"If you accept my proposal, it is possible you may succeed where your late husband did not. This man Kenyon, the man who was an associate of your husband. He is among those who seek the horn. I speak the truth when I tell you that these people, Kenyon and his colleagues, helped stir up feelings against me in Cairo. They feared my humble research into the curious history of these horns. They broke into my offices and removed my documents. Then they convinced certain religious zealots that I was engaged in dangerous work. Consequently, I was falsely accused of sedition."

"What do you mean — 'these people' — who do you mean, exactly?" snapped Grace.

"Kenyon, as you likely know, became a friend to your husband's father in Palestine during the British Mandatory Period in 1948. This acquaintance was a ruse which perhaps grew into a friendship. Or a friendship which grew into a ruse, only God can say which. But Kenyon is associated with an organization known as The Institute. He was, I am convinced, searching for the twin Frampton horns even in 1948, and has been after the horns ever since, even today. But he has always worked for The Institute, not for your husband's benefit."

"How do you know all this?" Grace wondered, not really believing she would receive a full answer. "And what is 'The Institute?' Why..." she began to say.

"I'm sorry, I don't know. There is also reason to believe that you cannot entirely trust your friend Mr. Hardman — or at least one of his acquaintances, a certain Jermaine Kidder."

"Jesus Christ," Grace spat, angry now, struggling to her feet, clutching the knapsack. "I've just about lost my goddamn patience with all of this. Don't trust so-and-so, oh, Mr. X is really Mr. Y. Oh, and by the way, Mrs. Muggins, sorry about your husband. Shit. How do I know I can trust you?"

"You do not," said Atrash. "But I am your best hope, my lady. And one twilight in the future you will look to the stars as I do on some desert nights, and you may see how small we really are compared to the greatness of God: the God who made the stars and the twilight and the desert. And you may wonder, as I often do, how many millions of days have come before this day and how many will come after. Now, let me reiterate my offer to you. Your husband's Sterner trumpet ..."

Some distance from The Manna, Kenyon and Eli were luncheoning at The Bell, slavering over courses of braised trake, funistrada, and buttered ermal.

"Let me tell you Aaron, what's happening at Dimona," Eli whispered. "They're using eight X-ray heads, tunnelling microscopy, diffraction, flourescent microscopy. The spectroscopic tests show 600,000 to 700,000 counts of iridium versus a 12,000 count of carbon arc background. The beauty is that once we know the monatomic structure of gold on the second horn, a five minute test is all that's needed to confirm the results of the first. And we already know where to find the richest deposit in the world for the sludge material."

"Don't tell me," said Kenyon. "Is it Wales or Lebanon?"

"Humph," said Eli. "Not bloody likely. Our South African friends near Schalltrichtervoeld are mining piles of the sludge, including all the platinum group elements. They go a half mile down into the ground and follow an eighteen-inch seam. I'm told there are about twenty-four hundred ounces per ton rather than the third of an ounce that is being recovered in the Negev. No one else knows it's there, and soon, very soon Aaron, no one but us will be able to analyse for the ghost gold in it.

"Now I'm going to let you in on something," said Eli, "even though you don't deserve it, since it seems your heart isn't in this work any longer. And when I make my report, well, both you and Thomas, speaking of whom, I should have heard from him by now and haven't — what idiots! You risk the entire operation through carelessness and curiosity and that shall be duly reported. But nonetheless I shall tell you in confidence that we have approached the Druze, about the ram's horn from Akko. And when the initial tests on the twins are complete, sometime in the next twenty-four hours, then we'll deal with the Druze. We offer them a bargain. The Frampton Horns, which will be worthless to us once we have thoroughly tested their gold, for the Shofar. Think of it, Aaron — an unexpected perk, is it not?

There was silence next between the two men, only the clinking of cutlery as they sliced through the thickly-breaded trake.

"Soon we'll turn out the newest and purest and fastest generation of computer chips," said Eli. "Are you listening? Think of he appications in our aircraft, our missiles, radar sighting technology. And even the civilian uses. Israel has the Hinnom Valley and the Kidron Valley and soon, very soon, we will have the new Silicon Valley of all the world. And we'll enforce the peace. Make friends with our Arab neighbours. With our technology and the Arabs resources, we'll unite to make the Middle East a real economic power.

"And then we can sit back and hear that ram's horn echo, loud and clear, near and far, all the way from Nahariyya to Naqquora, from Qiryat Shemona to Jericho — I want to hear it in Jericho."

Kenyon's mind drifted back to his most recent visit to Jericho — with Harry Holborn. And he thought sadly of Harry now, and a bitter taste rose with his braised trake. He took a sip of Chablis. But deep inside he cringed and his heartbeat increased with a gnawing fear that the day of judgment was, for him, coming all too soon.

"And this shall come to pass no matter what the price, eh Eli?"

"What happened in Cairo — that's unfortunate I'll grant you," said Eli, removing a morsel of ermal from a corner of his mouth. "The loss of an innocent or, if not entirely innocent, then a talented human life. It was a waste. The Swiss, well, he was disposable. He helped us but simply knew too much. Everyone else, the Americans, Germans, even the British will be falling over themselves to find old Sterner's files for the results of his spectroscopic analysis. But his files are gone. And the rest? Well it's done — a distraction, a footnote to history, nothing can be changed. We must focus on this. This is the future. Everything is at stake. We won't be foxed by that woman again. We need the second horn — now — and I'm going to get it."

It was mid-afternoon when Grace returned to The Bunker, smacking on the ornamental knockers of her own door. Hardman answered from the parlour where he'd been resting on the L-shaped sofa, medicated, his hands professionally bound and bandaged like boxing gloves.

He said nothing but his face foretold more was amiss. She stepped inside. Although the drummer had tried to tidy up, the home was in a ruin: the meandering edges of the Persian were torn, drawers emptied, jewelry scattered, pillows slashed, even the kitchen pantry had been rummaged.

A swell of blood-red anger swept through her, threatened to overwhelm the control she had fought so hard to achieve. She stood in the middle of the room, hands clenched, as the realization settled upon her heart that her quiet santuary, her last connection to Harry, lay smashed and violated.

Grace was beyond tears, her heart a spectral line on the cosmic cardiogram.

Hardman tried his best to console, but Grace waved him away. The drummer shrugged, walked over to the stereo and hit the reel-to-reel. *Solar Caustic*, the wild wind of Harry's Hart, began wafting through the room.

Grace listened vacantly for a few minutes, then rose, padded across the Persian away from the L, and pulled the Frampton Right from her backpack, undressing it from its woollen sweater wrap. She was surprised to see the Sterner still on the mantle. She took it down. And without a word, one horn in each hand, she went to the kitchen, turned on the gas for tea. She took off her jacket and felt a lump in the pocket — the slate stones from the crags above Gornhaffan. In one final wrenching gesture of hollowness and depletion, she flung the black shards around the kitchen.

Grace descended to her jewelry workshop on the lower level, gingerly placed the horns side by side on the work table, steadied the overhead lamp, and fired up the burner. She thought of the coming flight to her beloved. This must end. Prayers, desperate prayers flew everywhere: to the Grandfathers Manitou and Winnebago, to the strange Christian God of the Sisters of the Sacred Heart, to the Druid God and Sun God Re, to the God Mercury, the god of human hearts, of rain, of fire.

As she waited scant seconds for the flame to achieve its zenith, she placed her hands on either side of the glass vessel which fed the fuel up through a pelican into the burner. She meditated on the glass vessel, focusing her energies.

"Oh Harry my love," she said softly. "You have left me and there are no words for the emptiness that courses these aching vessels of my heart. But I cannot leave you. And if I must come to you, then I am willing."

She turned to the blue flame.

"Grace?" She could hear Hardman's voice shouting from atop the upstairs near the kitchen. "Gracey? Do you smell gas?"

She did not answer, but carefully now, urgently answering an inner voice, she brushed the bell of the Sterner against the fiery burner — braising the horn gently but definitely. Reaching into her Dreamweaver tools, she took a razor-blade and opened her middle finger so rivulets of her blood might lick the ripening metal.

As crimson drops trickled from her body, she prayed. And soon a brilliant shaft of light appeared around the Sterner and the light took the room in its thrall. And the liquid marrow of her bones seized and fixed forever to the hot brass, congealing and darkening the serpentined-G on the Sterner.

A mildewed gust seemed to swirl through the basement workshop, her sanctum, and she felt a lightening and quickening in her belly as she rushed to finish her work.

Then there was a thump upstairs, and a shout. With the Frampton under one arm and the Sterner in her left hand, she stopped to retrieve the key from the mannequin, ran to Harry's studio, and gently stuffed the Frampton into the safe.

She'd taken only a few steps upstairs when she smelled the smoke.

With the Sterner in hand she reached the kitchen doorway. One entire level of the house was engulfed in flame. She could see someone had entered from the garden, perhaps slipped on jagged shards of slate and ignited a spark in the kitchen where the stove spewed gas.

Through the smoke she saw Hardman, his torso flaring like a struck match, struggling with a figure in the parlour. Blue flames were spilling across the Persian like liquid fingers. She was transfixed. Everything was burning. She ran toward the parlour and her clothing crackled, bursting in a corona of flame. Drowning in fire, she was dancing, shouting, frenetic. She banged and careened forward, her nostrils dilated by the stink of burning hair. When she conquered the gauntlet of black smoke, she saw Hardman was on the floor, wrestling with the intruder, flames leaping everywhere. The furniture was engulfed in the pyre, the conflagration licked the walls. She became dizzy, sleepy somehow. Coughing. Her lungs were turned inside out like rubber gloves.

She stood, nailed to the floor as flames flowed toward her like a rising tide on a beach. A voice cried out. "I want to hear that horn!" A hand was raised crashing into Hardman's jaw. The drummer went limp on the floor.

The intruder rose to face Grace. She could not see his features, the smoke pinching her eyes, her throat constricting. The figure hovered before her, directed a blow to her solar plexus. "My dad would fix you, asshole," a voice within her said. Another blow came on the nape of her neck and she fell, stunned, to the smouldering Persian. The Sterner was ripped from her clutch and the figure retreated with the horn to the front door and wrenched it open.

A blast of cold outside air rushed into the parlour, breathing new life into the inferno which roared and screamed around her. The heat singed and washed and cleansed and she wanted to rise above. The smoke thickened, the flames licked and spat upon her bones. She could not move. She was serene, almost reconciled, drowning in an ocean of flame when now she saw her fingers move and she knew some far away place, some hidden reserve must be moving them.

She crawled her way to Hardman as flames sang all around her. She gripped his unconscious fingers, dragging him inch by inch to the hallway. Lighted ships breezed through her mind, flaming kiffs floating on the Nile. "I must do this, I must finish this," she said, dragging the drummer to the entranceway — to the door of The Bunker, pulling him through to the sweet cool pleroma.

When she awoke on the cobblestone drive she coughed until she thought she would deliver twins.

IOSIS

Near nightfall a few days later, they touched down in that faraway city, somewhere to the north of nothing, across the great psychological divide, the forty-ninth parallel, in Canada.

Sprawling, forgotten Winnipeg, bared on the steppes, was cast in its own autumn twilight, the sun hanging low on the horizon like a monolithic red orb.

The tinge of Arctic air was clear and deep as the place awaited capture by the cruel hush of winter. A final V of geese barked like flying dogs across the sky, trailing off beyond a frothy patch of grape-coloured cumulus.

Grace and the drummer had been treated for superficial burns. Nearly all their body hair had been singed away and their lungs were cooked but they were alive: cleansed by fire. The Bunker was gutted, irreparable.

And now on the prairie it was the light, Grace noticed, that was otherworldly. It was a sheer and splendid light she knew only on the plains: red, gold and purple, and its effect was to cast the spaces into a stark grey against pink chiaroscuro.

She hummed as she and Hardman climbed into the hotel limousine at the wind-swept and lonely air terminal. She carried one trumpet case, Hardman another, and they clutched them as the porter dropped their clothing bags into the rear luggage compartment of the limo.

Thousands of oaks and elms, their branches reaching to the heavens like scraggly arms pinned to a cross, had lost their leaves, mostly, and the gutters of the wide wind-blown October streets were choked with orange, green and brown droppings.

A flat, mud-brown river wandered as a martyr through the city, a few drunken homeless nested under the scrub oaks which lined the river's path in that flat, tumble-down metropolis: an old, lost, way-laying grain town where most of the inhabitants retired before they began to work.

As they turned toward the town core, Grace smiled at a sign boasting of the city's fifty-two pool-halls, thirty-nine swimming pools, twelve-hundred policemen and two dozen snowy owls.

"Can you put some of that hurtin' music on the radio — you know — country?" she asked the driver, who may have been Lebanese, Ethiopian, or from Uttar Pradesh — here, it mattered no more.

"You know Grace, I'm going to take a break from music for awhile," Hardman said definitively.

"You'll get a new agent?" Grace asked.

"Yeah. A new agent."

"What'll you do then?" she asked.

"From here? Well, I've sort of made up my mind," he said. "I think I'm going down to Mobile. I might do some research on that Madoc ap Owain guy. I think you should come, after things settle a bit."

"Nah, Spikey," she said. "I'm going back to London for a few days. Unload The Bunker I think, retrieve whatever is salvageable. Beyond that, I don't know. I'm not thinking about the future. It's weird but when you're happy time doesn't exist. Yesterday and tomorrow don't exist. But then something happens and you're full of either hope or despair. So I want to go where I have no hope or sadness."

They pulled up to the hotel, a modern five-star eccentricity in a cold, lowly place of crumbling, turn-of-the-century Edwardian. A man was peeing in the alley, steam rising from between his tattered gumboots.

A few hours later Kenyon waddled up to the same hotel check-in, having arrived on another flight. He unpacked, called Grace and Hardman on the house phone and arranged a meeting.

When the knock came they were ready.

"We won't put him on a lie detector, we'll just probe the whites of his eyes," Hardman said, as Grace answered the door. Dressed in a business-suit as always, Kenyon smiled, hugged her, proceeded limping to a chair by the desk.

"I have the official post mortem document," the old impresario announced, opening a leather attache case. "I think it sheds some fresh contours on precisely what has occurred here."

"Read," said Grace.

"This is the report of Dr. Robert Negroponte, taken at 07:40 hours in the City of blah, blah blah, in the Province of blah blah blah," reported Kenyon, his eyes skimming over the document. The autopsy listed the cause of death as drowning. And then it gave incidental pathologies. "Ah, here it is. I thought it anecdotally interesting: 'Subject deceased shows evidence of severe tinnitus caused by Meniere's Disease, a disorder of the labyrinth of the ear.'"

"What?" said Hardman.

"Meniere's Disease," said Kenyon, hoping to give them a snippet to chew on. "Sometimes accompanied by disabling attacks of vertigo, loss of balance, nausea, ringing or roaring in the ears, impaired hearing and an intolerance of loud noises. Apparently Van Gogh had it, prompting him to cut off his ear. There's been a suggestion Beethoven was a sufferer. Two other classical composers, Robert Schumann and Bedrich Smetana both were afflicted with Meniere's when they were in the tertiary stages of syphilis. Smetana tried to live with it, to make the terrible fiend his friend by incorporating his manifestation of the disease, which had a high E pitch, into a string quartet in E minor."

"Jesus," said Hardman, recalling his tiff with Harry in Cairo.

"Dr. Negroponte suggests this may explain Harry's recent distracted behaviour. And who knows — it may have something to do with his determination to unite both Framptons, which, as you know, are tuned to E rather than B-flat. Some relief may be gained if one avoids certain auditory frequencies — the key of E may be more generous to the ear than B flat. Van Gogh described his own affliction as 'auditory hallucinations' although the ancient Egyptians had a name for it: the curse of the bewitched ear: you can never have perfect peace and quiet."

Grace was silent. She could not believe one word which spilled from Aaron Kenyon's poisonous maw. She was seething, outraged, nauseated, disgusted. To calm herself she thought of old Twohearts and, strangely, of Pugh.

"And I have other news," Kenyon continued, reporting that his sources in Egypt had made further, private, enquiries as to how Harry met his end. "Although I'm sorry to say it's not necessarily good news," he said.

"It seems the evening following the final concert, Harry was taken by this taximan he'd occasioned to meet, 'Loot-Fee'," Kenyon said, dismissively exaggerating the name, "to a warehouse in one of the more dilapidated souks where they were met by a Professor Atrash, formerly of the Al-Azhar University in Cairo.

"Atrash had been sacked from the university for academic improprieties, something to do with offending conservative religious scholars. At any rate, in the soukh, near the river, Harry handed over the sum of $5,000 and was given an old beige trumpet case. Just as he was removing the horn someone confronted them — a group of local thugs likely — and these miscreants demanded both the money and the horn. These gangsters threatened to shoot everyone unless they complied in full and without argument. Harry apparently made a run for it, dove into the Nile, and, because he could not swim, took the Frampton Left to the bottom of the Nile with him forever.

"I suppose we could have it dredged, but who knows what we'd turn up?" Kenyon concluded.

"Never mind," said Grace, turning away.

"Hey, Aaron?" said Hardman. "How did you know that trumpet case was beige?"

There was no response. Kenyon blinked twice.

"I'd say you know too much. You were there at that warehouse, old man. Right there in Cairo the whole time. Jesus. What a snake." Hardman rose and semi-circled the small room.

The young drummer turned to Grace. "The man is low," he spit. "I bet he could crawl under the carpet and not make a lump."

Grace looked impassively as Kenyon, crushed — got up. Quiet and small now, he shuffled to the door, his neck glowing red behind him. His face flushed with blood as he tugged to release the doorknob and escape. He paused for just a moment, a tiny breath disgorging from his lips. The pride in his eyes had vanished. As he backed away from the room and into the hallway his eyes met hers, searchingly. The door closed with a polite click.

The drummer and widow sat for a time, quietly now. Then Grace stirred, smiled at her friend, her husband's friend, her lover. She told the drummer there was an errand awaiting her, something she must do alone.

She excused herself and locked the door of the bathroom. Grace washed her face and stared for a long time into the wall of shimmering, mirrored glass. Soon a lone tear trickled gently down her cheek. They had been betrayed, she and Harry. Fouled in every way. She pursed her lips and whispered to her reflection. Only Harry could hear her resentment, the anger at her own gullibility and foolishness. "Take this pain, oh God," she whispered. "And be with me. And with Harry."

Later, she had no idea how much later, she felt sufficiently composed to open the bathroom door. She discovered that Hardman had left. She took the elevator down, struggling with two cases and her carpetbag, and climbed into the rear seat of a waiting cab. The driver placed the cases beside her.

Fat flakes of snow were suspended in the biting frost outside. And as she rode through the lonely gush of chill on that dark night, she imagined the glistening-black casket where Harry rested. In her mind's eye she could see him stretched out in an unfamiliar suit and tie on white silk pillows.

The downtown streets were almost deserted as the cab slushed through the icyness and then came to a crawling stop at a red light. Idling. Waiting. Time was suspended.

Grace was alone and resigned to being alone. Harry was not there. And because he was not there tonight, tomorrow night, nor on any future night, she saw the only remedy. The only way to bring an end to her pain, her guilt, her restlessness, would be to forgive them — all of them, here and now. She looked at the cases on the seat beside her. This she could do for Harry. It struck her that there might be no other reason for her being. And she felt a lump rise in her throat, rise, rise — and disappear. Her anger was no longer on the horizon — it was no longer something to be turned over and over, to be polished like a stone. It was being given up. Although she was journeying to the end, she also was in the centre of her own humility and felt she was being whisked away into peace.

It was shortly after eight when the cab delivered Grace for a private viewing. The funeral director helped her through the entranceway with her bag and the two trumpet cases. He led her into a small room off the foyer, a room with two doors, and indicated that Harry's body would be on the opposite side of one door.

"I'll leave you, Ma'am," he said with a firm, solemn smile. "Take your time."

She sat for a minute gathering herself. She opened the door and slid one case, then the other, into the next room. She was so achingly tired yet more awake than ever as she pushed the cases toward the casket. Then she lit a few shoots of sweet grass, smudging smoke through the room. She hummed as she placed the contents of both cases, the twinned and blazing-gold Framptons, into each of Harry's hands. She took a long look, kissed him, touched his lips with her fingertips one last time, and lowered the lid.

And then Grace took her leave.

Early the next day there was the fresh dusting of winter's first snow.

The three of them, Kenyon standing behind, watched as the sparkling casket was lowered and a friendly pastor said a few words. Hardman, it seemed, couldn't stomach it and, leaving just a whiff of his vitamin fuel behind, dropped a pair drumsticks from his bandaged hands into the grave. He retreated to a waiting van with the final 'Amen'.

Grace turned from the hole, gripped Kenyon and pulled him along for a little stroll around the place, the brownish grass peeking through the snow.

It was all wide open space, bright blue sky and endless flat prairie. There was hardly any breeze, just a whisper, a breath of cooling wind. A wild black crow shivered, watching them from atop a nearby pine. They stopped and Grace removed her shoes and socks.

She could see the scrub oaks along the riverbank and the fresh snow felt so cool and friendly beneath her feet.

"Who are you, Aaron?"

There was silence. Grace snapped a small fir branch, split it open and inhaled the honey-like vapours. Her feet were planted firmly. Dark eyes shining she looked at the old man. Waiting.

"Is that an existential question?" he asked with a sigh. "Or rhetorical? Let's walk to that bench. My feet are killing me," he said, pointing with his cane to a seat that faced the river. He took her arm as they walked. She looked away, numb to the cool snow beneath her feet. The workmen were filling the grave with great clumps of thick prairie gumbo. She could hear the dull thumps.

Sitting. The air cold, clear, biting.

"My name is Kinneret, Aaron Kinneret," he said finally, hands folded, eyes down. "Since 1948 I have been engaged as a low-level courier for The Ancient Relics Directorate, an increasingly obscure and irrelevant sub-branch of 'The Institute' — the Mossad. The music business offered a more than perfect cover, you see."

He turned to her.

"In actual fact, I have not been called upon for a very long time for anything more than moving mail between dead letter drops. I am what's referred to in the espionage lexicon as a blind mule. I was used in an actual operation this one last time only because I knew Harry. Although I suppose you could argue that my only assignment for years had been to know Harry."

"You had time to get to know him, then," she said, probatively.

He paused.

"The Institute wanted the twins, you see. Needed them as much, more perhaps, than dear Harry. Oh yes, of course I was there when the horn was fetched from the Nile, we had to pry it from his fingers if you must know. And there was quite a struggle with the Arabs. But he over-reacted. He shouldn't have run. And no one expected him to dive in ... into that filthy river."

He sighed. "The business about the Meniere's was true."

"I know," she said. "I suspected. But that was not the whole story."

"No. Yes, we, well not I, but others, took the other Frampton from you — in The Bunker. The fire was accidental. Naturally, we could have recovered the one Frampton from your mantlepiece at any time but we were never certain of the location of the other. So we needed Harry to lead us to both."

Grace put her hand to her mouth, and turned away from the old man.

"Because you see on Saturday, the Sabbath Day," he said, "an exchange took place on the Golan Heights between Israeli authorities and representatives of the Druze: Israel gave over the twin Framptons for the Shofar of Akko. It is one more small step in the process of peace and reconciliation. Symbolic, perhaps, but nevertheless meaningful.

"We needed the twin horns to conduct some analysis. Do you see? After that, they became of no more use to us. So now the Arabs have the horns, the one Harry lost in the Nile and the one which was removed from you in London. They were used by certain people for certain experiments of a scientific and metallurgical variety. Those results should be complete in the fullness of time. A very good cause, I assure you. What the Arabs will do with the horns now, I cannot say."

There was an interregnum of silence, an emptiness that only a moment of forgiveness could fill.

"Aaron," she said slowly, taking a breath and staring at the ground beneath her feet. "I don't know why I'm going to tell you this, but I am going to tell you. Israel didn't give over both Framptons. Your friends never had them to give. The fire? They got the Sterner," Grace said, looking through him now, deeply, searchingly. The pain had not washed away, nor was her memory of anger and betrayal suddenly cauterized. But the pain had moved. It was no longer on the horizon for her, it was at the centre of all that was. And she could accept it.

Kenyon's pain, lumbering, burning, was just beginning to bubble. He stared at her, incredulous. Then, suddenly, tears welled in eyes and began to seep down his ancient cheeks.

She looked at him, surprised to see an old man cry so.

"I'm sorry Grace. I loved him too, in a way. I'm just so, so sorry."

And then it struck Grace, that inasmuch as her anger was irrational, so too was her forgiveness. And while the anger was sparkling and exciting, she saw that forgiveness was quiet and patient. Absolving him, she would have to give up her undisputed rightness. But only a moment of forgiveness, she saw too, might stop the deadly monster, the grotesque creature fed and fattened on her own bloodthirsty pain. And even in the consideration of this, there, on a bench, in a snowy graveyard, with a broken twig in her hands, it was too late to turn back — she had already turned.

"I forgive you, Aaron," she said, the words bursting from her lips as if notes from a golden horn. And this was a symphony which flowered from that silence beyond even justice, and it contained within it the peace that surpasses understanding, rare in any lifetime. She took him, and held him, and together they wept.

ESSENTIA
EXULTATA

It was a few more days before The Bunker and the Café Manna saw Grace again.

She first went to Peepeekissee to see her brother. And she walked across the cool prairie and drank from that good trout lake and licked the stones beside the cold water. At night she considered the stars and the number of days which had come before her. And the feelings these things bore within her, she trusted.

Joey took her to see Twohearts who told her of the Mandan and their secret language.

And Twohearts told her of the secret society of Itskinaks. He said her Grandfathers, members of the Horns, would plunge their finely carved feather totems into the ground to make a giant circle. He said snakes or serpents would destroy themselves trying to bang their way into the circle — there were many more snakes in those days — and the men would chant and re-tell in that sacred circle the secret stories of the beginning of the world.

"Sometimes the odd snake would sneak into the circle," old Johnny Twohearts said to her.

"Sometimes the Grandfathers would lift up a stone and find them snakes, or there'd be one snuck in under a split of wood. But there was so much powerful bewitch medicine in that circle that the snake had no choice — it had to change. It just couldn't be a snake no more. And the Grandfathers told that snake it had a duty to make a decision. And they'd pin his tail to a tree in the middle of the circle and wait while that snake decided. And sometimes that snake that got pinned either turned into a human being like the Grandfathers or sometimes it just got nailed to a tree and coiled up there and died."

And having heard these stories, and after offering the Grandfathers burning sweet grass and sage in memory of Harry, Grace went back to London to clean up The Bunker.

One crisp day, she lit a fire of autumn leaves and in the fire she burned some old pages of sheet music. And then she walked to the Café Manna and sat near the window to write a letter.

Rain began to fall, cold and hard.

She sifted tarry tea and saw the waiter had given her a cracked white cup. Though the grease-stained, mullioned glass she could see the flat across the road, where she and Harry had lived for so short and sweet a time.

A group of men were speaking in Arabic behind her at the tea counter. "I can hear them Harry, just here, maybe you can too," she whispered, writing on old music sheets.

And sometimes, my love, they ask if she is still crying. And one of them answers: "Not actual tears. But her dress, her shirt, and her shoes are crying. Her voice cries, and her hair, her nose, and her mouth are nothing but cries. Don't you know the look?"

The rain hammered like a drum on the window. And down the greasy pane her silhouette bends and droops, the droplets gathering into a pool, a river now, washing against a burning kiff which is floating down the Nile. And in that kiff, like Moses, is Harry Holborn.

Harry, I won't give away our secret. For you know better than all of them that the horns were meant for you. I took the Sterner and washed it with my blood, the ancient blood of the Grandfathers.

And Atrash made good on his bargain. He gave me that Left horn which they got from the Israelis and which you held in life for so short a moment. And I, Harry, have given it to you.

The Druze, you will be pleased to know, now have the Sterner which they have to scorn. They didn't really want your Hart, Harry, although I offered it as part of the bargain. They said, in the end, it was too precious to mock. So I gave it to Spike Hardman. He said he'd keep his sticks in it. Proudly. O, I know I could have kept the Hart, I could have, but the sight of it would only make me ache for you every minute of every hour. And every day for the rest of my life that you shall be away. O, that they all could take my heart also.

And Israel, I do not begrudge her the Shofar for the Day of Atonement. But you Harry, my love, you have your beloved Framptons. And the sound I hear you blow is both near and far.

Sleep beckons now and she rests, closing her eyes.

And before too long, Grace sees she is not in the Café Manna but she is in the air — flying, weightless.

And she raises her eyes, surprised to feel her foot bump on the trumpet case which is jammed under the passenger seat in front of her. Outside the oval window of the aircraft there is blackness on the final descent from Larnaca to London.

She is startled for a moment to know that she has been sleeping the cool dream-filled slumber of mourning. In the seat beside her a stranger rests soundly — his name, she sees on the boarding pass, is Atrash.

Turning to the window she sees below the amber glow of arrival. And far below the smell of burning leaves.